continued . . .

SCONES & BONES

Tea Shop Mystery #12

LAURA CHILDS

BERKLEY PRIME CRIME, NEW YORK

THE BERKLEY PUBLISHING GROUP
Published by the Penguin Group
Penguin Group (USA) Inc.
375 Hudson Street, New York, New York 10014, USA

Penguin Group (Canada), 90 Eglinton Avenue East, Suite 700, Toronto, Ontario M4P 2Y3, Canada
(a division of Pearson Penguin Canada Inc.) • Penguin Books Ltd., 80 Strand, London WC2R 0RL,
England • Penguin Group Ireland, 25 St. Stephen's Green, Dublin 2, Ireland (a division of Penguin
Books Ltd.) • Penguin Group (Australia), 250 Camberwell Road, Camberwell, Victoria 3124, Australia
(a division of Pearson Australia Group Pty. Ltd.) • Penguin Books India Pvt. Ltd., 11 Community
Centre, Panchsheel Park, New Delhi—110 017, India • Penguin Group (NZ), 67 Apollo Drive,
Rosedale, Auckland 0632, New Zealand (a division of Pearson New Zealand Ltd.) • Penguin Books
(South Africa) (Pty.) Ltd., 24 Sturdee Avenue, Rosebank, Johannesburg 2196, South Africa

Penguin Books Ltd., Registered Offices: 80 Strand, London WC2R 0RL, England

This is a work of fiction. Names, characters, places, and incidents either are the product of the author's
imagination or are used fictitiously, and any resemblance to actual persons, living or dead, business
establishments, events, or locales is entirely coincidental. The publisher does not have any control over
and does not assume any responsibility for author or third-party websites or their content.

PUBLISHER'S NOTE: The recipes contained in this book are to be followed
exactly as written. The publisher is not responsible for your specific health or allergy
needs that may require medical supervision. The publisher is not responsible
for any adverse reactions to the recipes contained in this book.

SCONES & BONES

A Berkley Prime Crime Book / published by arrangement with Gerry Schmitt & Associates, Inc.

PUBLISHING HISTORY
Berkley Prime Crime hardcover edition / March 2011
Berkley Prime Crime mass-market edition / March 2012

Copyright © 2011 by Gerry Schmitt & Associates, Inc.
Excerpt from *Postcards from the Dead* by Laura Childs copyright © 2012
by Gerry Schmitt & Associates, Inc.
Cover illustration by Stephanie Henderson.

ISBN: 978-0-425-24664-1

BERKLEY® PRIME CRIME
Berkley Prime Crime Books are published by The Berkley Publishing Group,
a division of Penguin Group (USA) Inc.,
375 Hudson Street, New York, New York 10014.
BERKLEY® PRIME CRIME and the PRIME CRIME logo are trademarks of Penguin Group
(USA) Inc.

PRINTED IN THE UNITED STATES OF AMERICA

10 9 8 7 6 5 4 3 2 1

ALWAYS LEARNING   **PEARSON**

For Elmo, dear departed family dog, who
served as the model for Earl Grey.

ACKNOWLEDGMENTS

Many thanks to Sam, Tom, Niti, Bob, Jennie, Dan, and the fine people at Berkley who handle design, publicity, copywriting, bookstore sales, and gift sales. A special thank-you to all tea lovers, tea shop owners, bookstore owners, librarians, reviewers, magazine writers, websites, and radio stations who have enjoyed the ongoing adventures of the Indigo Tea Shop gang.

This may be book twelve, but there are many, many stories yet to tell and so many marvelous teas to be brewed!

1

❦

A smirking human skull, all hollow eye sockets and pronounced parietal bones, grinned diabolically at Theodosia. A second skull, this one with crooked teeth clenched in an agonized grimace, wasn't quite as mirthful.

"Some of these images are a little bizarre," Theodosia murmured to Drayton.

"Jolly Roger flags were meant to frighten," Drayton replied. "The pirates who flew them wanted their designs to inspire fear and dread."

Theodosia took a step backward and gazed at the diverse collection of antique pirate flags that hung inside the shallow glass case. There were skulls and crossbones, full-sized skeletons, even skeletons dancing a jig.

"Actually," said Theodosia, a smile twitching the corners of her mouth, "they're just the kind of thing today's graphic designers and tattoo artists would groove on."

It was Sunday night at the Heritage Society in Charleston, South Carolina, and the grand opening of the Pirates and

Plunder show. Theodosia Browning, proprietor of the Indigo Tea Shop, had been cajoled into attending the event by Drayton Conneley, her master tea blender and all-around Heritage Society booster.

"Take a look at this drinking cup," said Drayton, nudging her with the shoulder of his tweedy jacket. "It's the one that was featured in the Charleston *Post and Courier*'s arts and entertainment section a few days ago."

Theodosia moved to a freestanding glass display case to gaze at what was certainly a bizarre curiosity—a genuine human skull that had been transformed into a drinking cup. The cranium had been pared away, a silver web surrounded the skull on four sides, and a silver handle jutted out. But the pièce de résistance was the enormous diamond snugged beneath the skull's chin. A diamond that, to Theodosia's curious eyes, had to weigh at least ten karats, if not a whopping twelve.

"This piece was owned by a pirate as well?" Theodosia asked. She pushed back her tousle of auburn hair and bent even closer to get a good look. Set on a black velvet cushion, the skull cup was horrifying, sensational, and awe inspiring, all at the same time.

"I assume this bizarre little beauty belonged to a pirate," said Drayton, "though a diamond of such magnitude was no doubt plucked from the necklace or bracelet of some hapless noblewoman who ventured onto the high seas." He straightened up and gave a quick smile.

"Gives new meaning to the phrase *killer diamond*," Theodosia responded. She could just imagine standing on the foredeck of one of His Majesty's clipper ships, bound for Charles Town and a new life in the New World. Then gray mists parted, a giant black galleon rose up, and screaming pirates bore down upon you. Grappling hooks clamped the rails, murdering brigands swung onto your ship to . . .

Theodosia shook her head, aware that her overactive imagination had carried her far, far away, into a different, high-adventure realm. Then again, Theodosia looked like she might have slipped in from an earlier century. Her abundance of auburn hair could have inspired Raphael; her fair English skin seemed tempered by the cool, rainy weather of the Salisbury Plain. Theodosia's blue eyes sparkled with barely contained energy, and her face, with its high cheekbones and full mouth, was agile and expressive. Theodosia never bothered to keep a tight rein on her passions, whether they be ire or mirth. She wore her heart and her feelings on her sleeve and crashed through life at full tilt.

Drayton slipped on a pair of tortoiseshell half-glasses and inclined his dignified, graying head. "Let's read the description card for this oddity," he mumbled to himself. He was a sixty-something history buff who loved nothing better than to delve into the provenance of an obscure object.

"What's it say?" asked Theodosia. She smiled to herself at Drayton's bounding enthusiasm. He was an almost-partner, dear friend, and quirky sidekick. Not necessarily in that order.

"Whoa-ho," said Drayton, nodding his head with approval. "This wasn't just owned by a pirate, it *is* a pirate!"

"Excuse me?"

"Says here it's reputed to be Blackbeard's skull." Drayton took a step backward and blinked in surprise. "My goodness."

"Are you serious?" said Theodosia. Blackbeard was, after all, the big daddy of pirates. A man with dozens of grisly legends attached to him and a fierce and fascinating character who'd entertained and inspired for practically two centuries.

Growing up in Charleston and the surrounding low country, Theodosia had heard endless tales about the swashbuckling pirates and brigands who'd plied the Carolina coast right up until the nineteenth century. Many had roamed all the way from South America up to Canada, terrorizing merchant and passenger ships and enjoying a wild, freewheeling life on the high seas. Some had been captured by U.S. naval ships and met their fate on a gallows just a few blocks from here, on the Battery near White Point Gardens. Of course, the gallows was long since gone, while the gardens were now a frothy riot of magnolias and dogwood.

"I had no idea Timothy possessed such an amazing collection of pirate memorabilia," said Theodosia. Timothy Neville was the director of the Heritage Society, a crusty octogenarian who had a knack for twisting donors' arms and a keen, calculating memory that could recall exactly which old skeletons lay in uneasy repose in which Charleston attics.

"Although the Heritage Society owns a few of these pieces, most are actually on loan," Drayton explained. "Cajoled from antique dealers and private collectors."

"Really quite spectacular," said Theodosia, leaning forward to admire gold doubloons that spilled from an old wooden chest, a parchment map that depicted the Carolina coasts and shipwreck locations, and other maps that hinted at where treasure might still be buried. And, of course, there was that ubiquitous collection of pirate flags.

"I'm also told," said Drayton, "that this show was inspired by one of the curators stumbling upon an interesting stash of pirate memorabilia in the downstairs storage rooms. Items they didn't even realize were in their possession!"

"This show really does have the wide appeal of a museum blockbuster," said Theodosia. "I mean, who doesn't like pirates?"

"They *are* fascinating," agreed Drayton.

"Blackbeard and Bluebeard," said Theodosia. "And Captain Jack Sparrow." She chuckled as she glanced around. Though Theodosia had been immediately swept up in pirate legend and lore, most of the guests here tonight seemed much more focused on the champagne and hors d'oeuvres that were being served by tuxedoed waiters out in the great hallway.

As if to underscore her thoughts, a piercing shriek suddenly echoed through the almost-empty gallery.

"Good grief!" said Drayton.

Theodosia and Drayton turned in unison to find Delaine Dish and her crazy sister, Nadine, running playfully toward them. Close on Nadine's heels was Bill Glass, the scummy editor of an even scummier weekly tabloid known as *Shooting Star*.

"Theo-*do*-sia!" Delaine demanded, in her strident, pay-attention-to-me voice, "you're missing all the fun!" Delaine was the owner of Cotton Duck clothing boutique and a confirmed social gadabout. With her heart-shaped face, swirl of dark hair, and piercing eyes, Delaine was a striking beauty. Yet her appeal was undermined by her abrasiveness and constant need to know.

"You're missing the show," Drayton replied in a curt tone.

Delaine gave a clumsy shrug, splashing a few drops of champagne onto her pale yellow suit. "Oops. Clumsy me," she said, obviously a little tipsy.

Nadine, who was dressed in a bright purple suit, giggled loudly. "Maybe you should give us a quick lecture, Drayton. After all, you're on the board of directors here."

"Yeah," said Bill Glass, gesturing offhandedly at one of the displays, "tell us about these crazy black-and-white flags."

"The Jolly Roger," said Drayton, pulling himself to full height, "is derived from the French phrase *jolie rouge*, meaning 'pretty red.'"

But they really weren't listening. Instead, Delaine had her nose pressed tightly against a glass case, gazing starry eyed at a glittering array of gold doubloons.

"Pirate's booty," she murmured.

At which point Bill Glass slung his arm around Nadine's waist and gave a wolfish grin. "This is *my* idea of booty!"

This was followed by shrieks of uproarious laughter from both Delaine and Nadine.

That did it for Drayton. Disorder and double entendres in the hallowed halls of the Heritage Society were high treason to him. He clenched his jaw so tightly the muscle quivered and his brows shot up. With a stoic yet pained expression, he turned to Theodosia and said, "Time for a refreshment?"

Theodosia immediately agreed. "My thought exactly."

"A terrific show," Theodosia told Camilla.

"Very impressive," offered Drayton.

Camilla Hodges, the Heritage Society's office-manager-slash-secretary-slash-membership-director gave an appreciative smile. "Thank you," she said. "It took a fair amount of work to pull this off." Camilla was fifty-something with a waft of bluish hair and thighs that were permanently encased in Lycra. She was also enveloped by a constant cloud of perfume. But always a classic scent, like Shalimar by Guerlain or Joy by Jean Patou.

"You received some great publicity, too," said Theodosia. Before she stepped off the business merry-go-round to become chief bottle washer and proprietor of the Indigo Tea Shop, Theodosia had worked as an account executive in a large Charleston marketing firm. She'd waged constant war to snag her fair share of publicity and newspaper articles, so she knew how important the photo and accompanying blurb in the *Post and Courier* had been for the Heritage Society.

"Thank you," said Camilla, raising her champagne glass and clinking it against Theodosia's and Drayton's glasses. "Now that our budget's been snipped yet again, I think they've added the title of PR director to my already long list of responsibilities."

"Well, you did a masterful job," said Drayton.

Camilla reached out and grabbed the arm of a young man who was standing nearby and pulled him into their circle. "This is Rob Commers," she told them. "One of our history interns and all-around good guy who pretty much functioned as my right-hand man."

Rob, a string-bean, earnest-looking college kid who couldn't have been a day over twenty, blushed furiously.

"You're getting your degree in history?" Theodosia asked him.

"I am," said Rob. He had cropped dark hair and long dark eyelashes, the kind Theodosia would have killed for. "And since I've been interning here, I found out how much I don't know." He gave a rueful grin. "Which means I should probably go on for my master's."

"Nothing wrong with that," said Drayton.

"Rob was an enormous help in organizing this show," Camilla continued. "He did a fantastic job at handling the mailing list and invitations."

"It worked," said Theodosia. "Because you got a great turnout." Indeed, they were standing elbow to elbow in the great hallway.

"I just wish more guests were looking at the displays," said Camilla. Her brows puckered in a frown, and she shrugged. "What can you do?"

"I'm afraid it's see and be seen," said Theodosia. Much as she loved Charleston, it was largely populated by social animals. Folks who wanted to go out, rub shoulders with others, be recognized, and get their photo in the society section. Nothing wrong with that, of course, except for the fact that you could end up rubbing shoulders with the same old shoulders week after week.

"Maybe we could somehow cajole a few guests to take a quick peek in the gallery?" suggested Drayton.

"Better wait until Delaine and Nadine come out," said Theodosia. Then she caught sight of Delaine's heart-shaped face and flashing violet eyes and said, "Oh, here she comes now."

"What if we turned down the lights in the gallery?" suggested Rob. "Make it a little more sexy and inviting."

"Not a bad idea," said Theodosia. "Just have the overhead pinpoint spots on." She recalled the spectacular jade exhibit in Chicago's Field Museum where the lights were positively cocktail lounge low. But the moody, intimate atmosphere packed visitors in like crazy.

Camilla grabbed Rob's elbow and said, "We'll be back in a minute. As soon as we find the rheostat."

"We'll save you a lobster roll," said Drayton, eyeing an approaching waiter who carried an overflowing tray of appetizers.

"And maybe a cream cheese wonton," said Theodosia, as the waiter stopped and tilted his tray toward them.

"Fantastic!" exclaimed Drayton, helping himself to a small, golden roll.

"Better yet," said Theodosia, grabbing a bright blue toothpick, "I'm going to have one of these lovely pink shrimp." But just as she stabbed a giant cooked shrimp, there was a loud shatter of glass followed by a bloodcurdling scream!

2

❧⚜❧

Stunned, Theodosia dropped her shrimp and shoved her champagne glass into Drayton's outstretched hand. Then she spun about and sprinted for the gallery. Just as she reached the doorway, she collided head-on with Nadine, who had rushed out, screaming bloody blue murder and jigging wildly as if possessed by demons.

"She's, she's, she's . . . !" jabbered Nadine.

What's going on?

Theodosia placed her hands firmly on Nadine's shoulders and shoved her to one side. She was faintly aware of an exit door slamming and a loud security buzzer going off.

"Don't g-g-g-g-g—go in!" Nadine stuttered as she dropped to her knees.

Theodosia stared into the newly dimmed gallery and took in the horrific scene. Camilla Hodges was sprawled on the floor, moaning and making feeble motions with her legs, as if she were trying to run in slow motion.

Rob, the intern, lay in a crumpled heap just beyond Camilla!

"Dear Lord," muttered Theodosia. She was at Camilla's side in a heartbeat, grabbing her hand and feeling for a pulse. Camilla had one, but her eyes were fluttering and she seemed about to descend into unconsciousness.

"Call 911!" Theodosia barked out, then turned to see a dozen terrified faces staring blankly at her. "Call 911 now!" she barked again. "We need an ambulance!" She glanced over at Rob. "Two ambulances!"

The security buzzer was still buzzing frantically as everything seemed to descend into slow-motion chaos. Feeling like she'd suddenly fallen down an unwelcome rabbit hole, Theodosia pulled herself up, stumbled to Rob, and tried to do a quick assessment. Tried to remember what she'd learned in her long-ago Girl Scout first-aid course.

Because the situation wasn't good.

Rob was barely breathing and blood seemed to be leaking from his side in copious amounts.

Stabbed? He's been stabbed?

The notion finally registered in Theodosia's overstimulated brain. "He's been stabbed!" she shrilled.

Drayton was suddenly kneeling beside her, ripping off his Brooks Brothers tie.

"Use this," he told her. "Try to squelch the bleeding."

Theodosia fumbled with Drayton's tie, rolling it into a ball, then pressing it firmly against Rob's side. "Ambulance?" she asked, her teeth chattering.

"On its way," Drayton told her.

Blood continued to leak out. "This is bad," Theodosia told him. "It's real bad." She knew she was babbling a little bit herself. "Got to keep the pressure on. Got to keep . . . is the ambulance coming?"

"On its way," Drayton said again. He looked gray and stricken, as if he'd been injured himself.

Theodosia pushed the bunched-up tie harder against Rob's wound. "Camilla?" she asked.

"Being taken care of," said Drayton.

"This kid is barely breathing," Theodosia murmured. "Blood's leaking out of him like crazy!" Drayton's tie was warm with blood and completely soaked through now. "We need something else, something better. A towel maybe . . ."

Somebody passed her a black pashmina, and Theodosia hastily wadded it up and pressed it against Rob.

But like sand from an hourglass, the blood continued to ooze from Rob's injured body. Fifteen seconds later, Theodosia stared down at his ashen face, at his long, soft eyelashes, and felt the life go out of him.

"Noooo!" Theodosia moaned, rocking back on her knees. "Noooo!" Just as she let loose her mournful howl, the buzzer suddenly, mercifully stopped.

Drayton's hand was on Theodosia's shoulder, pressing gently. "The boy's gone, Theo. You did everything you could. You did everything right."

"Maybe the ambulance guys . . ." Theodosia cried, unwilling to give up. "The EMTs, they're trained for . . ."

Drayton reached a hand forward and gently closed Rob Commers's eyes.

"You're sure?" asked Theodosia. "You're absolutely sure?" Her voice was racked with emotion, her face damp and streaked with tears.

Drayton nodded silently.

"But why?" Theodosia wailed.

"That's why." The scratchy, otherworldly voice of Timothy Neville floated above her. Timothy might have run the Heritage Society with an iron fist, but no amount of will or power could undo this terrible deed. He'd stumbled into the gallery, looking like a broken old man.

"Dear Lord!" Drayton cried to Theodosia. "Timothy's right. Look at the case!"

Startled, reeling from the assault on Camilla as well as Rob's bizarre, untimely death, Theodosia lifted her head and gazed at the glass case.

The square display case was shattered, as if it had been battered with a heavy instrument. The lower shelves were littered with shards of glass.

And the skull cup with its large diamond was nowhere in sight!

Theodosia was aware of people pressing close to her, of whispers and anguished murmurs. She stared at Drayton. "This is bad."

His head bobbled in agreement.

"I mean," she stammered out, "this is a crime scene. We have to get everyone out of here."

As if she'd commanded it, three uniformed officers suddenly rushed in.

"Thank goodness," Drayton muttered, as the officers took charge and the crowd was pushed back.

"Camilla!" Theodosia cried suddenly. She turned from where she was still kneeling and saw a woman on the floor next to Camilla, holding her hand and whispering to her. "Is . . . is Camilla all right?"

"She's in and out of consciousness," said the woman. "Looks like she got a very nasty knock to the head. I'm a nurse," the woman added. "I'll stay with her until the ambulance arrives."

Theodosia looked down at Rob. One of the officers was kneeling across from her, checking vitals. "Gone," was all he said.

Theodosia turned pleading eyes on Drayton. "Where's the ambulance?"

He pulled himself to his feet, then helped Theodosia up. "Should be here any second."

There was the sudden, sharp wail of a siren, then Timothy said, "It's coming, it's coming." He looked frail and nervous, almost on the verge of collapse.

The dozen or so people left in the room seemed to hold their collective breath in anxious anticipation. There were three short yips from the siren, signaling an impending approach, and then a tremendous screech of brakes and grinding clash of metal!

"Good grief!" exclaimed Drayton.

Theodosia touched a hand to her heart to find it beating like a timpani drum. Please, she prayed to herself, don't let another person be hurt! She tottered two steps, then hesitated as Delaine suddenly flung herself into the gallery.

"There's been an accident!" Delaine keened. "A three-way collision!"

"Oh, no!" Theodosia murmured.

"What now?" said Drayton.

There were a few more minutes of pandemonium, and then two EMTs rushed in with a clanking gurney. As everyone watched silently, one of the EMTs put a stethoscope to Rob's chest, then shook his head. They moved on to Camilla, who was barely breathing, hastily put an oxygen mask on her face, then carefully transferred her to the gurney and carried her out.

Poor Rob still lay where he'd been felled.

"We need another—" Theodosia called after the departing crew, then suddenly snapped her mouth shut.

Like an angry bull in a china shop, Detective Burt Tidwell lurched into the gallery. He was a big bear of a man with a weather balloon stomach and bullet-shaped head. Bushy brows topped slightly protruding and belligerent eyes. Head of the Robbery-Homicide Division, Tidwell was short-tempered, blunt, and a pit bull of an investigator.

But tonight, as he took in the gallery scene, Tidwell looked seriously shaken up. His legs quivered unsteadily and his eyes seemed slightly unfocused. An angry gash split one side of his wide forehead and bright red blood trickled down.

"What happened?" Theodosia cried.

"What happened *here?*" Tidwell demanded. He staggered backward two steps, his beady eyes taking in Rob's body and the shattered display case.

"Murder," said Theodosia.

"And theft," added Drayton.

"Detective," said Timothy Neville, regaining some composure as he approached Tidwell, "you were in an accident?"

Tidwell shrugged and waved a pudgy hand. "Got sideswiped . . . it was nothing. Stupid. An ambulance, my car . . . another guest attempting to leave."

Theodosia stepped forward. She knew Tidwell and liked him. Respected him, in fact. But this was no time for him to gut it out. He was bleeding and looked ready to collapse.

"Detective," said Theodosia, "I think you need medical attention."

"Nonsense," Tidwell replied, in a brusque but quavering tone.

But Tidwell was growing paler with every second that ticked by.

"Can we get another EMT in here?" Theodosia asked Timothy.

Timothy nodded and spun away.

"It's *nothing*," Tidwell reiterated, looking angry and annoyed. "Just a silly, stupid accident." He took a step forward, looking at the fallen body of Rob Commers. Then he reached inside his jacket and pulled out a white hanky. He held it to the side of his head for a few moments, then took it away. Red, sticky blood clotted the hanky.

"Perhaps," said Theodosia, "we should call in another homicide detective. Just for the time being."

Irritation and agreement were mingled on Tidwell's broad face as he swayed unsteadily. Then he said in a hoarse voice, "Possibly . . . you're right."

Another ambulance arrived within minutes. The EMTs ministered to Tidwell first, while two crime-scene guys bagged, tagged, and photographed Rob's body as well as the shattered case. Theodosia, Drayton, and Timothy looked on silently from the hallway. Finally, the EMTs were allowed to file into the gallery to load Rob's lifeless body onto a gurney. Slowly, silently, they slid it past the cadre of onlookers and out to the ambulance.

"What a night," breathed Drayton, turning his back on the gallery.

"Awful," sighed Timothy. "Our patrons are going to . . ."

Theodosia didn't hear the rest of Timothy's words. She stood there, staring morosely into the empty gallery, letting everyone file past her. When the voices had faded completely, she reentered the gallery, walking stiffly, her heart heavy. She stared at the shattered case, the bloody carpet, and the pirate flags that winked slyly at her.

"Shocking," she muttered, then turned to go. The pin-point spots glimmered overhead, turning the hundreds of tiny glass shards that lay underfoot into brilliant crystals.

Plus one small flash of orange.

What?

Theodosia bent down and swiftly scooped up a small piece of paper. She stared at it and frowned. It looked like a ticket.

A ticket? Whose ticket? Who could have dropped this?

And, suddenly, like a light piercing the wilderness, her brain responded with a nasty possibility. *The murderer?*

3

Awful," Timothy Neville murmured in a thin, reedy voice. "Simply awful."

Monday morning had dawned sunny and bright in Charleston with a dazzling blue sky. A lazy breeze wafting in from the Ashley River brought delicious hints of springtime warmth and stirred palm fronds up and down historic Church Street. But inside the Indigo Tea Shop, the mood was morose.

"More tea?" asked Drayton. Without waiting for anyone to answer, he hefted a Chinese red teapot and poured a steady stream of amber liquid into Timothy's cup. "A Grand Pouchong from Taiwan," he said in a quiet voice, "meant to calm the nerves and fortify the spirit."

"I think we could all use a little fortifying today," Theodosia agreed. Timothy had shown up at their front door first thing this morning, dressed impeccably as always in a dove-gray suit and yellow Versace tie. His mood hovered somewhere between mournful and despondent, yet he was obviously eager to talk. So now, instead of prepping the tea shop for a busy Monday morning and looking forward to a busy week, Theodosia and Drayton were seated at a small round table next to the stone fireplace, puzzling through last night's terrible events.

Timothy lifted a gnarled hand to his forehead and touched it softly, as if to indicate mental stress or the stirrings of a nasty migraine headache. "What is my board of directors going to say?" he asked with a downward-turned mouth. "Donations have slowed to a trickle these last couple of years. And now, with last night's fiasco . . ." He let loose a deep and mournful sigh.

Theodosia didn't much care about Timothy's board of directors. Boards came and boards went, and not much fundamentally changed within an organization. Rather, she was consumed by thoughts of Rob's death as well as the terrible beating poor Camilla had sustained.

"How is Rob's family going to cope?" Theodosia asked in a slightly arch tone. "Will Camilla make a full recovery?"

Drayton nodded. "Theodosia's correct. Our immediate thoughts should be with the two of them."

"I *know* that," Timothy said, in a testy voice. "I'm just trying to get a grasp of the total picture."

"As are we all," said Drayton.

Timothy pursed his lips. "There'll surely be repercussions and . . ." He stopped short as Haley Parker, Theodosia's young chef and baker par excellence, arrived at their table and breathlessly presented them with a plate of scones. This was followed by a footed glass bowl filled with poufy mounds of Devonshire cream.

"Sorry to interrupt," said Haley, giving a quick shake of her head and tossing back stick-straight blond hair. "Just thought you might enjoy some caramel scones." She ducked her head and added, "They're fresh from the oven."

"Thank you, Haley," said Theodosia. "They look wonderful." She reached for a fat, golden scone drizzled with sticky caramel and bits of chopped pecan and set it on her plate. It wasn't going to erase the terrible memory of last night, but it was going to be a lovely accompaniment to her tea.

Haley edged closer to the table, shifting her slim body from one Capezio-shod foot to the other. "Figure anything out yet?" she asked. Her youthful curiosity seemed revved to a fever pitch.

"No," said Timothy, in a flat, dismissive tone. He fluttered his fingers in an offhand wave, as if to shoo Haley away.

But Haley hung in there. Over the years, she'd exchanged her fair share of words with Timothy Neville and, unlike many of his big-buck donors, Haley wasn't the least bit intimidated by Timothy's money, power, or brusque manners.

"Because I was just wondering . . ." said Haley.

"Wondering what?" asked Theodosia. Officially, on paper, she was sole proprietor of the Indigo Tea Shop, but her little enterprise was run as an equal-opportunity tea shop. Everyone who worked there had a voice; everyone was treated with the utmost respect.

"I know you're awfully upset about that fellow who was killed last night," Haley continued.

"Rob," filled in Drayton.

"Right," said Haley. "And you're crazy worried over Camilla . . ."

Timothy stared at Haley with red-rimmed eyes. "Do you have something to add to this discussion? If so, kindly spit it out!"

To her credit, Haley kept her cool. "But nobody has a clue as to what really happened?" she asked.

"A murder happened," said Drayton. "And a very close call."

"Do you know what Detective Tidwell's take was on the whole thing?" Haley asked. "You mentioned that he was there last night, that he got the call out personally." Theodosia and Drayton had filled Haley in on most of last night's events just before Timothy had shown up.

"Detective Tidwell was involved in a car accident!" Timothy snapped. "And required medical attention. How helpful was that?" he asked, in a petulant tone.

"Tidwell *was* a sort of casualty," acknowledged Drayton.

"Then who do you think will head the investigation?" asked Haley.

"Search me," said Drayton. "Hopefully the Charleston Police have a whole roster of smart detectives."

"I think Tidwell will be back on the job," offered Theodosia. He hadn't looked like he'd been badly injured. A scrape and shaken up for sure, but more of a bruised ego than actual body bruises.

"Tidwell will have to play catch-up," predicted Timothy.

"That's not good," said Drayton.

Haley's eyes danced crazily. "But Theodosia wouldn't."

"Excuse me?" said Timothy.

"I mean, she was there, right?" said Haley.

"What are you getting at, Haley?" asked Drayton.

But Theodosia already knew.

"Oh, no . . ." said Theodosia. She set her scone down and brushed her hands nervously against her black Parisian waiter's apron, focusing on tiny particles of sugar that danced and twinkled and caught the light like a miniature galaxy.

Timothy swallowed his sip of tea with a gulp and suddenly fixed his eyes hungrily on Theodosia. "Yes," he said. "You were right there. First one in, in fact."

"No," Theodosia said again.

But Timothy had grasped the notion like a bird dog with its teeth set into its quarry. "Theodosia, we need your help. *I* in particular need your help. You're . . ." Timothy paused, looking contemplative for a few moments, then finished his sentence with, "You're good at puzzling things out."

"She certainly is," agreed Drayton.

Theodosia shot Drayton a warning look. A look that said, *Kindly leave me out of this!*

"Sorry, Theo," said Drayton, "but the fact remains, you *do* have a certain nuanced way of looking at things. At solving puzzles."

"Nuanced?" said Theodosia. What the heck was that supposed to mean?

"Focused, then," said Drayton. "Strategic."

Theodosia picked up her knife and busied herself by splitting her scone lengthwise, then slathering on a little too much Devonshire cream. "Oh, that," she said in a soft voice. "The truth of the matter is, I get lucky sometimes."

But Timothy was shaking his head. "No, it goes well beyond luck," he told her. "You're clever. And blessed with a real knack for figuring things out."

"Detective Tidwell doesn't think so," said Theodosia. "He thinks I'm a meddler."

"That's *his* point of view," said Timothy. "Being a trained professional, he pretty much has to vehemently oppose any civilian who has the same skill sets he does."

"Precisely," said Drayton.

"You really do need to get involved in this," Haley urged Theodosia. "I mean . . . jeez . . . have you guys seen this morning's headlines?"

All three gazed at her with blank expressions.

"Oh, boy," said Haley, her eyes going wide. She held up a forefinger, then dashed to the front counter, grabbed the *Post and Courier*, and returned. Grimacing, she unfurled the paper with a reluctant flourish. The four inch-high headline, BLACKBEARD'S CURSE, jumped out at them. And under it in slightly smaller type, BLOODY MURDER AT PIRATE EXPO.

"Ghastly!" exclaimed Drayton. "Exactly what we don't need."

"My directorship is finished now," sighed Timothy. He dropped his head in his hands and remained motionless for a few moments.

"Timothy?" said Theodosia. "Are you okay?"

Timothy lifted his head and faced her with a defeated expression. "No. Not in the least."

It broke Theodosia's heart to see Timothy so upset. She knew he was terrified of losing his position as director of the Heritage Society. Knew if that happened, it would mean the end of him. Timothy was a proud old man who carried out his duties with every fiber of his being. To strip him of his directorship would surely send him into a downward spin. And at his age . . .

Theodosia sat for a minute, thinking. Then she took a big gulp, a reluctant gulp, and said, "Um . . . what would you actually want me to do?"

A spark seemed to ignite in Timothy's slate-gray eyes. "Perhaps just . . . look into things?" he asked in a hopeful voice.

"Dear girl," said Drayton, turning to face Theodosia, "if you can help in any way . . ." He removed a pair of tortoiseshell half-glasses from the pocket of his jacket, perched them owlishly on his aquiline nose, then took the paper from Haley. After fifteen seconds of scanning the front page, Drayton said, "According to the police commissioner, they haven't narrowed it down to any particular suspect."

"That's because they don't have *any* suspect," said Haley.

"Typical," said Timothy.

"I can't believe that," said Theodosia. "They must have some clue about where to start looking." At least she hoped they did.

"No," said Drayton, as he continued to mutter over the article, looking more and more unhappy. "It says here they may have a witness, but that witness seemed slightly befuddled." He stabbed at the paper with his index finger. "Befuddled. That's quoting the writer verbatim."

Theodosia knew they had to be referring to Nadine. And they probably weren't far off. Nadine had been crazy and overwrought last night, and that was putting it mildly.

"Then it's all over," said Timothy, in a defeated tone. "Over before we've even begun."

Haley edged closer. "What about the skull drinking cup?" she asked in a quiet voice.

Theodosia's brows pinched together. "What about the skull cup, Haley?"

"Maybe that's where you should start," said Haley. "That's what the thief—the murderer—was really after, right? I mean, you said it belonged to Blackbeard."

"*Was* Blackbeard," said Drayton. "The cup was supposedly created from his actual skull."

"What are you all getting at?" Timothy asked, in a tremulous voice.

"Haley may be right," said Theodosia, as a tiny spark of an idea ignited in the back of her brain. "If we knew a little more about the skull cup, we might be able to look at last night from a slightly different perspective."

"You mean from a historical perspective?" Drayton asked. "Or look at a possible motive and try to track down the killer?"

"We really don't want to attempt apprehending a murderer on our own," said Theodosia.

"Good point," said Drayton.

"But we could look at the basics," said Theodosia, warming up to the idea. "We could study the facts at hand and see where they take us. For instance, could the skull cup possibly be authentic? If so, where did it come from? Is it a rare collectible? And, if so, who would want it?"

Drayton threw Timothy a questioning glass. "Where *did* the skull cup come from?"

Timothy took a quick sip of tea. "You mean initially? Before it was donated to the Heritage Society?"

"That's right," said Theodosia, putting a note of encouragement in her voice.

"No idea," said Timothy.

Theodosia shook her head. How could he not know? He

was the director of the Heritage Society and the thing had been pulled from his own vast storeroom. "You must have *some* knowledge of the piece," she said. "After all, you thought it was significant enough to include in your show. And someone typed up a fancy little description card."

Timothy pursed his lips, suddenly looking put upon. "To the best of my knowledge, that skull cup was donated some forty years ago, long before I even assumed directorship of the Heritage Society. Apparently it had been rattling around in storage until one of our curators pulled it out for the Pirates and Plunder show."

"Which curator?" asked Haley. "That guy Rob?"

"No, no," said Timothy. "Rob wasn't a curator, he was one of our interns. A good boy, working toward his degree in American history. No, he only assisted George Meadow. Meadow curated the show while Rob did the grunt work—sending out invitations, checking guest lists, that sort of thing."

"We have to look at that guest list," said Theodosia.

"Not a problem," said Timothy.

"So Rob had nothing to do with the skull cup?" Theodosia asked. She wondered, could an intern, working for little or no money, have hatched a dramatic robbery plan? Then could he have gotten burned in carrying out that plan? Could an unknown accomplice have done a one-eighty on him?

"None of us had much to do with the skull cup in general," said Timothy. "Except agree that it was an interesting piece."

"Are there other interns?" asked Theodosia.

Timothy nodded. "Yes."

"We need to talk to them," said Theodosia.

"Where are you going with this?" asked Timothy.

"A skull with that kind of history attached to it," said Theodosia, "embedded with a diamond that size . . ." She closed her eyes halfway, trying to conjure up a visual reference of the skull and fix it in her memory. "It must be worth a small fortune."

"Though the piece was truly dreadful," Drayton murmured.

"But more than a few people were aware that skull cup was in your collection," said Theodosia.

"They were since last Wednesday," said Timothy, "when the *Post and Courier* featured the skull cup in a photo montage."

"Just bad luck," said Drayton.

"You told me it was *good* publicity," Timothy snapped. "You seem to have changed your tune drastically!"

Drayton's mouth opened and closed soundlessly, and then he regrouped and said, "Perhaps someone attended the pirate show, saw that massive diamond, and . . . bam! They were spurred into action by simple greed!"

Theodosia leaned back in her chair, looking thoughtful. "For some reason, this doesn't feel like an impulse crime."

Timothy's head snapped in her direction. "Are you referring to the murder or the theft?"

"Both," said Theodosia. "Although my best guess is the theft was primary, while the murder was a spur-of-the-moment mistake. Committed out of . . . necessity."

"Excuse me?" said Drayton.

"So the thief could make a hasty and unimpeded escape," said Theodosia. "Through that fire door that, unfortunately, led out to your back patio."

Drayton put an index finger to his temples and rubbed, as if he suddenly had a splitting headache, too. "I hate to hear you talk like that."

"You were the one who wanted me to get involved," said Theodosia.

"And you're humming along already," said Haley, a note of pride in her voice. "Spinning some interesting theories."

"Do you have any information on that skull cup?" Theodosia asked again. "Any paperwork that might shed some light? Give us a place to start?"

Timothy looked dour. "Doubtful."

"Well, take a look anyway, will you?" said Theodosia. "It's important."

"Yes," said Timothy. "Of course."

"Then there's the matter of the ticket," said Theodosia.

Timothy's brows shot up. "Ticket?"

Theodosia reached into the pocket of her apron and pulled out the pale orange ticket. "I found this in the gallery last night." She twiddled it between her fingers. "Know what it is?"

"No idea," said Timothy.

"A ticket," said Haley. "For what?"

"I don't know," said Theodosia. "It looks to be homemade, possibly run off on a laser printer. Along with a seven-digit number, all it says is COMPLIMENTARY MEMBERS PASS."

"But a members pass to what?" asked Drayton.

"That," said Theodosia, "is what I intend to find out."

4

Theodosia *finally busied* herself with tea shop preparations, getting ready for the flurry of activity that pretty much occurred like clockwork every single day.

Battered wooden tables were graced with white linen tablecloths. Flickering tea lights were placed in glass votives. Antique sugar bowls, gleaming bone china plates and teacups, and tiny silver spoons and butter knives were arranged on each table.

Early this morning, Haley had stopped at the Church Street farmer's market and bought several bunches of white daisies. Now those cheery flowers bobbed their heads in crystal vases.

"Perfection," said Drayton, gazing out over the tea shop. "As always."

"The tea shop does look lovely," agreed Theodosia, "but my heart still feels heavy from last night."

"Understandable," said Drayton. "But at least we've taken the first step toward a resolution." His eyes fluttered, and then he corrected himself. "Actually, *you* have."

"Let's hope it's a step and not a stumble," said Theodosia, as the bell over the front door tinkled merrily, announcing the arrival of their first customer.

Except it wasn't a customer after all, but Leigh Caroll, the new owner of the Cabbage Patch Gift Shop. Leigh was an African American woman in her middle thirties, fairly close in age to Theodosia. She was tall, with beautifully burnished skin, sepia-toned hair, and almond eyes that turned up slightly at the corners, giving her an upbeat, mischievous look.

"Come on in, Leigh," said Drayton, giving a big wave from behind the counter.

"Leigh!" said Theodosia, delighted to see her friend. "Can I offer you a scone and a cuppa? We could brew your favorite peach oolong if you'd like."

"Excuse me," said Leigh, putting a hand on her hip and assuming an inquisitive expression, "but you've got some explaining to do, girlfriend."

"About . . . ?"

"I just talked to Lydia at the Chowder Hound who talked to Carol Ann at Boynton's Frame Store. And the word up and down Church Street is that you were at the Heritage Society last night when that poor boy was killed!"

"I *was* there," said Theodosia, "and it was awful! And Camilla Hodges, the office manager, was badly injured as well."

"You were a witness?" asked Leigh, curious now.

"Not really. I just sort of caught the tail end of the excitement."

Leigh's face crumpled, and she shook her head. "How could something like that happen?" she asked. "In the Heritage Society of all places? If you're not safe in a *museum*, then where are you safe?"

"I don't know," said Theodosia. "But it's a little terrifying when you feel . . . I don't know, the brush of death's wings against you?"

Leigh lowered her voice, since Drayton was still working

nearby, measuring out tea. "You went there last night with Drayton?"

Theodosia nodded. "You know how much he loves that place, since he's on the board and all."

"So I imagine Drayton's fairly shaken up? He being the strong yet sensitive type?"

"Pretty much," said Theodosia. "So's Timothy Neville. He stopped by earlier to toss his lamentations into the mix."

"Have the police worked up any theories?"

"Not according to this morning's paper," said Theodosia. "I guess we'll just have to keep our fingers crossed."

"And our doors locked," said Leigh. She inclined her head, and the two of them moved over toward an antique highboy that held a fine display of antique teacups, tins of tea, and jars of DuBose Bees Honey. "I got that Fitz and Floyd teapot you were interested in," Leigh said in a whisper. "The Florentine design with the fruit and gold inlay."

Theodosia reached out and grabbed Leigh's hand. "The one that's been retired for more than twenty years? The one you thought you'd never be able to locate?"

Leigh chuckled. "It took some doing, but I located one. But only one."

"You're a wonder!" said Theodosia. Then she lowered her voice again. "It's for Drayton, you know. For his birthday this Saturday."

"I know, honey," said Leigh, "which is why I went out of my way to hunt it down."

Twenty minutes later, the tea shop was more than half filled with customers. Then, a brightly painted red-and-yellow horse-drawn jitney clip-clopped to the front door and six more visitors came scrambling in.

Theodosia served caramel scones, zucchini bread, and

blueberry muffins, while Drayton brewed pots of English breakfast, Darjeeling, and Prince of Wales tea.

And just when the tea shop was all warm and cozy and redolent with the mingled scents of tea and scones, just when Theodosia was feeling decidedly optimistic, the phone rang. Her boyfriend, Parker Scully, was calling.

And he wasn't one bit happy.

"Are you *kidding* me?" Parker screeched loudly into Theodosia's ear. "Somebody was killed at the Heritage Society last night?"

"Afraid so," said Theodosia. She was hunched next to the front counter, whispering quietly into the phone, trying not to let her guests overhear—or guess at—the gist of her conversation.

"Theo, you go out for a quart of milk and somebody gets axed!" he shrilled.

"That's not true," she told him. "That's so unfair."

"Just do me a favor," said Parker. "Don't get involved."

Theodosia glanced down and saw that her knuckles were turning white as she gripped the phone.

"Did you hear me?" Parker asked.

"Um . . ." Theodosia stalled.

"No amateur sleuth investigations, okay?"

"Nothing amateur," she told him.

He seemed to breathe a sigh of relief, even though Theodosia was now firmly entrenched in a little white lie. *Oh well, it won't be my first and it surely won't be my last.*

"So, anything else on your mind?" Theodosia asked, hoping to sidetrack any more questions concerning last night's murder.

"Now that you mention it," said Parker, "there is. I know we talked about hitting that new oyster bar tonight, but it looks like I have to run down to Savannah. Remember that restaurant I told you about . . . the one I was thinking about buying a stake in?"

"Brandywine's?" She thought the name was corny, but she'd eaten there once and the food had been terrific.

"That's it exactly," said Parker. "Anyway, it seems the place is on the auction block sooner than expected. So I'm going to mosey down to meet the owner and talk terms."

"Sounds exciting."

"It is, and I promise I'll be back in time for your house-warming party."

"You're sure?" asked Theodosia. She had finally taken a giant leap of faith and bought a charming little English cottage a few doors down from the Featherbed House B and B. After months of wrangling and negotiations, she'd finally closed the deal and moved in. Though still in the throes of unpacking, decorating, and updating a ho-hum kitchen, Theodosia was bound and determined to throw a house-warming party this coming Wednesday evening.

"Theodosia?" said Drayton. He stood before her, a teapot clutched in each hand, obviously needing help. But Theodosia had one more call to make.

"I'm sorry," the woman at the hospital switchboard told her, "but at the moment we're not able to put any calls through to that patient."

Theodosia bit her lip. Did that mean Camilla's condition had worsened overnight? Or were the doctors just being guarded? "Do you have any information at all on Camilla Hodges?" Theodosia asked.

"Let me check," said the switchboard operator. There was a rustle of papers and then she came back on the phone. "Apparently her sister is with her and Ms. Hodges has shown some improvement. But there's a hold on all incoming calls until tomorrow."

"So I can call tomorrow," said Theodosia. "That's good news, right?"

"I would think so," said the operator in a kind voice.

Hope so, thought Theodosia.

* * *

"Here's the deal," said Haley. "For lunch we've got chive egg salad tea sandwiches on marble swirl bread, popovers stuffed with chicken salad, strawberry and field greens salads with citrus vinaigrette, and lentil soup." Haley dipped her wire whisk into a bowl of batter as they spoke, whipping it around frenetically like the rotor blades on a helicopter.

"That's it?" asked Drayton.

"And chai tiramisu for dessert," said Haley. She looked up suddenly. "Oh . . . if anybody's interested, the lentils are a special Orano variety. They exude a sweet, subtle flavor that's slightly reminiscent of chamomile."

"Then I shall brew a pot of chamomile tea," said Drayton. "As a charming accompaniment."

"With all that chamomile in the air, we're going to be so mellow we won't know what to do," said Theodosia. She and Drayton were hunkered in the doorway of their postage stamp–sized kitchen, while Haley did her daily chef's ballet of leaping from cutting board to cooler to their enormous black industrial stove. She was a baking whiz who could probably find work as a pastry chef at any number of Charleston's elegant hotels or B and Bs. Yet Haley remained a stalwart fixture at the Indigo Tea Shop, whipping up lunches, scones, and quick breads, as well as dessert treats that included such frothy offerings as chocolate mousse, rice pudding, and crème brûlée. To their regular tea shop customers, Haley was a quirky young woman with prodigious baking skills. To Theodosia she was a national treasure.

"So we can start taking orders now?" Drayton asked. The titles on his business cards may have been catering manager and master tea blender, but luncheons were squarely in Haley's domain.

"Go for it," said Haley. "But don't bring me all the orders at once; I don't want to get all befuddled and swamped."

"Haley says one thing but means another," Drayton said out of the corner of his mouth, as he and Theodosia headed back into the tea room. "She adores being busy because it challenges her multitasking skills. Gives her an incentive to try for her personal best."

Theodosia's eyes flitted toward the wavering glass panes of the front door, where two familiar shadows hovered. "Are you up for a challenge, too?" she asked.

Drayton's chin lifted a few millimeters. "I have no fear of trial by fire."

"Oh, no?" said Theodosia, as Delaine and Nadine suddenly charged into the tea room like a thundering herd of water buffalo.

"Oh, no," echoed Drayton. Then he managed a quick attitude adjustment and said, with a warm and friendly smile on his face, "Ladies, welcome!"

But murder was foremost on their minds, and Delaine and Nadine didn't waste any time bringing it up.

Delaine flipped open her copy of this morning's newspaper and crowed, "What a story! Now the Heritage Society will be on the tip of everyone's tongue!"

Drayton gazed at her with slightly hooded eyes. "And you think that's a *good* thing?" He was just this side of incredulous.

Delaine stabbed at the headline with a bloodred fingernail. "Publicity, any publicity, is highly beneficial."

"No," said Drayton, "it really isn't. In light of the fact than an intern was killed, poor Camilla was badly injured, and a valuable artifact was stolen."

Mouth pinched, eyes narrowed, Delaine gazed at Drayton with open hostility. Nadine immediately took up the cause and followed suit, glaring with all her might.

Seeing this as a bit of a standoff, Theodosia stepped in. "Let's get you two seated at a table, shall we? Are you interested in a little lunch? Perhaps a pot of Drayton's special Darjeeling tea?"

"Tea?" said Nadine, her hostility crumbling.

"Lunch?" said Delaine. Then she said, in a slightly grudging tone, "I suppose. As long as we're here."

"Step right this way," said Drayton, hustling them along now, trying to smooth things over. "We have a lovely table over here by the window." He pulled out captain's chairs, plumped up the cushions, and fussed appropriately as Delaine and Nadine settled in.

Theodosia hurriedly brought out a plate of scones and a small bowl of jam while Drayton skittered off, then appeared seconds later with a pot of tea. "Chun Mei organic tea with a sweet plumlike aftertaste," he told them.

"I think we're all a little jumpy because of last night," said Theodosia, still trying to inject a note of calm.

Letting loose a little shiver, Nadine suddenly grinned widely and said, "They said I saw the killer!" Her tone was just this side of boastful.

"Excuse me?" said Theodosia, as Drayton carefully poured out tea.

"In the newspaper article," said Nadine. "But you have to turn to where it's continued on the second page."

"The sidebar," said Delaine, trying to be of help.

"Nick Van Buren reported that I saw the killer!" said Nadine, giving another self-satisfied smile.

"Seriously?" said Theodosia. Somehow she'd missed that part.

Delaine thrust her newspaper toward Theodosia. "If you don't believe my sister, then see for yourself. Read the article!"

Theodosia shook her head. "No, it's not that I don't believe what's in the article, it's just that I didn't realize Nadine witnessed the . . . um . . . murder."

"Oh," said Nadine, a mousy grin creeping onto her face, "I really didn't."

"Am I missing something?" asked Drayton. "Either you saw the murder take place or you didn't. And if you were an actual witness, you should be huddling with the police and not whiling away your lunch hour here."

Delaine's high-pitched laughter suddenly overshadowed everyone's words. "Don't you people *get* it?" asked Delaine. "Nadine didn't really see *any*thing."

"That's right," Nadine giggled, "I just told the reporter that I did. I thought it would make for a juicier story."

"And you have to admit it does!" finished Delaine. The two sisters grinned at each other like a couple of pro athletes ready to high-five each other after the game-winning score.

"So you fibbed to the police, as well?" asked Theodosia. Seriously, was she missing the humor in this? *Was* there humor in this or were these two women totally bonkers?

"Oh, no," purred Nadine. "I didn't say word one to the police, since it was basically just a made-up story."

"Ah," said Drayton, "I see." But his wary tone indicated he really didn't.

Delaine's gaze slid sideways. "But she kind of saw *some*thing."

Nadine shrugged. "Maybe someone in a gray jacket."

"Did it ever occur to you," said Theodosia, feeling a rush of heat, "that the killer might be avidly reading the *Post and Courier* right this very minute?"

"Theo," said Delaine, her brows pinching together, "what *are* you getting at?"

How to explain this? Theodosia wondered. Then she decided to say it outright, to not mince words. "If the killer thinks Nadine was a witness to his crime, then he just might come back to take care of her!"

5

Delaine stared at Theodosia for a long moment as she digested her words. Then she made an airy, offhand gesture with her hand and said, in a clipped tone, "Doubtful."

"*I'm* not worried in the least," Nadine chimed in. "Fact is, fabricating my little story was just a fun thing to do. Case in point, we've been fielding dozens of calls all morning."

"Our customers at Cotton Duck find this quite exhilarating," said Delaine. "True crime and all that." She giggled, pleased with herself. "In fact, this sort of high drama is probably advantageous for business, considering I've got my Silk and Syrah event coming up in a matter of days."

Theodosia stared at Delaine, wondering how anyone who rescued stray cats, tirelessly raised money for the Alzheimer's Association, and glibly cajoled stodgy millionaires into contributing funds to the city's various food banks could be such a philistine concerning last night's murder at the Heritage Society.

Delaine, seeming to sense a hint of Theodosia's unease, said, "Don't be so glum, Theo! It was all in good fun."

"Fun," said Theodosia, in a flat tone.

Delaine dimpled prettily and said, "After all, we really came here to deliver some good news—news that will surely perk you and Drayton right up!"

"And what news is that?" asked Drayton, still wary.

Delaine smiled a conspiratorial pussycat grin at Nadine and said, "We want the two of you to help us plan a wedding!"

Theodosia took a step backward. "Who's getting married?"

Delaine's grin expanded as she leaned sideways and playfully nudged her sister. "Our dear, dear Nadine here is the lucky bride!"

"Goodness," said Drayton, obviously taken aback. "And the lucky groom is . . ."

"Bill Glass, of course," Nadine piped in, blushing crimson now.

"Really?" said Theodosia. Nadine and Bill Glass? Somehow, the two of them didn't exactly strike her as a match made in heaven. After all, they'd only been dating for . . . what? Two months? Which might be perfectly acceptable if they were keeping track in dog years.

Drayton was the first to recover his composure. "Congratulations are in order then, dear lady. Tell me, have you set a date?"

Nadine ducked her head. "Nooooo."

"Truth be told," said Delaine, "she's not *technically* engaged."

"Ah," said Drayton, nodding, "still picking out rings. That's certainly understandable."

"Actually," said Delaine, "Bill Glass hasn't asked her yet. But he will," she added hastily. "He will."

Up at the front counter, measuring scoops of Keemun tea into a blue-and-white Chinese teapot, Drayton said, "Did I miss something or am I just turning dotty in my old age? A wedding without a groom? An eyewitness who really didn't witness much of anything?"

"I don't think either story contains a kernel of truth," said Theodosia.

"You don't think . . . ?" Drayton glanced over his shoulder at Delaine and Nadine. "That fellow Glass . . . ?"

"If you ask me," said Theodosia, "Bill Glass exhibits all the telltale signs of a confirmed bachelor. He lives in a one-bedroom condo, uses his cheesy made-up press pass to mooch free drinks whenever he can, and never, ever dates a woman for more than a few weeks."

"And he publishes that awful tabloid," said Drayton. "Which makes him a terrible sleaze."

"I'm not saying there's *never* going to be a wedding," said Theodosia, "but I'm sure not going to hold my breath."

Ten minutes later, with Delaine and Nadine happily munching salads and tea sandwiches, Theodosia made another pass at them. She pulled the orange ticket from her pocket and asked, "Does this belong to either of you?"

Nadine glanced at the ticket and shook her head. Delaine peered suspiciously at the ticket and said, "Why are you asking?"

"Because I found it in the gallery last night," said Theodosia.

Now Delaine just looked bored. "You're thinking there was an actual witness?"

"Possibly," said Theodosia. "Or maybe the killer dropped it." She focused her gaze on Nadine. "Nadine, what can you tell me about last night? What did you actually see? Or think you might have seen?"

Nadine nibbled at her lip. "To tell the truth, I'm not completely sure. Everything happened so fast."

"Just relax," said Theodosia. "Let your mind go back to those last few moments in the gallery."

Nadine frowned and said, "Someone was wearing gray. I do seem to recall a gray jacket, so a man perhaps?"

"Or an unfashionable woman," said Delaine.

"A gray suit?" asked Theodosia. "Or maybe more casual, like a sweater?"

Nadine suddenly threw up her hands in frustration. "I don't know! Stop pressuring me! All your questions just make me feel stressed and uncomfortable!"

"Perhaps this can wait?" asked Delaine, blotting a linen napkin against her lips and leaving a greasy red smear. "It's not exactly the best time for questions."

"I'd say it's the perfect time," said Theodosia. "While things are still fresh in Nadine's mind."

But Nadine was shaking her head furiously. "Honestly," she said, "my head's completely spinning." When Theodosia looked dubious, Nadine added, "Probably from being swept off my feet!"

Swept off her feet? Theodosia thought to herself. *By Bill Glass?* This was a man who was boorish, rude, insensitive, and sexist. And those were some of his better qualities.

Nadine touched a hand to her head. "It's just so very difficult to think," she mumbled.

"Try," said Theodosia. But Nadine clamped her lips together and refused to answer any more questions.

Theodosia was sitting at her desk in the back office, pondering the clutter atop her desk, sipping a cup of chamomile tea, when Timothy Neville called.

"I did manage to find a few bits of paperwork," Timothy told her.

"Paperwork . . ." Theodosia said, struggling to put his words into context.

"Concerning the skull cup," said Timothy. "Donation forms, that sort of thing."

"Oh, of course!" said Theodosia, straightening up in her chair. "That's great news. Can you bring everything over right away?"

Silence spun out for a few moments, and then Timothy said, "I'm afraid I can't manage that since my afternoon is completely jammed. Obviously, I need to stop by the hospital and check on Camilla, then speak with that poor boy's family."

"Okay," said Theodosia, thinking. "What about if you scanned everything and e-mailed it to me?'

More hesitation. Then Timothy said, "E-mail?" He said it as though he'd been asked to explain quantum physics in relation to black holes.

"Those interns you have?" said Theodosia. "They're young?"

"Just kids, really," said Timothy.

"Have them do it," said Theodosia. "They'll know how."

Theodosia hung up and flipped open a Marks & Madewell catalog. It was time to place another order for tea strainers, bamboo tea scoops, and tea thermometers. And she couldn't forget the organic sugar cubes that Haley loved to decorate. A couple of times a month, Haley would whip up her favorite frostings and fondants and squirt out miniature hearts, fleurs-de-lis, and floral motifs on top of sugar cubes. Adorable, of course, and always a delight to their tea party guests.

"Theodosia?"

Drayton stood in her doorway, looking a little grim.

"Now what's wrong?" she asked.

"That reporter is here," said Drayton. The word *reporter* rolled off his tongue as though he were talking about the Ebola virus. "Nick Van Buren. And get this, Haley thinks he's cute. In fact, she's plying him with tea and sandwiches and sugar cookies even as we speak." Drayton touched a nervous hand to his bow tie. "We have to do something."

"You're right," said Theodosia, "we can't have Haley making nice with our customers."

"You know what I mean," said Drayton, rolling his eyes.

"Van Buren's not a customer in the true sense of the word. He's here to poke and prod and ask questions. Make our lives miserable."

Theodosia stood up, untied her apron, and pulled it off. "It was only a matter of time, Drayton."

"Be nice," Haley called, as Theodosia whizzed past the kitchen door.

"I'm always nice," said Theodosia.

"Okay," said Haley, holding a wooden spoon in one hand and a jar of lemon curd in the other. "Just don't let Drayton start hissing and spitting like a crazed wombat."

"Drayton wouldn't do that."

"Sure he would," Haley called to her, as Theodosia continued on her way to meet the intrepid young reporter.

"Miss Browning!" Van Buren exclaimed, popping up from his chair like a manic gopher. "Great to see you. Thanks so much for your hospitality." Van Buren was in his late twenties and built like a football player, with dark hair and olive skin. He gestured to the luncheon plate Haley had fixed for him. "I didn't have time for lunch, so your chef Haley kindly rustled up some grub for me."

Theodosia glanced sideways toward the front counter and saw Drayton visibly flinch at the word *grub.*

"Haley's a charmer," Theodosia said, sliding into the chair across from Nick. She fixed a warm smile on her face and said, "Now, what can I do for you?"

Van Buren bobbed his head, as if that were the exact opening he was looking for. "I thought maybe I could pick your brain about the Heritage Society murder. I'm trying to find a new angle for tomorrow's story."

"Story," Theodosia said, in a neutral tone.

"Our Facebook and Twitter pages have been getting an unusually high number of hits and reader commentary, so my editor wants to keep churning this thing." Van Buren smiled, the dazzling smile of a young reporter who believed it was his God-given right to lob as many questions as he saw fit. "You know, keep running with it."

"I doubt I can add a single word to your story," said Theodosia. "From what I've read so far, you've pretty much covered everything." *And then some.*

But Van Buren was used to encountering roadblocks. He took his own sweet time and pulled a black leather-bound notebook from his jacket pocket and a pen from his shirt pocket. Then he flipped his notebook open and squinted at the page, as if he were lost in thought. Finally, he glanced up at Theodosia and said, "Who exactly did you see in the gallery when you went running in?"

"Rob Commers and Camilla Hodges," said Theodosia. "And, of course, Nadine . . . um . . ." Delaine's sister had been married and divorced so many times, she wasn't sure which last name Nadine was currently using.

"No," said Van Buren, smiling and shaking his head, as if he were amused, "I'm not talking about victims or witnesses, I mean anyone else."

"There wasn't anyone else," said Theodosia.

"From what I understand, you were the first person to actually respond," Van Buren persisted. "You rushed in fast and tended to Mr. Commers, so surely you saw *something.*"

"Just an exit door closing."

"The killer making his getaway," said Van Buren, putting a note of drama in his voice.

"Or *her* getaway," said Theodosia.

"You think it was a woman?"

"I really couldn't say," said Theodosia. "I didn't see enough to make a judgment call either way. People were injured, so that's where I focused my efforts."

"Are you aware that Nadine Dish was able to give a fairly decent description?"

"I know that's what you reported," said Theodosia.

"No, she actually *saw* someone," said Van Buren. "Which makes her the number one eyewitness."

"Okay," said Theodosia. "Sure."

"You don't believe me?" asked Van Buren.

"I believe you just fine," said Theodosia. "It's Nadine who worries me."

"Did you know," said Van Buren, "that the skull cup was reputedly used by a secret society that was located in either North or South Carolina?"

"Really," said Theodosia.

"That's right," said Van Buren. "I also discovered there are apparently three different skull cups."

"Let me guess," said Theodosia, "the owners all claim to own the original Blackbeard's skull?"

"How did you know that?" asked Van Buren.

"Just a wild guess," said Theodosia.

"But we don't know if the one stolen Sunday night was the real Blackbeard's skull."

Theodosia thought for a few seconds. "What we *do* know is that it had an enormous diamond embedded in it." She paused. "I'll bet the other skulls don't have that."

Van Buren gazed at her for a few long moments. "No, they don't."

"You didn't answer any of his questions," Haley said to Theodosia, once Nick Van Buren had left.

"But he answered one of mine," said Theodosia.

Haley frowned. "Which was . . . ?"

"I was wondering if there were any other so-called Blackbeard skull cups out there," said Theodosia. "And the answer is yes."

"So you kind of used him," said Haley.

Which caused Drayton to jump into the conversation. "Just because you're suddenly sweet on him, Haley, doesn't mean Theodosia has to dredge up an answer for every impertinent question."

Haley put her hands on her hips in a confrontational gesture. "Every time I'm remotely pleasant to someone, you're convinced I want to jump into a relationship with him. And that the guy is up to no good."

"That's because he probably is," said Drayton.

"Not true," said Haley. "Besides, I'm an adult. I make good judgment calls all the time."

"What about that motorcycle fellow you dated last year?" asked Drayton. "The one with the black leather jacket and ripped jeans who wanted you to ride to Alaska with him?"

"Smike," said Haley, smiling. "He was a really sweet guy."

"He was a homicidal maniac," said Drayton.

"Haley," said Theodosia, "could you check on our last table of customers? See if they need anything?"

"You're just trying to get rid of me," said Haley, but she cast her eyes toward Drayton.

"We wouldn't do that," said Theodosia.

"Sure we would," said Drayton.

"I'm going to go check my e-mail," said Theodosia, "and when I come back I hope the two of you will have reached a very friendly détente."

"Drayton and I don't need détente," said Haley, giving a snarky grin. "We get along like peas and carrots."

"I wish," Theodosia murmured, as she pushed her way through the velvet celadon-green curtain into her office.

A quick check of her e-mail revealed that Timothy, or one of his interns, had indeed sent the information over. She hit a button and her printer whirred for a few seconds, then spit out six pages of documents. Gathering them up, she carried the pages out to Drayton.

Haley was pouring tea and chatting happily with the two women still seated at the far table, so Theodosia slipped into a seat and beckoned for Drayton to join her.

"A cup of tea?" he called from behind the counter.

"Love one," she told him.

Drayton fussed for a few minutes, then brought two cups of tea to her table. "The Yu Huan tea," he told her as he sat down. "Jade Ring."

Theodosia took a quick sip. "White tea scented with . . . jasmine?"

"Well done," said Drayton, a note of approval in his voice.

Theodosia was building her tea repertoire and vocabulary by leaps and bounds, but still worried that she'd never know as much as Drayton. Of course, he'd grown up in Canton, China, the product of missionary parents, and had then worked for Croft & Squire Tea Ltd. in London. In his job he'd regularly commuted to Amsterdam, where the great wholesale tea auctions of the world were held.

"Let's see what we have," said Theodosia, spreading the papers out on the table. "Let's take a look at this stuff Timothy sent over and see if we can glean a few more bits of information."

They shuffled through the pages, reading hastily, passing them back and forth to each other.

"Listen to this," said Drayton, a note of excitement coloring his voice. "The skull cup was donated in 1968, as part of the Hector Pruett estate."

"The skull cup was donated by Hector Pruett himself?" Theodosia asked.

Drayton's brows pinched together as he continued to scan the papers. "No, his grandson. A man by the name of Sidney Pruett."

Theodosia tilted her head, thinking. "So who was this Hector Pruett to have such a crazy thing in his possession? Some kind of collector or antique dealer?"

"Don't know," said Drayton, still reading.

"Maybe the grandson, Sidney Pruett, is still around?" Theodosia proposed.

Drayton lifted his head. "Possibly. I've run across this name before and I'm positive there are Pruetts still living in Charleston. Maybe they're even . . ." He hesitated, thinking. "Donors to the Gibbes Museum of Art?"

"Could be," said Theodosia. She'd heard the name somewhere, too.

"Wouldn't it be weird," said Drayton, "if this Sidney Pruett or the Pruett family had wanted the skull back?"

"And masterminded the murder and heist last night?" said Theodosia.

Drayton tilted his head, thinking. "Mmm . . . something like that."

"Sounds far-fetched," said Theodosia. "I think it'd be a whole lot easier to simply petition the Heritage Society and get them to deacquisition the piece." She hesitated. "You can do that, right?"

Drayton's shoulders edged up a notch. "Search me."

"So what have we got so far?" Theodosia asked. "Nadine's somewhat foggy recollection of a man in a gray jacket. Or maybe a taller woman in a gray jacket . . ."

"And Timothy's paperwork," said Drayton. "Concerning the Pruett donation.

"And here's the guest list," said Theodosia, shuffling a couple of pages.

"Lots of invited guests," said Drayton, peering at it.

"Everybody and his brother," said Theodosia. "Plus, it was a public event, so anybody could have just waltzed in."

"Not much help," said Drayton, pushing the guest list aside.

"Here are the donation papers," said Theodosia.

Drayton pushed his glasses up onto the bridge of his nose and read. "Oh my," he said, after a minute had ticked by.

"What?" said Theodosia.

Removing his glasses, Drayton pinched the bridge of his nose between his thumb and forefinger. "I think Grandfather Pruett tried to sweeten the pot and make the Heritage Society more amenable to his donation."

"How so?" asked Theodosia.

"There's a sort of bio here on the skull," said Drayton. "It's basically a summary of how Blackbeard was defeated by a Lieutenant Robert Maynard at Ocracoke Inlet and got his head lopped off." He shook his head. "That much we know for a fact, but then it veers into supposition."

"You mean about the skull being made into a drinking cup."

"Right."

"Does it say whose imaginative idea that was?" asked Theodosia.

Drayton shook his head. "No."

"Anything about the diamond?"

"Again, no," said Drayton.

"So just a rousing good story," said Theodosia. "Which probably helped net the old man a decent tax write-off."

"Something like that," said Drayton.

"But still, not much to go on," said Theodosia. She'd hoped there'd be something in the Heritage Society's papers that would propel her in the right direction, but that didn't seem to be the case.

"Disappointing," said Drayton.

Theodosia thought for a minute. "We've still got the dropped ticket."

"There's that," said Drayton, but he didn't sound hopeful.

"What we need—" began Theodosia.

Bang. Bang. Bang.

"Is for that noise to stop," finished Drayton, a touch of irritation in his voice. "Whoever's out there should respect my CLOSED sign! After all, it's printed quite clearly in the King's English."

Another loud *bang* followed.

"We're closed," Drayton called.

Then the doorknob turned and the wooden door swung slowly open. And like a burly bear scouting a cave for hibernation, Detective Burt Tidwell stepped gingerly into the tearoom. His strangely shaped head swiveled as he scanned the room, revealing a large white bandage.

"Good heavens!" said Theodosia, jumping up. "I didn't expect to see you! Looks like you got quite a nasty bump last night! I hope you don't have a migraine or anything!"

"According to the doctors," said Tidwell, "I sustained an MTBI, also known as a mild concussion. Nothing to be unduly concerned about."

"Are you sure?" said Theodosia, "because anything with the word *concussion* attached to it sounds serious." She pulled out a chair for Tidwell and made a welcoming gesture. "Please, Detective Tidwell, sit down. Relax."

Tidwell took her advice and eased his bulk into the captain's chair. But he looked far from relaxed.

"A cup of tea?" Drayton asked, jumping into solicitous mode.

Tidwell gave a tacit nod.

"How about a caramel scone?" asked Theodosia. "I know we have a couple left."

Tidwell's nod was a bit more enthusiastic this time.

A few minutes later, as Tidwell slathered gobs of Devonshire cream onto his scone, they chatted about last night's murder.

"This is not a courtesy call," Tidwell informed them. "I'm interviewing everyone who was at the Heritage Society last night."

"Lots of interviews then," said Drayton.

"Let's say I'm talking to those who were in close proximity to the scene of the crime," Tidwell amended.

"Ah," said Drayton.

"We had a visit from Nick Van Buren earlier today," said

Theodosia. "He was asking questions as well, though I daresay he appears to be a step ahead of you."

"The press," snorted Tidwell. "I doubt they're breaking any new ground. But, pray tell, what exactly did you tell him?"

"Nothing," said Theodosia. "There's nothing to tell. Neither of us has a shred of information concerning last night."

"You disappoint me, Miss Browning," said Tidwell. "Usually by now you've ferreted out a clue or two."

"Nope. Sorry," said Theodosia.

"Except . . ." said Drayton, then quickly closed his mouth.

Tidwell stopped in midbite and let his beady eyes shift toward Drayton. "Except for what?"

"The ticket?" Drayton said, in a raspy voice. He glanced at Theodosia and added, "You really have to show him that ticket."

Theodosia reached into her pocket, felt around for it, then carefully placed the orange ticket in the center of the table.

Tidwell gave it a cursory glance, then went back to slathering more Devonshire cream on his already overloaded scone. A veritable tsunami of Devonshire cream.

"I found it in the gallery last night," Theodosia explained. "After everyone had left. I thought maybe . . . the killer had dropped it."

"Possible," said Tidwell, as he took an enormous bite then chewed thoughtfully, looking like an overgrown yet thoughtful chipmunk.

"All it says is COMPLIMENTARY MEMBERS PASS," said Theodosia. "No venue, no date."

"Mmm," said Tidwell, still chewing.

"Do you think you could take it back to your crime lab?" Theodosia asked. "Check for fingerprints or glue-fume it or something?"

Tidwell's enormous head moved from side to side in a gesture of pure exasperation. Then he swallowed hard and said, "You really have to stop watching *CSI*."

"Oh, please," said Theodosia. "You're just upset that I stumbled upon an actual clue."

Tidwell made a noise in the back of his throat, somewhere between a grunt and a groan.

"The thing of it is," said Theodosia, "we've made headway in other areas, too. We found out a few details about the missing skull cup."

"The one from the Hector Pruett estate," said Tidwell.

Theodosia rocked back in surprise. "You already know about that?"

"I was inconvenienced," said Tidwell, "not incapacitated." He popped the last bite of scone into his mouth and chewed thoughtfully.

"Well," said Theodosia, "maybe you could do some sort of search on the skull cup, too. Maybe look through police records, see if it was ever reported stolen?"

Tidwell stared at her. "And why would I do that?"

"Because," said Theodosia, "there are apparently other skull cups floating around. Owned by other museums. Maybe . . . well, maybe this is one of those."

"Excuse me," said Tidwell, drumming fat fingers on the table. "Who's running this investigation?"

Theodosia let loose a deep sigh. Why did it always have to be like this? Why did Tidwell always stall when it came to giving out the teeniest amount of information?

Tidwell's frown turned to a glower.

"You're running the investigation," said Drayton, stepping into the fray, trying to dispel some of the tension that hung sticky and electric in the air above their heads.

"Exactly," said Tidwell.

"You know," said Theodosia, deciding to come at Tidwell from a different angle, "Timothy Neville is awfully upset."

"Is he," said Tidwell.

"He's scared to death he might lose his directorship," said Drayton.

"Which is why," said Theodosia, "we'd appreciate being kept in the loop on this."

"There is no loop," said Tidwell. "I head the Robbery-Homicide Division, and I decide how each and every investigation is carried out." He wiped his lips delicately, pulled himself to his feet, then seemed to totter slightly.

Theodosia instinctively reached a hand out. "Are you sure you're okay?" she asked.

"Couldn't be better," Tidwell responded. He took a couple of moments to steady himself, then turned and slalomed toward the door.

"Detective Tidwell," Theodosia called after him.

Tidwell hesitated, his hand gripping the doorknob.

"I'd love it if you came to my housewarming party on Wednesday night."

Tidwell's head swiveled around. "You don't have enough guests already?"

"Of course I do," said Theodosia, "but the more the merrier."

Tidwell pursed his lips. "Doubtful."

6

❧

"I'm loving this," said Theodosia, as she stacked a pile of tinder in her fireplace, touched a match to it, and watched an orange finger of flame waver, then ignite into dazzling shades of yellow, blue, and orange. "Are you loving this?" She smiled into the soft, expressive brown eyes of Earl Grey, her canine buddy and Dalbrador mix. "Are you happy we finally have our own little home?"

Reclining on a slightly frayed blue-and-gold Oriental rug, Earl Grey cocked his head to one side and gave a speculative gaze.

"I realize," Theodosia continued, "that this is a far cry from our old apartment above the tea shop. But, if you recall, you did cast a yes vote toward our moving. Specifically, you were in favor of the fenced backyard. So you're still okay with everything, right?"

Tilting his muzzle up slightly, Earl Grey replied with a contented "Rwwr." *Right.*

"Thank you," said Theodosia, "because I think this place

is perfect for both of us." She added a slightly larger chunk of wood to her already blazing fire, then reached over and stroked the dog's right paw. "More room for you plus a very cozy home that's steeped in history. And you know what else?"

Earl Grey gazed at her with doggy seriousness.

"We're going to have a housewarming party here Wednesday night. So if you want to invite any doggy friends, please feel free. As long as they're exceptionally well mannered, that is. As well-mannered as you are."

Theodosia stood up, pulled her yellow cashmere shawl tighter around her shoulders, then looked around her living room and smiled.

She was hopelessly in love with her new home. But who wouldn't be? Gazing at it from the street side, it appeared as though a classic English cottage had been magically transported from the Cotswolds and plunked down smack-dab in the middle of Charleston. Rough cedar tiles replicated a thatched roof, the asymmetrical design lent a quirky appearance, and architectural details included a stone chimney, cross gables, arched doors, and a lovely turret. Whatever term you used to describe the little revamped carriage house—Hansel and Gretel cottage, Tudor, or Anne Hathaway style—the place was simply adorable.

Of course, the interior had also captured Theodosia's heart. A brick-floored foyer had walls of hunter green with antique brass sconces. The living room featured a high beamed ceiling, polished wood floor, and brick fireplace set into a wall of beveled cypress panels. And now that she'd arranged her chintz sofa and damask chairs, flopped out the Aubusson carpet, and hung a few paintings, the place had literally sprung to life.

"Remind me," said Theodosia, "to move the highboy in here for the party. We can use it as a kind of serving station for wine and cheese and things."

Earl Grey rose to his feet and stared at her.

"Oh," she said, "time to go?" She looked at her watch. "Wow. It's later than I thought."

Every night around ten, the two of them enjoyed an evening constitutional. Sometimes Theodosia pulled on her leggings and running shoes and they did a fast dogtrot through the tangle of back alleys that wove through the historic district. Sometimes they just strolled along leisurely, peeking into some of the fantastic Charleston courtyard gardens along the way, marveling at pattering fountains, crumbling antique statuary, and lush foliage that had been lovingly cultivated by various owners of the various neighboring mansions for well over a century and a half.

Tonight it was a ramble. Theodosia clipped a red leather leash to Earl Grey's red-and-blue plaid collar, what she called his business-casual collar, and together they headed out the back door. Winding their way through the small backyard that was crowded with dogwood trees and magnolias, they crept past a leafy web of vines that crawled up the back wall. As the pièce de résistance, a tiny fountain tumbled and burbled into a tiny oval pond that had been recently stocked with wriggling goldfish.

Stepping out into the alley, Theodosia carefully latched the gate to safeguard against marauding raccoons that might lumber in to stare beady-eyed at the fish and decide to make it their own personal sushi bar.

The night was chilly as Theodosia and Earl Grey set off. During the day, with the sun out in full force, spring was coming on like gangbusters, coaxing the local flora and fauna to bud and blossom like crazy. But evenings were still cool and damp, thanks to the fog that rolled in from the crashing Atlantic. Though this so-called marine layer softened the lights and gave everything a romantic, soft-focus appearance, the dampness could also cut to the bone.

"How was your new dog walker today?" Theodosia asked Earl Grey, as they quickstepped down the alley.

Earl Grey tossed his head, looking spunky.

When they'd lived above the Indigo Tea Shop, Theodosia could easily steal moments here and there for a quick stroll with Earl Grey. Now that she was a few blocks away, she'd hired a dog walker to drop by afternoons. Mrs. Berry, a retired schoolteacher from down the block, had lamented that she wanted to drop twenty pounds and saw Earl Grey as her ticket to daily enforced exercise.

"Did Mrs. Berry teach you your ABCs?" Theodosia asked him as they cut across Orange Street and headed down Tradd. "Is she secretly homeschooling you?"

Darting left, she cut down a narrow alley that had been built back in the days of the horse and carriage. Then they popped back out on King Street. This was the heart of the historic district, where grande dame homes hunkered shoulder to shoulder in grand and gracious splendor. Lovely Italianate homes with their arches, balustrades, and verandas. Victorian homes with their fanciful gables and gingerbread trim. And austere Gothic Revival homes with their pointed arches, buttresses, and stone tracery.

Amid all this grandeur was a labyrinth of back alleys and brick pathways that wound past carriage houses, service entrances, and gazebos. And there were narrow cobblestone walks that snaked between yards and outbuildings, too, making everything picturesque, contemplative, and a little mysterious.

Theodosia was thoroughly warmed up but breathing easy as they finally turned and headed down their own back alley. But twenty feet in, she suddenly became aware of footsteps.

Footsteps where? Behind me?

Hunching her shoulders forward, she continued walking, noting that Earl Grey, ears perked and crab-stepping slightly, had heard them, too.

Someone following me?

As Theodosia picked up the pace, the person behind her did, too. Though not easily prone to worry or panic, Theodosia kicked it into an even higher gear. And when she arrived at her back gate, she threw it open, ducked into her yard, drew breath, and paused. She glanced around, saw a garden spade glinting in the dark, and rested a hand on its wooden handle.

The footsteps came closer and closer until finally someone was directly across from her. Not wanting to panic, yet still not knowing all the local denizens, Theodosia called out a loud "Hello?"

She also tried to inject a note of authority along with a questioning tone. A tone that asked, *What exactly are you up to, anyway, out there in the dark?*

"Hey," answered a gruff male voice. Then a tall, dark-haired man swam into focus, and Theodosia breathed a small sigh of relief.

It was Dougan Granville, her neighbor, hotshot attorney-at-law, and the man she'd bought her home from. The seller. Granville had a well-deserved reputation as a pit bull in court and a man who was woefully short on any niceties. He was a tough negotiator who threw up tricky barriers and distractions. In other words, slippery when dry.

"How are you?" Theodosia asked Granville, trying to be friendly and feeling slightly guilty that she might have clobbered him by mistake.

Granville's answer was to stick an enormous cigar in his mouth, flip open his gold Cartier lighter, and puff mightily.

Argggh! Awful!

Blue plumes of smoke billowed from the suddenly lit cigar, polluting the night air and canceling out any subtle hints of magnolia that might have drifted across from her back garden. Granville continued to puff, his cheeks sucking in and out like a dying fish. Finally, he deigned to give an answer.

"Thank goodness you've done some planting," said

Granville, lobbing an offhand wave in the direction of her backyard.

"Excuse me?" said Theodosia. *How rude was this?*

"That sure was a mess with your backyard all dug up."

"Not my doing," said Theodosia, who'd had to deal with the State Archaeology Office over a few strange items that had turned up in her garden. "Although the electrical certainly needed doing." Granville, as absentee landlord, had let things go and then been forced to pay for needed repairs. Though, of course, he'd dragged his feet like crazy.

Granville shrugged. "Whatever."

He stood in the darkness, staring at her. But Theodosia was unable to make out his eyes or fathom the expression behind them. All she saw was the glowing red tip of his cigar.

"You're working late," said Theodosia. Somehow she felt the need to fill this awkward conversational void.

"More like having fun," said Granville. "I was just over at DG Stogies, my new cigar store."

"Cigar store?" said Theodosia. "You have a retail business?" Not that she was all that interested.

"Cigar smoking's still huge," commented Granville, puffing some more to underscore his sentence. "We do a brisk business in Cohiba, Carlos Torano, and Kristoff Maduros. Course, it's still tough to get the good stuff from Cuba, but that's bound to change any day now."

"It all sounds very exotic," said Theodosia.

"Eh, not really," said Granville, pluming out another noxious glut of smoke.

"You know," said Theodosia, waving a hand, trying to deflect the smoke as best she could, "that smoke is really awful."

Granville let loose a loud, amused snort, then turned and walked away.

"What a bozo," Theodosia muttered, as she tugged Earl Grey across her backyard. "Doesn't he realize he's polluting the entire neighborhood?" She unlocked the back door and shepherded Earl Grey inside.

Then she stopped. And checked herself.

If she had to live next door to Granville, shouldn't she try to remain on decent footing with him? Yeah, maybe.

So no nasty cracks about stinky smoke or air pollution?

"Doggone," she muttered, standing in the doorway. "What do I do now that I've completely alienated him?"

Earl Grey turned to look at her and said, "Rrrrmm."

"Are you serious?" said Theodosia. "Invite him to our housewarming?"

Earl Grey gazed stolidly at her.

Theodosia considered this for a few moments. "Okay, you're probably right. It's good PR."

Feeling slightly resigned but resolute, Theodosia pulled her back door shut and marched back across the yard. Okay, she'd make nice with Granville. Knock on his back door, smile graciously, and invite him to her housewarming party. If the planets were properly aligned, he'd say no and she'd be off the hook. But in the end, she'd have scored some "good neighbor points" for extending the invitation.

Worst-case scenario, if Granville *did* accept her invitation and showed up, she could pawn him off on Tidwell and let the two of them bore each other to death.

Theodosia ducked out into the alley, pulled open Granville's back gate, and walked lightly up his back walk.

Unlike her postage stamp–sized yard, Granville's yard was enormous. It was a decorator-done showcase garden that complemented his enormous mansion. A rectangular pool was surrounded by flower beds, shrubbery, and trees while statuary stood everywhere, glowing a faint white in the darkness.

Creeping up to Granville's back door, Theodosia searched for a buzzer or knocker. Not finding one, she rapped her knuckles hard against the door. The wood, a sturdy Carolina pine, barely telegraphed her tap.

Huh.

She rapped again, flinching this time. Nothing.

"Mr. Granville?" she called out. "Dougan?"

Still nothing. He was either ignoring her or just not hearing her.

Theodosia shuffled her feet and thought about this. Probably the latter; Granville just couldn't hear her. So now what?

Placing a hand on the brass doorknob, Theodosia turned it and pushed the door, letting it swing open a foot. She called again, her voice echoing eerily through the home. Still no response.

She took one tentative step into the back hallway, which, upon closer inspection, was quite cozy and elegant. Wine-red walls; a black-and-white tiled floor; nice paintings on the wall; a small wooden bachelor's chest that held keys, briefcase, a bowl of coins, and a brass lamp with a glowing green shade.

"Mr. Granville?" she called again.

Theodosia decided Granville must have gone directly upstairs. Or maybe he was in the front of the house, in a home office, talking on the phone?

Probably puffing away like a chimney, too.

Turning to go, Theodosia took a step, stopped, then stared at the painting on the wall. Only it wasn't a painting at all, but a framed print of a fierce-looking pirate. Wild hair swirled about the man's head, a flamboyant red cape billowed out behind him, and he brandished a wicked-looking saber. At the bottom of the frame, printed in flat copperplate writing, was the name EDWARD TEACH.

The name of the subject or the illustrator? Theodosia wondered. *Has to be one of them.*

Slipping out and pulling the door shut, Theodosia retraced her steps. A few minutes later she was snuggled in front of her fireplace, her shawl pulled around her, a book in her lap.

She read a page, then two more pages. But she didn't seem

to be absorbing the words or story line tonight, because the name Edward Teach kept tickling gently at her brain.

Why? Had she heard the name before? Or maybe she was still jazzed from last night's Pirates and Plunder show—and subsequent murder.

Theodosia let all of this percolate in her brain for a few minutes, then banished it from her thoughts. Thirty seconds later it was back at her like a bad case of heartburn. So she reached for the phone.

Drayton picked up on the second ring. "Hullo?"

"You're still up," she said.

"Just doing a little reading," said Drayton. "Catching up on my *Beowulf*, if you must know."

"I have a strange, slightly obscure question for you," said Theodosia.

"Fire away," said Drayton. "There's nothing better than a rousing game of Twenty Questions just as you're off for bed."

"This has to do with pirates again."

"Of course it does," said Drayton.

"Did you ever hear of a rather flamboyant pirate by the name of Edward Teach?"

There was a short intake of breath on the line, then silence. In fact, Drayton was silent for such a long time that Theodosia figured he was pretty much stymied.

"Sorry," said Theodosia, finally filling the void. "I knew it was a long shot. Correction. Long, long shot."

"No," said Drayton, "that's not it at all. You simply caught me off guard. Fact is, I *have* heard of Edward Teach."

"Seriously?" Theodosia's voice rose in a squawk.

"Yes, but Mr. Teach was better known by another name," said Drayton.

"Which was?" said Theodosia, puzzled at Drayton's some-what dodgy response.

"Blackbeard. Edward Teach was Blackbeard."

Now she was the one who was suddenly silent. "The

pirate?" she finally asked. "The one whose skull was just stolen?" She was too shocked for words!

"One and the same."

Theodosia rested her head against the soft padding of her chair and thought for a long minute. "I wonder," she murmured, "why everyone is suddenly so nuts about pirates?"

7

⚜

"*What's the deal* with pirates?" Haley asked, as she gently patted out a wedge of dough, sprinkled a small amount of flour onto it, then positioned her scone cutter and gently pressed down.

"I don't know," said Theodosia. She was standing in the kitchen with Haley, using a wire whisk to whip fresh cream into peaks and froths.

"That's all you and Drayton have been talking about," said Haley. "Who stole the skull cup at the pirate show? Who murdered that poor intern and clobbered Camilla?"

"You were the one who wanted me to get involved," Theodosia pointed out.

"I know, but now you're puzzling about why your neighbor has a pirate picture hanging in his powder room."

"Back hallway," said Theodosia.

"Whatever," said Haley. She picked up a piece of dough, laid it on her baking sheet, then asked, "You don't think your neighbor is involved, do you? After the little bit you've told me about him, you wouldn't just randomly leap to that conclusion, would you?"

"No, I wouldn't," said Theodosia. In the cold, clear light of day, she decided she'd probably overreacted. Dougan Granville wasn't involved because he hadn't even been at the Heritage Society on Sunday night. Or had he? Hmm, maybe she'd better check that guest list again.

"I have to admit," said Haley, "the skull cup thing is intriguing. I mean, who would abscond with the ratty old skull of some dastardly eighteenth-century pirate, then have it set in silver by a jeweler or silversmith? The whole thing is totally whacked out!"

"I agree," said Theodosia, continuing to whip away.

"You can set your whisk down now," said Haley. "I'd say you've pretty much beaten that cream into submission."

"Okay," said Theodosia, sticking a finger in and taking a taste. "I can't believe you always do this by hand. Aren't you afraid of getting carpal tunnel syndrome?"

"Naw, I'm a pro."

"You sure are," Theodosia agreed, reaching for a bright red carnival glass dish.

"What I think you should do," said Haley, cutting out her final scone and placing it on her baking sheet, "is get in touch with that archaeologist we know, Tred Pascal. Try to pick his brain." She smiled at her handiwork, slid the whole shebang into the oven, set the timer, then wiped her hands on her apron.

"You just want to date him," said Drayton.

Theodosia and Haley both glanced over to find Drayton standing ramrod straight in the doorway.

Haley cocked her head to one side and shrugged back her long blond hair. "What is it about my social life, Drayton, that has you so whipped up?"

"Not a thing," said Drayton. "You can see whoever you please. Doesn't matter to me."

"Sure it does," said Haley. "You're like one of those old families in the social register. All in a tizzy about finding a proper escort for their debutante daughter. For the grand cotillion ball or something equally stupid."

"I'm not, either," protested Drayton.

"You kind of are," said Theodosia.

"Anyway," said Haley, "why shouldn't we call Tred and ask him about that skull cup?"

"Because," said Drayton, "that skull cup's connected to a murder. And we've got enough going on without tossing somebody else into the mix!"

Theodosia grabbed Drayton by the arm and pulled him back out into the tea room. It was always better to give Drayton a defined task to do, to keep him *occupado*.

"I'm thinking of brewing a pot of Indian spice tea today," said Drayton, once he'd squinted at the myriad of tea tins that were stacked floor to ceiling on wooden shelves behind the counter.

"Sounds perfect," said Theodosia. She glanced at the clock overhead and saw they had maybe ten minutes before they opened for business. "And what about Formosan oolong? That's always a big hit."

Drayton reached up to the top shelf and grabbed a tin. "Then I shall indulge you."

"Not me," smiled Theodosia, "our customers."

"Of course," said Drayton, taking a Brown Betty teapot off a shelf, then rethinking his choice and grabbing a yellow floral teapot instead. "Don't forget," he said, "we have that group of antique dealers coming in at noon."

"How many again?" Theodosia asked.

"Four or five, at least," said Drayton. "And I'm thinking of doing a blue-and-white theme. For the table decor, I mean."

"Always a classic look," agreed Theodosia. She was dithering over candles and knew it. The small white votive lights or the tall pink tapers?

Drayton shifted his teapot from one hand to the other. "You're preoccupied," he said. "No doubt still mulling over that Edward Teach painting."

"Print," said Theodosia. "Fact is, I'm not a big believer in coincidences, but . . . seeing it was a little strange."

"You think your next-door neighbor is a pirate aficionado?"

Theodosia reached up with an index finger and scratched her nose. "Maybe. Or he just likes that particular image. Or maybe it's just there to hide a crack in the wall."

"I wonder," said Drayton, "was Granville at the Heritage Society Sunday night?"

Even though she'd entertained the same thought, Drayton's question suddenly made Theodosia uneasy. "Where are you going with this?" she asked.

Drayton's stared at her. "It's a simple question."

"Maybe not so simple," said Theodosia. "In any case, I haven't the foggiest idea. I didn't see his name on the invited guest list, but that doesn't mean much since the event was open to the public."

"Then you have to call Granville," Drayton said. "Find out for sure, so you can put your mind at ease."

"Are you crazy?" said Theodosia. "I can't just call Granville and ask him a question like that. He'll think I'm a complete and utter nut job!"

Drayton let one eyebrow quiver for a millisecond. "But you're more than a little curious. Admit it."

"Yes," said Theodosia. "Who wouldn't be? In light of . . . well, *you* know."

"So call and ask."

"Come on," said Theodosia, "it's the absolute wrong thing to do."

"Why do you say that?" asked Drayton.

Theodosia searched her mind for a really good reason.

Finally she found one. "Okay, here's the thing. What if Granville *was* somehow involved? If I call and ask about Sunday night, he'll think I'm running some kind of investigation."

"Which you are," said Drayton. "But if Granville *wasn't* at the Heritage Society . . ."

"Then he'll just think I'm a nosy neighbor."

"Which you also are," said Drayton, looking pleased. "You're the one who crept up his sidewalk and peeped in the back door. Opened Pandora's box, so to speak."

Still, Theodosia was reluctant. "You want me to just call Granville and ask him flat out if he was at the Pirates and Plunder show?"

"Absolutely not," said Drayton, "I'd be shocked if you did anything that obvious. But I have great faith in you. I'm sure you'll figure out a clever, disarming way to phrase your question."

Just as Drayton predicted, Theodosia *did* find a way to broach the subject to Granville.

"There's something I should have asked you last night when I ran into you," Theodosia said to Granville, once she'd made it past not one but three different gatekeepers at his law firm and finally had her neighbor on the phone.

"What's that?" asked Granville. He sounded busy. Harried, even.

"I have something of yours," said Theodosia, trying to sound friendly and even a little coy.

"What?" snapped Granville. "What are you talking about?"

"Something you must have dropped," said Theodosia. "When you were at the Heritage Society on Sunday night." She paused. "You were there, right?"

"Unfortunately, yes," said Granville. "A waste of time though, considering the evening ended so badly."

"I think you might have dropped a ticket," Theodosia continued, trying to sound breezy and casual, even though her heart had started to hammer in her chest. "An orange ticket? Um, it maybe fell out of your pocket?"

"No," said Granville. "If you found something, it's not mine."

"Really," said Theodosia. "You're sure?"

"I'm sure," he said.

"Okay then," said Theodosia, trying to figure out how to keep Granville on the line. How to ask him another question. Finally she stuttered out, "I take it you're a pirate fan?"

"I am," Granville grunted, "in fact, I'm a card-carrying member of the Jolly Roger Club."

"You mean like . . . a pirate club?" She giggled, to make her question seem silly. "With secret handshakes and a real hideout?"

"No, no," said Granville. "We're basically memorabilia collectors."

"And you have lots of pirate memorabilia?"

"I lent two of my own Jolly Roger flags to the Heritage Society's exhibition."

Theodosia paused and decided to take a wild stab. "If you're a collector, I'll bet you would have loved to get your hands on that skull cup."

Granville hesitated for a split second, then said, "You have no idea."

"*The Jolly Roger* Club," said Theodosia.

Standing at the counter, enveloped in an aromatherapy-like swirl of malty Assam, sweet, earthy Yunnan, and fragrant oolong, Drayton stared back at her. Clearly, he hadn't expected Granville to be involved at all.

"It's a kind of club," Theodosia told him. "That Granville belongs to. In fact, he's actually one of the memorabilia collectors you mentioned."

"I mentioned them only in the abstract," said Drayton, giving a quick, pinched frown.

"Yes, but now it's poured in concrete," said Theodosia. "Granville just told me so, like ten seconds ago." She glanced sideways to survey the tea room. The early-morning customers had come for their scones and cuppa and since departed. Now they had the folks who'd "come for elevenses," as Drayton so aptly phrased it. But only three tables were occupied at the moment, so they had a little latitude to ponder this new wrinkle before the luncheon crowd came charging in.

"Interesting," said Drayton.

"And a little creepy, right?" said Theodosia.

"Though Granville did offer a logical reason for why he was there."

"But when I mentioned the stolen skull cup, he went a little gaga," said Theodosia. "I had the feeling he would have loved to add it to his collection."

"Obviously someone already did," said Drayton.

"They certainly did," said Theodosia. "Now we just have to figure out who."

"Okay, you two," said Haley, emerging from the kitchen with a pen and spiral notebook, "it's time to stop swanning around and go over today's luncheon menu." She flipped a page and looked at them with dancing, mischievous eyes.

"Haley," said Drayton, "you're a stickler for efficiency."

The corners of Haley's mouth twitched. "You taught me well, Drayton."

"What wonderful offerings will we be serving our customers today?" asked Theodosia.

"I just pulled two pans of eggnog scones from the oven," said Haley, "and are they ever good!"

"That's a brand-new recipe?" asked Drayton. "Eggnog scones?"

"From my grandma's receipt book," said Haley, "and they're delicious if I do say so myself. We'll serve 'em piping hot with plenty of strawberry jam."

"What else?" asked Drayton.

"White bean soup," said Haley, "with broth a little on the creamy side. Smoked turkey and cranberry cream cheese tea sandwiches. And a baby field green salad with avocados, white asparagus, candied walnuts, and blue cheese. Customers can order each item separately, or as a soup and sandwich combo, or they can have all three."

"The Full Monty," said Drayton.

Haley glanced at Theodosia. "Theo, you can work out a special price for the full complement, right?"

"Of course," said Theodosia. "And you know about the antique dealers coming in at one o'clock?"

"Drayton's already briefed me," said Haley. "In fact, I'm baking some special pumpkin walnut bars from a recipe he gave me."

"So we're set," said Theodosia.

"Not quite," said Haley.

"Now what?" asked Drayton.

Haley's eyes narrowed and she said, "Tell me more about that orange ticket you found."

8

True to Drayton's word, his table setting incorporated a blue-and-white theme. White linen tablecloth with white napkins edged in blue. Spode blue-and-white salad plates supplemented with a variety of teacups, small plates, and rice bowls, all ranging from the palest blue to deep cobalt blue and decorated with Chinese tea house scenes, florals, and chintz patterns.

"All it took was that first frigate loaded with blue-and-white export ware," said Drayton, standing back to make a final inspection of his table. "Once Europeans caught sight of those magnificent pieces, the love affair was on."

"And still is," said Theodosia. "Of all the antique teapots and teacups we sell out of our gift corner, Chinese blue-and-white pieces are by far the most popular."

"But not the easiest to find anymore," said Drayton.

"Getting tougher and tougher," agreed Theodosia. When she'd first opened the Indigo Tea Shop a few years back, she'd scoured the surrounding counties, hunting through antique shops, tag sales, and rummage sales for antique tea ware. Back then, it was fairly easy to find orphan teacups, teapots, and the odd piece of silver that she could wash, polish, and use in the tea room or sell for a small profit. And the blue-and-white pieces had been simple to find. Now it seemed like there was a plethora of florals and chintzes, but blue-and-whites were fewer and farther between.

"And I put together a lovely centerpiece," said Drayton, placing a large blue-and-white pitcher filled with white peonies in the center of the table.

"Perfection," said Theodosia, as she lit a pair of tall white tapers.

And then they were off and running. Customers drifted in, some with reservations, some who'd just been walking the historic district and been drawn in by the fragrant aromas that wafted out the door.

Now every table but the center circular one was filled, and the Indigo Tea Shop buzzed with activity. Theodosia stepped deftly between tables, delivering lunch plates, offering refills on tea, getting seconds on scones, and refilling small bowls of lemon curd and Devonshire cream. She noted that Haley's eggnog scones were a huge hit and decided she'd have to snatch one before the whole lot was just a fragrant memory.

At ten minutes to one, their first antique dealer arrived. A man by the name of Stephen Pembroke who ran a military relics store. That pretty much broke the dam. A few minutes later, four more antique dealers shuffled in and took their seats.

Drayton saw to his guests personally, while Theodosia took care of the rest of the customers. A fairly easy task, since most were still sitting happily at their tables, sated from Haley's delicious food and lulled into a heavenly carbohydrate haze.

Drayton, on the other hand, was a whirling dervish of activity. He poured tea, ferried scones, and even sat down for a few minutes at a time, joining in spirited conversation with the dealers.

"What we want to do," said Pembroke, a large man with a florid face who seemed to be a sort of spokesman for the group, "is hold a large antiques expo this September. Possibly at the civic center or municipal auditorium. And I mean reasonably large and highly prestigious, something on the order of the International Fine Art and Antique Dealers Show in New York."

Overhearing his words, Theodosia leaned in to insert her two cents' worth. "I think you have a wonderful idea. It's a great way to draw upscale visitors and highlight the fact that Charleston really is a huge antique center."

Indeed, when it came to antiques, Charleston was the mother lode. Thousands of old families of British and French descent had settled here, bringing with them to the New World many of their finest pieces. As Charleston grew and prospered with its indigo and rice plantations, it also became a thriving center for cabinet and furniture makers, silversmiths, artists, and glassblowers. The large showcase homes that were built demanded equally elegant furniture and finery, so the flurry went on for decades. But as the plantation era gradually faded away, fortunes rose and fell, and older generations handed down their antiquities to successive generations who weren't quite as enamored of such things. And so a huge antique trade sprung up. As attics were emptied, large homes converted into B and Bs, and descendants lost interest in family heirlooms, antiques poured into the marketplace, suddenly making Charleston the go-to hot spot for antique collectors in the know.

"Perhaps," said Drayton, "we might even persuade Theodosia to come out of retirement and handle our advertising."

"I'd be happy to help," said Theodosia. She was still thrilled about leaving her crushingly stressful marketing job to run the Indigo Tea Shop. And, much to her credit and fortitude, she had never looked back.

"Nice of you," said Pembroke.

Haley suddenly popped out from the kitchen and thrust a tray of bars into Theodosia's hands.

"Thank you," said Theodosia, but Haley had already scurried back into her lair. Theodosia shrugged, slipped her hands around a pair of silver tongs, then placed a pumpkin walnut bar on Pembroke's dessert plate, followed by two large lush strawberries dipped in white chocolate.

As Theodosia worked her way around the table, happily dispensing sweets, she was suddenly aware that the dealers had switched their topic of conversation to the murder at the Heritage Society. And, of course, the missing skull cup.

"The disappearance of the Pruett cup is a real tragedy," said one of the men, an antique dealer Theodosia recognized as Thomas Hassel. He was a tall, pinch-faced man with a tangle of gray hair who wore silver rings on several of his fingers. Hassel was sole proprietor of The Silver Plume, an antique shop that specialized in estate jewelry. Theodosia supposed Hassel was a sort of rival to Brooke Carter Crockett, her friend who owned Heart's Desire just down Church Street.

"You knew about this skull cup?" Theodosia asked him.

Hassel looked up at her with a slight amount of surprise in his eyes, then gave a quick nod. "I've heard rumors about skull cups for years—there's more than one, you know. But I always figured the diamond-encrusted skull had been snatched up by some European collector." He emitted a laugh that sounded more like a sharp bark. "Who knew it was languishing in the basement of our own Heritage Society? Collecting dust and dispensing bad karma."

"Why do you say that?" asked Theodosia, moving closer to him and placing an extra pumpkin walnut bar on his plate. "About the bad karma?"

"Oh," said Hassel, his eyes flicking back and forth, "that skull cup has a rather delicious history."

"Tell me," said Theodosia, leaning in. "Start from the beginning."

"Well," said Hassel, "after Blackbeard was defeated by Lieutenant Maynard and the Royal Navy in Ocracoke Inlet, North Carolina, his head was sliced off and suspended from a large oak tree. Eventually, probably out of respect for their dear departed captain, one of Blackbeard's compadres cut the grisly head down and commissioned a local silversmith to turn Blackbeard's skull into an ornate drinking cup. That's when the diamond came into the picture, too. It was supposedly from a huge cache of treasure that Blackbeard's crew had amassed." Hassel now had the rapt attention of everyone at the table. "But get this," he continued, "the diamond used to adorn the skull cup reputedly came from a dagger that had been used by Louis XIV of France."

"Seriously?" said Theodosia. *The Sun King? What a story!*

"There are several variations on the story," Hassel told her. "But the Louis XIV rumor is the one that seems to carry the most credence. Apparently, the original diamond was as large as eighteen karats, but was split over the years. Broken down into three smaller stones."

"The diamond in the skull cup was . . . what?" asked Theodosia, "maybe nine or ten karats?"

"Possibly even twelve," said Hassel.

"So after hearing all the wild legends," said Theodosia, "you finally got a chance to see the skull cup in person." She paused. "I take it you were there Sunday night?"

"I was," Hassel said, nodding.

"And you believe it was the actual skull of Blackbeard?" Theodosia asked.

"Again, it's only rumor," said Pembroke, from across the table.

"Why wouldn't it be real?" Hassel asked, gazing back at him with fiery eyes. "Embedded with the diamond and all.

Obviously that's why it was included in the show. It's rumor based on fact. Close enough for jazz, as they say."

A chill ran down Theodosia's spine. "The actual skull of Blackbeard," she murmured. "Along with a diamond owned by the King of France. And now it's all disappeared again. Gone down the rabbit hole."

"For how long, we'll never know," said Hassel. He turned sharp eyes on Theodosia and asked, "What exactly is your interest in the skull cup?"

"Anything that inspires murder," said Theodosia, "is of interest to me."

"Can you believe those antique guys are still blabbing away out there?" asked Haley. Lounging in the doorway of Theodosia's office, she looked vaguely at odds and ends. "They're probably bragging about the size of their andirons or something."

"If they're not gone by the time we close," said Theodosia, "we'll just lock them in."

"Hah!" said Haley, stabbing a finger at her. "Good one."

"You want me to order another couple of dozen wooden spoons for you?" Theodosia asked, as she thumbed through a restaurant supply catalog. "You seem to like them. You seem to run through them fairly fast." Whatever it was, the soups and chowders Haley concocted or her penchant for endless stirring, she chewed through them relentlessly.

Haley tilted her head thinking. "Sure, why not." She shifted from one foot to the other, then asked, "Can I bring you anything? Sandwich? Cup of tea?"

"Nope."

Haley scrunched up her face. "Think I could leave early?"

"I don't see why not," said Theodosia.

"Drayton can clean up?"

"Or I will."

"You're a dream boss, you know that?" said Haley, as she skipped out the door.

But Theodosia was far from finished. The discussion at lunch concerning the skull cup had only served to ratchet up her interest. And now she was about to indulge in a little investigating that would hopefully yield an answer or two.

Pulling her mobile phone from her bag, Theodosia clicked a couple of buttons and brought up the photo she'd made of the ticket. She studied it. COMPLIMENTARY MEMBERS PASS with a seven-digit number that she figured had to be today's date. Hmm.

Spreading the *Post and Courier* on her desk, she paged through it until she came to the arts and entertainment section. Maybe, if she could find an event that was happening tonight, an event that required a ticket, she'd be able to put two and two together and . . .

Theodosia ran an index finger down the Happenings column, noting that it was divided into "Happening Today" and "Happening This Week."

Because of the big Charleston Food and Wine Festival that kicked off tomorrow, there were tons of listings under "Happening This Week." But only three events were listed under "Happening Today."

Okay, good. Let's see what this ticket might get me admission to.

There was the Ozone Dance Troupe at the Lebeau Theater. A book reading at a local Barnes & Noble. And a concert tonight at the Gibbes Museum of Art.

She took a deep breath as well as a wild guess. Maybe the concert at the museum?

Theodosia tapped a finger against her desk, thinking. Then she slid open her bottom drawer, grabbed the Charleston phone directory, paged through it, and found the museum's general information number.

The phone was immediately answered by a chirpy receptionist. "Hello?"

"I wonder if you could help me," said Theodosia. "I had a pair of tickets for your concert tonight. But, silly me, I've gone and lost one of them. And I'd planned to bring a guest . . ."

"Were they members tickets?" asked the woman.

"The orange-colored tickets?" said Theodosia, winging it now.

"That's a members ticket," said the receptionist in a smooth, appeasing tone. "So there shouldn't be a problem. The orange tickets we send out are really just a sort of courtesy. The concert tonight is actually open seating, and I know for a fact there are lots of available seats."

"So I can bring my guest and just show up?" Theodosia asked.

"We'd be delighted to have you," said the receptionist. "We're always happy to entertain a member."

Dashing out into the tea shop, Theodosia found Drayton staring at the detritus of an empty table. Dishes were strewn haphazardly, candles had guttered low, and even the flowers looked droopy.

"What we should do now," he said, "is sell the place. Start fresh."

"No," said Theodosia, "what we're going to do is attend a concert tonight."

Drayton stared at her. "We are?" He narrowed his eyes, suddenly suspicious. "It's not a rock concert, is it? You and Haley wouldn't run some crazy con on me, would you?"

"That's right, Drayton," said Theodosia, "the Rolling Stones are playing at the Gibbes Museum tonight and they're going to blow the roof off." She paused and smiled. "You know I'd never be that sneaky. I realize that anything besides a string quartet playing a sedate Vivaldi sends you into complete and total apoplexy."

"Then what's the concert?" asked Drayton, still looking hesitant.

"It really is a string quartet," said Theodosia. "That ticket I found in the Heritage Society gallery? I did a quick check and it turns out it's for a concert tonight at the Gibbes Museum of Art. Not only is it a members ticket, but there's no problem in bringing a guest." She paused. "And you're the guest."

Drayton stared at her. "Let me get this straight. You're saying that, theoretically, our killer might have dropped that particular ticket?"

"It's possible."

"Which means," said Drayton, "that our killer could conceivably *be* there tonight. At the Gibbes Museum."

Theodosia nodded. "That's a whole lot of theoreticals, but yes, I suppose he could be."

Drayton was silent for a few moments, and then something behind his hooded gray eyes seemed to click into place and he made up his mind. "Then I think we should go."

"Great." Theodosia picked up a second gray plastic tub and began stacking dirty plates into it. "Did you learn anything more?" she asked. "Talking with the dealers? About the skull cup, I mean?"

"Not really," said Drayton. "The only thing I found slightly disconcerting was how knowledgeable Hassel was."

"That struck me as slightly odd, too," said Theodosia. "I got the feeling that he'd almost . . . I don't know . . . *researched* it." She grabbed another plate. "What do you know about Hassel, really?"

"We're just acquaintances." Drayton was carefully lining up spoons with spoons, knives with knives. "Fellow history buffs."

"Do you trust him?" asked Theodosia.

Drayton made a slight grimace. "I don't know him well enough to make that kind of call." He picked up a teacup and placed it in the plastic bin, where it made a tiny clink against a stack of plates. "But I can see *you're* suspicious. Hassel's keen interest in the skull obviously raised your proverbial hackles."

Theodosia shrugged. "Sort of. It might help if we knew someone who had dealings with him. Like another antique dealer or collector."

"Someone to vouch for him?" asked Drayton. "Is that what you're saying?"

"I guess it is," said Theodosia.

"Nobody comes to mind," said Drayton. "The only thing I really know about Thomas Hassel is that he's not as involved with antiques as he is with jewelry and old silver."

"It just so happens," said Theodosia, "I know someone who's an expert in old silver."

9

Brooke Carter Crockett was hunched over her workbench when Theodosia pushed her way into Heart's Desire. The shop, so elegant with its Oriental carpets, glittering chandeliers, and sparkling glass cases, was filled with tasty diamond, ruby, and pearl jewelry—some of it brand-new, much of it estate pieces.

"Theodosia!" said Brooke, lifting her head. "Thank goodness. I thought it might be that awful Amy Lou Wiggins coming in here to try to sell me her grandmother's emerald necklace again. I keep telling her the stones are really tsavorite, but she doesn't want to believe me."

"Lots of that going around?" asked Theodosia, stepping to the counter.

Brooke spun her task chair around to face Theodosia. She was slim and slightly elfin, with a white cap of hair and a perpetual smile. "You have no idea. It's the economy, you know. Still in the trash can, so everyone's desperate to raise extra cash."

"I hear you," said Theodosia.

"On a similar note," continued Brooke, "I'm just back from the Palm Beach Jewelry, Art and Antique Show."

"How was that?" asked Theodosia.

"Heartbreaking," said Brooke. "I can't tell you how many estate pieces were being offered for sale. Trays and trays filled with Cartier, Tiffany, and Bulgari pieces, as well as hundreds of diamond rings and bracelets from Harry Winston, Chopard, and Neil Lane. And you just *know* many of those pieces were owned by women who'd lost money in those big Wall Street Ponzi and hedge fund debacles."

"They're still feeling fallout from that?" asked Theodosia.

Brooke nodded. "Oh, sure. They lost the big money when the market imploded a couple of years ago, and now they've run through their savings accounts, too. All that's left of consequence are their homes and jewelry."

"Let me guess," said Theodosia, "the jewelry is being sold off in order to maintain the homes."

Brooke nodded. "Property taxes and electric bills just keep coming due. To say nothing of groceries, lawn care, or popping for the occasional face lift."

"See why I opted for a smaller home?" said Theodosia, smiling.

"Honey, me, too. I'm the original cocooner. Give me my little Charleston single house and my dog Toby and I'm happy as a clam, even if I did turn my guest bedroom into a shrine for my ceramic dog collection." She reached for her teacup and took a quick sip. "Want some tea?"

Theodosia shook her head. "I've already hit my quota."

"Thanks to you," said Brooke, "I think I've turned into a complete tea addict."

"There's a twelve-step program for that, you know," said Theodosia.

Brooke looked surprised. "There is?"

"Never be more than twelve steps away from your teakettle," said Theodosia.

"Oh, you!"

Theodosia pointed toward Brooke's workbench, where a number of half-finished charm bracelets lay. "Those pieces are adorable; can I see one?" Brooke was a master at charm bracelets, and her handcrafted charms depicting palmetto trees, churches, oysters, and sailboats were always in big demand. Recently, she'd started crafting South Carolina state symbol charms, too, such as the loggerhead turtle, which was the state reptile; yellow jessamine, the state flower; and Carolina wren, the state bird.

Brooke turned and picked up a half-finished bracelet. It was a silver link bracelet strung with pieces of twisted red coral, white quartz, and pale blue chalcedony. "Something different," she said, handing it to Theodosia.

"Beautiful," said Theodosia, admiring it and thinking it would be a perfect summer accessory. "And so much going on." The bracelet was a perfect mix of warm and cool colors integrated with polished silver.

"It's getting there," said Brooke. "I'm starting to love working with chalcedony. Especially the blue and the pink." She set a tiny silver teaspoon on the counter in front of Theodosia. "How do you like this?" She was grinning as she said it.

Theodosia touched the spoon with her index finger. Brooke had crafted a tiny silver teaspoon with a twisty handle that resembled a living piece of sea coral. "I love it! How soon can I get fifty for the tea shop?"

Brooke reared back. "Fifty? Are you serious?"

"We could sell these," said Theodosia. "My customers, especially the dedicated tea drinkers, would go bonkers for them."

"No kidding," said Brooke, clearly surprised. "I really just made it as a lark." She shook her head. "Fifty. Is that an actual order?"

"Absolutely it is," said Theodosia. "Do you want me to sign something? Issue a purchase order?"

"You're such a buttoned-up businesswoman," said Brooke. "I just scrawl things on Post-it notes. That's my system."

"If it works, that's all that matters," said Theodosia. She leaned forward and stared down into the glass case. A diamond brooch, a strand of Polynesian black pearls, and a contemporary-looking diamond-and-amber necklace sparkled back at her.

"That's a gorgeous piece," said Theodosia, her eyes riveted on the amber.

Brooke slid the back of the case open, then reached in and lifted the amber necklace from its black velvet pillow. "It would go beautifully with your auburn hair," she said as she handed it to Theodosia.

Suddenly self-conscious, Theodosia lifted a hand and patted her hair. "It's humid today, so I'm afraid it's looking a little wild." Whenever the humidity climbed above sixty percent in Charleston, which it did on an almost daily basis, Theodosia's hair reacted big-time. Lifting at the roots, it fluffed out around her like a golden halo. Haley referred to it as big Southern hair; Drayton kidded her about being a friendly Medusa. Both were right.

"Honey," said Brooke, "I'd kill for your hair." She pushed a mirror toward Theodosia so she could try on the necklace. Then she said, "I heard about that murder at the Heritage Society. Pretty nasty."

"That's for sure," said Theodosia. She lifted the necklace to her collarbone, feeling its coolness against her skin. "One minute Drayton and I were lifting a glass of bubbly and having a moment, the next minute people were screaming bloody blue murder."

"And that boy was killed," said Brooke, "and poor Camilla got conked on the head. How is Camilla?"

"Okay. Better," said Theodosia. She fastened the amber necklace, then glanced in the mirror. It was definitely a killer piece, all fiery and gorgeous as it encircled her neck. "And the skull cup was stolen," she added.

"I heard about that, too," Brooke said, a thoughtful note in her voice. "I saw the photos in the paper. A rather strange item. Not exactly your understated little collectible."

"It's fairly hideous," said Theodosia. "And it's supposed to be Blackbeard's skull."

Brooke looked surprised. "They didn't mention *that* in the article."

"No, they didn't," said Theodosia, "Plus I found out there's a nasty story attached to it."

"Tell me," said Brooke.

So Theodosia quickly related the story Thomas Hassel had told her at lunch—about the skull being cut down to make into a cup, the diamond being added, and the bad karma—and finished with, "And that's why I wanted to talk to you."

Brooke looked perplexed. "About the skull cup?"

"No, about Hassel. What do you know about him?"

"From what I know, he's primarily a jewelry dealer," said Brooke. "He's been in business for quite a while."

"Anything else?"

Brooke wrinkled her nose and made a face. "Not much, just an occasional rumor here and there."

"Okay," said Theodosia. This is what she came for. "What can you share with me?"

Brooke lifted her shoulders. "Just that Hassel's maybe, um, a little unethical?"

"How so?" asked Theodosia.

"Let's just say when a grieving son or daughter brings in their dearly departed mother's old mine diamond ring for appraisal and sale, Hassel doesn't exactly pony up top dollar."

"Ah," said Theodosia, "he drives a hard bargain."

"He errs on the side that favors him," said Brooke.

"Okay, here's another question from way out in left field. What do you know about pirates?"

Brooke gave a slow reptilian blink. "Johnny Depp?"

"There's that," said Theodosia. "But what I'm really asking about are the real-deal aye-matey-walk-the-plank kind of pirates."

"Like your pal Blackbeard," said Brooke. "I don't know much about pirates at all. Except they were cranky, drank more than they bathed, and tended to pester early Charleston residents." She gave a quick smile. "Not necessarily in that order."

"Huh," said Theodosia.

"You're interested because this has to do with the missing skull cup?" asked Brooke. "Or the murder?" She hesitated. "Or both?"

"A little of both," Theodosia admitted. "Timothy Neville over at the Heritage Society is all freaked out, and I told him I'd noodle things around."

"Sounds like you're doing more than noodling," said Brooke. "I just wish I could be of more help."

Theodosia gazed at the amber necklace one more time, than took it off. There'd be no jewelry splurges right now, not when her kitchen needed updating.

"You know," said Brooke, "I do know someone who's rather pirate literate."

"Who's that?" asked Theodosia.

"Professor Irwin Muncie over at the College of Charleston."

"A pirate professor?" Theodosia asked, half in jest.

"History," said Brooke. "Pirates are just his sideline."

By the time Theodosia got home, she was late, late, late. She fixed a quick bowl of kibble for Earl Grey, then shuffled the pup as well as his dinner and a bowl of fresh water into the backyard.

Upstairs, whirling around in the small room she'd converted to a walk-in closet, Theodosia was faced with a fashion dilemma. What to wear?

Since tonight's concert featured classical music, did that mean semiformal or elegantly casual? That is, a little black dress or maybe silk slacks and a slithery tank top? Theodosia gazed at herself in the full-length mirror and gave a rueful smile. It would be a lot easier to just wear what she had on—khaki crop pants and a silk T-shirt. But Drayton would undoubtedly show up in something tweedy with his ubiquitous bow tie, so she should follow suit, right?

What to do?

Only one thing to do. Call Delaine. After all, she was the self-proclaimed expert and arbiter on all things fashionable.

Sighing, because she knew Delaine would probably give her a lecture and a mild scolding, Theodosia dialed the phone, hoping to catch Delaine at her shop.

And she did.

"You're asking me what to wear to the Gibbes Museum?" Delaine shrilled in Theodosia's ear.

"It's a concert," said Theodosia. "A string quartet."

"I *know* it is," said Delaine. "I'll be attending as well. I'm dating the PR director, remember?"

Theodosia didn't remember. "You'll be there?"

"Is there an echo?" asked Delaine. "Didn't I just say that?"

"So it's a fancy event?" asked Theodosia.

"Obviously," said Delaine. "There'll be the usual big-shot museum donors and board members scattered in with the riffraff. And the de rigueur cocktail party afterward."

"Cocktails?" said Theodosia. It did sound like a fancy event.

"That's right," said Delaine as she continued to needle Theodosia. "Mixed drinks in stemmed glasses with bits of fruit poised on the rim, or perhaps a floating olive."

"So what exactly are you saying?" asked Theodosia.

"That it's always better to be a little bit overdressed than underdressed, dear," said Delaine, who sounded like she was really enjoying this little tête-à-tête.

"So I should wear . . . what?" asked Theodosia. She stared at her hanging racks of clothes, rubbing bare toes against the dark blue Aubusson carpet. The pile felt lush and smooth and deep, and she was beginning to wish she'd never called Delaine in the first place.

"Wear your black cocktail dress," Delaine instructed. "The one with the little bow on the shoulder. But, for goodness' sake, throw some accessories on. You don't want to look like you're dressed for a funeral!"

No, thought Theodosia, *that will happen a couple of days from now.*

"Remember those black mules you bought from me, the ones with the poufy red silk flowers on the toes?" asked Delaine. "They're just right for tonight. And maybe some pearls. But don't just loop them around your neck in a single strand like some dowdy old dowager," Delaine cautioned. "Do something kicky and fun. Wind them around your neck a couple of times, then secure them to your dress with a sparkly pin." She paused to grab a quick breath. "Can you do that?"

"Those are all great suggestions," said Theodosia. "Thanks so much."

"Who's your date?"

"Drayton."

"Oh," said Delaine.

"Does that change things?" asked Theodosia.

"No," said Delaine, "but when the photographers start snapping pictures for the society pages, try to get in the picture with me. And for goodness' sake, don't forget to *smile*! You always look like some poor frightened animal caught in the headlights!"

10

꧂

The Gibbes Museum of Art at 135 Meeting Street was a Beaux Arts building of extraordinary charm. Established in 1905 by the Carolina Art Association, the Gibbes Museum offered not only a distinguished collection but a full program of gallery talks, lectures, and seminars as well.

"Where's the concert being held?" Drayton asked as they strolled through the main door into an ornate corridor hung floor to ceiling with magnificent eighteenth-century oil paintings.

"I think maybe . . . the rotunda," said Theodosia. As they continued across the marble floor, their heels clacking sharply, she could see a gathering of people straight ahead of them.

"Ah," said Drayton. "Almost a perfect sound chamber."

"See anyone you know?" Theodosia asked as they drew closer to the group that had converged there.

"No," said Drayton, "but I'm sure there'll be . . ."

"Theodosia!" came a shrill voice.

Theodosia and Drayton hesitated for a millisecond, long enough for Delaine to furiously elbow her way through the crowd and essentially waylay them.

"Delaine," said Drayton, offering a reserved smile.

"I was wondering when you two chickens were going to show up," said Delaine, giving a little pout. "I so want to introduce you to Max."

From somewhere behind Delaine, an attractive man suddenly materialized. Tall and thin, with a tousle of dark hair, Max had an olive complexion and wore a slightly sardonic grin. Probably, Theodosia decided, you needed a sense of humor to keep company with Delaine. Max, the new boyfriend and PR director, was also a couple of years younger than Delaine. A couple of years younger than she herself was.

"This is Max," Delaine announced with a fair amount of pride. "Max Scofield, the director of PR here at the museum."

"Newly appointed director," said Max, as Delaine completed the introductions and they all shook hands. "As yet unproven."

"Theodosia used to be in PR," said Drayton, as the foursome moved slowly toward the rotunda, where four empty music stands awaited tonight's musicians and a hundred or so chairs had been arranged in a semicircle.

"Is that so?" asked Max. He smiled at Theodosia, looking interested.

"Please, let's not get into past lives," said Delaine, grabbing on to Max's arm and clinging for dear life. "That can be so tiresome."

"No," said Max, "I'm interested."

"My background's more marketing than PR," Theodosia told him. "In the financial and technology sectors. But I have to admit that's a few years in the past. Now, with Drayton's help, I run the Indigo Tea Shop."

"Which I've heard wonderful things about," said Max, focusing on Theodosia.

"From me," said Delaine, trying desperately to insinuate herself in the conversation.

"And we handle catering for special events," Theodosia finished.

"You'll have to drop by for tea some time," Drayton invited.

"I believe I will," said Max.

Delaine suddenly slid directly in front of Max and went wide-eyed. "Did I tell you two about Nadine's awful predicament?" she asked.

"Now what's wrong?" asked Theodosia.

Delaine looked pained. "My poor, dear sister has been thrown into a complete and utter tizzy. The police decided to question her about the murder Sunday night and they don't believe her even though she *swore* she didn't see a single thing!" Delaine's sentence ended in a plaintive wail.

"Maybe they're grilling Nadine because she told that Van Buren person from the *Post and Courier* that she'd been an eyewitness?" Drayton offered.

"Obviously," said Theodosia, feeling that Nadine had certainly earned her predicament, "the police subscribe to the *Post and Courier*, too."

"Whatever the case," snapped Delaine, "she's being prodded mercilessly." She shook her head. "It's just not the proper way to treat a citizen in good standing."

"Neither is murder," said Theodosia.

They'd arrived at the rotunda now, where most of the guests had already taken their seats.

"There are four seats together over there," said Drayton, pointing.

Delaine gave Max's arm a sharp yank. "Thanks anyway, but we're sitting over *there*." She waggled her fingers at Theodosia and Drayton and sang out, "Bye-bye, lovies."

Max gave a good-natured shrug and said, "Talk to you later." But he looked pointedly at Theodosia.

Theodosia and Drayton found seats in the second-to-last

row, just as the musicians filed out. It wasn't a large crowd, so they had an optimum view of the musicians as well as the patrons.

"Keep a sharp eye out," Theodosia whispered to Drayton.

"What am I looking for?" he asked, as he joined the crowd in light applause.

"Maybe . . . someone who was also at the Pirates and Plunder Show?"

"In that case," said Drayton, "Thomas Hassel is sitting right over there."

Theodosia's head spun from side to side, in search mode. "Where?"

"Far right, second row from the front," said Drayton.

"I'll be darned," said Theodosia, finally catching sight of him. "When I quizzed Brooke about him, she seemed to think Hassel's business dealings were a trifle shady."

"I wouldn't be surprised," said Drayton.

"And you always see the good in people."

"I do when they're good people," responded Drayton.

"Brooke also gave me the name of a pirate expert," said Theodosia. "Professor Irwin Muncie at the College of Charleston."

"You're thinking he might shed some light?"

"About the skull cup, yes," said Theodosia. "Maybe he can. At any rate, I think we should go talk to him." She sat there, formulating questions in her mind, then asked, "Do you see Dougan Granville anywhere?"

"He of the pirate painting?" said Drayton, crossing one leg over the other and smoothing his gray trousers. "I've never actually met your Mr. Granville. I know him only by reputation, mostly from the little innuendos you choose to share with me."

"Okay," said Theodosia. "Point taken."

"About Delaine's friend Max . . ." said Drayton.

"Max wasn't at the show Sunday night," Theodosia said, a little too quickly.

"No, but he's certainly interested in you," said Drayton, a slight cat-that-ate-the-canary grin slipping onto his face.

Theodosia's brows arched. "You're not serious! He's dating Delaine. Has been for a couple of months."

"Don't be surprised if he calls you."

"You're crazy," said Theodosia. "That's never going to happen."

Oh," said Drayton, "I think it might."

The concert was just right. About forty-five minutes of Mozart with a little Beethoven tossed in for good measure. And just as Drayton had predicted, the rotunda with its high dome and ancillary small galleries was acoustically perfect.

Afterward, there was a cocktail party. And as everyone chatted and crowded en masse toward the small bar that had been wheeled in, Theodosia got separated from Drayton.

No matter. She soon found herself rubbing shoulders with Thomas Hassel.

"We meet again," she told him.

He gazed at her sharply, then said, "You. I almost didn't recognize you."

"I come out from behind the teapot once in a while," Theodosia joked.

"Lovely concert, wasn't it?" asked Hassel.

"Terrific." Now that she was conversing with Hassel, he didn't seem like the big bad wolf she'd tried to make him out to be. Still, she decided to quiz him on the ticket. "You're a member here?" she asked.

Hassel nodded. "A member for life. You, too?"

"No, I'm not," said Theodosia. "But a friend gave me a couple of her members tickets." She paused. "Although nobody ever collected them. At the door." She paused again. "Did you have to turn in your orange ticket?"

"Hmm?" said Hassel. He'd been glancing around during her ramble, losing interest. "Excuse me," he said, "there's someone I need to say hello to."

"Smart," Theodosia muttered to herself. "Really peachy."

"I don't think they're serving anything peach-flavored," said a warm baritone voice behind her.

"Hmm?" Theodosia spun around to find Max Scofield smiling at her. For some reason, she was receiving a low-level electrical buzz from him. It made her a little nervous, but it was interesting, too. She supposed it was simply good old-fashioned . . . chemistry?

"Museums are only allowed to serve WASPy drinks like martinis and gimlets," said Max.

"And cheap white wine," laughed Theodosia. "Trucked down from New Jersey in tankers."

"Good one," said Max. He reached out and gently put a hand on her shoulder as they chuckled together.

Theodosia stopped chuckling. "Where's Delaine?" she asked. Sharp-eyed Delaine had certainly noticed the way Max had seemed to connect with her. It wouldn't do to make it appear like a two-way street.

"She's getting her picture taken," said Max. "Some photographer from the *Post and Courier* is over there, snapping away for the society pages."

"Shouldn't you be over there, too?" asked Theodosia. "Isn't that part and parcel of your job description? To pose with the patrons and drink with the donors?"

"Gosh, I hope not," said Max. "Besides, that nutty friend of Nadine's is here tonight, too. Stalking people."

"You mean Bill Glass? He's here taking pictures?"

"That's the guy," said Max. He put a hand to his forehead and pushed back an adorable tousle of dark hair. "What's his magazine again?"

"*Shooting Star,*" said Theodosia.

Max gave a snort. "Seems like a real rag."

"You know," said Theodosia. "I think you're going to make a great PR director."

"*What did I* tell you?" said Drayton, when Theodosia finally hooked up with him again. "That Scofield character finds you fascinating." Drayton seemed both amused and a little taken aback. He knew she was dating Parker Scully, but he also knew there'd been no major commitment. From either side.

"Give me a break," said Theodosia. "He's a PR guy, so that's his shtick. It's his job to be friendly and make everyone feel important."

"And raise money?" asked Drayton.

"There's always that," said Theodosia. "You know as well as I do that places like this are black holes for money. Every donor wants to believe they helped put a Rembrandt on the wall. They don't want to think that their money might be spent on necessities like lightbulbs and toilet paper."

"You're such a killjoy," laughed Drayton. "A smart cookie, but a killjoy."

"I'm a realist," said Theodosia. She glanced around and saw that Bill Glass was snapping photos like crazy and slowly moving their way. "Let's go get that drink," she said.

"Lead the way," said Drayton.

The crowd had thinned a bit, so they were able to make their way to the bar. Drayton ordered two white wines, then stood patiently while the overworked bartender popped the cork on yet another bottle of Chardonnay.

As Theodosia waited, she turned around and studied the crowd. She was still on the lookout for someone who'd been at the Pirates and Plunder show. Someone who might have dropped an orange ticket. Someone who . . .

A gold-and-diamond skull ring on a woman's hand caught the light and flashed like a lighthouse beacon.

Theodosia blinked, stared, and did a double take.

The ring wearer was a tall, predatory-looking blonde who clearly wasn't a natural blonde. Dark roots made her hair look exotic and wild, like it had been colored and retouched for a role in some futuristic movie. Her clothes were edgy, too. Black leather slacks and a low-cut red silk blouse. But it was her ring and the rest of her jewelry that drew Theodosia's eye.

The woman was dripping in skull jewelry. An enormous skull pendant set with a sprinkle of bright red rubies dangled from her neck. Two large skull rings flashed on either hand. Her gold stud earrings carried tiny skull images.

"Drayton," said Theodosia, giving him a sharp nudge, "do you . . ."

At that exact moment, the exotic-looking woman turned her head and caught sight of Drayton. Her broad face flickered with recognition and her mouth turned up in a smile. "Drayton!" she called out, "is that you?"

"You *know* her?" Theodosia hissed.

Drayton, who'd been juggling dollar bills and wine, almost fumbled the glasses as he aimed a friendly nod toward the woman and murmured to Theodosia, "It's Scarlette Berlin, the art dealer."

Scarlette Berlin made a beeline for Drayton, cutting through the crowd like a battleship on cruise control. She planted herself in front of him and proceeded to administer a series of air kisses accompanied by noisy chirps. Finally, when Drayton had been sufficiently greeted and pecked, he was able to say, "And this is Theodosia Browning."

Scarlette turned her effusive grin on Theodosia. "You're the tea lady, of course. Lovely to finally meet you."

"How do you two know each other?" Theodosia asked. How indeed?

"Heritage Society," said Scarlette, in a voice that was both booming and gregarious. "Drayton and I first met at a board meeting a couple of months ago."

"Scarlette gave the Heritage Society a rather generous donation," said Drayton.

"You're an art dealer?" Theodosia asked, clearly fascinated by this eccentric, colorful character.

"Berlin Fine Arts," said Scarlette. "Located on Philadelphia Alley in the French Quarter."

"And you like skulls," said Theodosia. She couldn't resist.

"Oh, dear me, yes," crooned Scarlette, fluttering her fingers, the better to show off her rings. "You might say I'm a connoisseur of the bizarre and fantastical. Give me a Damien Hirst or a Christian Audigier and I'm happy as a clam."

Theodosia recalled reading about the diamond-encrusted skull the artist Hirst had created and sold for something like one hundred million dollars and decided this lady ran with a pack of extremely well-heeled collectors.

"You must be curious about the murder and theft at the Heritage Society," said Theodosia.

Scarlette's face turned serious and she leaned in close, so close Theodosia could see tiny particles of mica in her midnight-blue eye shadow. Then, as if she were sharing some deep, dark secret, Scarlette said, "It's fascinating! Not the murder, of course, that's just too awful for words. But the disappearance of Blackbeard's skull." She snapped her fingers and said, "Poof! Once again it's managed to disappear."

"Except someone managed its disappearance," said Theodosia. "It didn't just slip away on its own."

"Well, yes," said Scarlette.

"So you were at the Heritage Society Sunday night?" Theodosia asked.

"No," said Scarlette, frowning and shaking her head. "I missed all the Sturm und Drang. I was in Savannah, delivering a painting to an important client."

Theodosia nodded, trying to get a read on this colorful and exotic woman. She was clearly interested in skulls. So . . . could she somehow be connected with the Blackbeard skull?

"You realize," Drayton said to Theodosia, "that Scarlette's your next-door neighbor. She practically lives down the block from you."

"Is that so?" said Theodosia.

"My home is on Lamboll Street," said Scarlette. "Where are you?"

"Just down from the Featherbed House," said Theodosia. "The cottage next to the Kingstree Mansion."

"Oh, I know it!" exclaimed Scarlette, "a darling little place. So quaint and cute. Must be easy to furnish a cottage that size."

"It's coming along," said Theodosia, her jaw going a little tighter.

Scarlette rolled her eyes. "My place is such a white elephant. Enormous rooms, twenty-foot-high ceilings . . . it's a good thing I'm an art collector."

"You know," said Theodosia, "I'd love to visit your gallery some time." *And I'd love to know more about you.*

Scarlette flashed a megawatt smile. "Then come visit us Friday night! We're having an art opening in honor of the Food and Wine Festival." She smiled. "Of course, I'd love to visit your tea shop sometime as well."

"Then come by tomorrow," said Theodosia. "We're having an opening as well. All day, in fact."

11

❧

"Miss Josette!" Theodosia exclaimed. "I didn't know you were coming in today." She was having a little trouble getting into the swing of things this Wednesday morning. For some reason, dreams about grinning skulls had haunted her all last night. And now, this morning, she seemed to be afflicted with a weird dream hangover.

"If you're busy, I can come back," said Miss Josette, still hovering in the doorway. She was an African American lady in her midseventies who lived on the outskirts of Charleston. Her nimble fingers and fine design aesthetics had won her acclaim as one of the premier weavers of traditional sweetgrass baskets. Elegant and utilitarian, the baskets were fashioned from long bunches of sweetgrass, pine needles, and bulrush, then bound together by strips from native palmetto trees.

"No, no," said Theodosia. "We asked for flat baskets and I see that's exactly what you've brought us. So . . . fantastic."

Stepping all the way into the tea shop, Miss Josette set her stack of baskets on the nearest table. "I brought you eight," she said. "Think that will do?"

Drayton, bustling into the tea shop proper from the back, caught sight of the baskets and hastily switched direction. "Splendid!" he exclaimed, clapping his hands together. "Our baskets have arrived."

Theodosia picked up the top basket, a flat elephant ear basket, and handed it to Drayton. "It's perfect, right?"

"They all are," proclaimed Drayton. "Perfect for our tea and cheese tasting event."

Miss Josette shook her head, a little puzzled. "Tea and cheese? That's a new one for me."

"For me, too," said Theodosia, grabbing a star basket to admire, "but Drayton assures me it's the hot new gourmet trend. He also says he knows just how to do the pairings."

"If Drayton says cheese and tea go together, then it must be so," said Miss Josette. She had a special place in her heart for Drayton, who, with his courtly manners and carefully done bow ties, could do no wrong in her eyes.

"So we'll take all of these," said Drayton, gathering up the baskets with great enthusiasm. "We'll protect the bottoms with linen napkins and use them as trays for our breads, crackers, and cheeses."

"Come by tomorrow night, if you can," Theodosia urged Miss Josette. "We're one of the kickoff events for the Food and Wine Festival. Bring that sweet nephew of yours, too."

"I might just do that," she replied.

"*This is going* to be our best Food and Wine Festival ever," declared Drayton. He was bustling about, setting the tables with small cream-colored Haviland plates that were embossed with a tree-and-well design. "Don't you love these plates?" he asked, holding one up to catch the morning rays that twinkled in through leaded glass windows. "With their marvelous crinkly edges?"

"You're using some of our good china," Theodosia remarked.

"Just felt like it," said Drayton. "And I'm going to set out some of the Capo di Monte porcelain figures for centerpieces."

"No flowers today?"

"Just figurines and candles," said Drayton. "And jam in cut crystal bowls to add some bits of sparkle." He paused. "I really am upbeat about the Food and Wine Festival. It's good for the food industry in general and a great way for local restaurants to get a much-needed boost."

"I can't believe how many events have been scheduled," said Theodosia. "Something like thirty-five?"

Drayton nodded. "Counting ours, there's ten different kickoff events tomorrow night alone."

"Parker's hosting one of the Friday evening events. A tapas buffet and Spanish wine tasting."

"Plus there's an oyster roast, champagne tasting, gourmet dinner, and Gullah foods dinner scheduled that same night."

"Get out the Pepto-Bismol," said Theodosia.

"And don't forget the big seafood grill Saturday afternoon," said Drayton as he carefully placed a porcelain swan in the center of a table.

"And Timothy's party on Saturday night," said Theodosia. It was all very hush-hush, of course, but Timothy's party was also supposed to double as a birthday party for Drayton.

"I hope Timothy's still moving ahead with his party," said Drayton, "seeing as how he's agonizing over the murder."

"I'll give him a call," said Theodosia, "offer any help I can." She reached out and straightened a butter knife. "I just wish I had some sort of answer for him. Or news."

"Well, you don't, and that's just the way it is."

"Not a lot of clues to work with," said Theodosia.

Drayton gave her a sideways glance. "Knowing you, something will turn up."

"Hope so."

"Oh," said Drayton, "don't forget we're leading that tea tour Friday morning." As yet another event for the Charleston Food and Wine Festival, Theodosia and Drayton had agreed to lead a tea tour through the historic district. They were going to start at the Redcliffe House, where a cream tea would be served; visit the Charleston Library Association; then lead their group on a rambling walk down King Street and Gateway Walk. They'd dispense a few historical sound bites, then continue on to the Indigo Tea Shop for lunch.

"Are we doing too much?" asked Theodosia. Then she shook her head. "Of course we are, we always do too much. We try to cram everything in."

"Yes, we do," said Drayton. "But catering events and hosting special parties keeps things interesting. You really don't want to stand around all day and tickle teacups with a feather duster, do you?"

"Might be nice for a change," said Haley, emerging from between the velvet curtains, "because we really are hip deep in alligators."

"If you need help, Haley," said Theodosia, "we can always bring in—"

Haley lifted a hand, palm toward Theodosia.

"—an assistant," finished Theodosia.

"You know what?" said Haley. "I'm sure I can manage. I always do."

Drayton threw her a sharp look. "You just don't relish the idea of an assistant puttering around in your kitchen. Helping prep the food and—"

"Stealing my recipes," said Haley.

"They wouldn't steal your recipes," said Theodosia. Honestly, Haley was almost phobic about her recipes, or *receipts* as they were so often called in the South.

But Haley was suddenly serious. "Don't be so sure about that. You know that recipe I have for lemon scones?"

Theodosia and Drayton gazed at her. Haley in one of her rants was really quite interesting.

"People have offered me *money* for it," said Haley, in a passionate, almost reverent tone. "The food critic from the *Post and Courier* said it was like eating ambrosia."

"High praise," said Drayton, though he still wasn't taking her all that seriously.

"And Constance Brucato, that TV producer, invited me to come on air and do a baking demo," said Haley. "She said they'd even put my recipe on their website." She frowned and shook back her hair with youthful energy. "But I'm not that easily enticed. After all, my recipes are proprietary information."

"Are you taking another business class?" asked Theodosia. Haley sporadically earned college credits, only to switch majors at a rapid-fire pace.

"I've taken enough business classes," said Haley. "Now I'm focusing on real-world experience."

"Such as you get here," said Drayton. "So you can run your own tea shop some day?"

"Well, maybe," said Haley. Then hastily added, "But not in this market. I would never try to cannibalize your audience, Theo."

"You *are* taking a business class," Theodosia murmured. She wasn't worried about Haley jumping ship. Haley had received dozens of job offers in the last couple of years. But nobody was ever willing to give her free rein in their kitchen. Nobody but Theodosia, that was.

"Enough," said Drayton, glancing at his antique Piaget watch, then giving it a quick tap with his index finger. "We have less than five minutes before throwing open our doors to the world. So tell us, Haley, what sublime culinary treats will be gracing our menu today?"

"Good stuff," said Haley, switching back into business mode and flipping open her notebook. "For morning tea we have brown sugar streusel muffins, pumpkin bread with cream cheese frosting, and golden raisin scones."

"Sounds like I should be readying pots of English breakfast tea and Moroccan mint tea," said Drayton, doing a quick perusal of his shelf of tea tins. "And for lunch?"

"Chicken pâté tea sandwiches and prosciutto with asparagus tea sandwiches," said Haley. "Plus mixed green salads with red pepper dressing, and chilled peach soup with ginger."

"Wonderful," murmured Theodosia.

"And here come our customers," said Drayton, gazing out the front window. "Like clockwork."

They all got busy then, seating customers, brewing tea, and serving the muffins, pumpkin bread, and scones.

Theodosia hustled to the front counter, where Drayton was working away in a fragrant cloud of steam. "I need a pot of Earl Grey," she told him.

"The organic?" he asked. "With a hint of citrus?"

"Works for me," said Theodosia. She arranged three teacups on a tray while she waited for Drayton. "When are the cheeses supposed to arrive?"

He measured tea into a red ceramic teapot, added hot water, then popped the pot into a red paisley tea cozy. "After lunch. Then we'll sit down and match them to the appropriate teas."

"And you're sure you can do that?"

Drayton gave her a baleful look. "Oh, please."

Theodosia threw up her hands in mock surrender. "Just checking. You realize our entire event rests squarely on your shoulders."

"Just what I need," said Drayton. "More pressure."

* * *

When they were busy and filled except for two small tables, Scarlette Berlin burst in on them.

"Surprise!" she cried, her voice booming across the tea room like approaching thunder, causing more than a few customers to frown and turn their heads to see what the commotion was all about.

"Scarlette," said Theodosia. "Miss Berlin."

"Bet you didn't think I'd come, did you?" said Scarlette, shaking a finger at her. Today she was turned out in tight black slacks, a red skull T-shirt, and a black suede jacket. The same skull rings flashed on her constantly moving fingers.

"We're delighted you took time from your busy schedule to visit us," said Theodosia, recovering her composure. She hadn't really expected Scarlette to show up at all. The woman struck her as more of a coffee-fueled Type A versus a laid-back take-your-time-and-enjoy-it tea drinker.

"I even brought a guest," said Scarlette, gesturing to an older, gray-haired man who stood next to her. "Rudolph, a dear friend and fellow art dealer." As Scarlette spoke, her head rotated like a periscope, taking in every nook and cranny of the Indigo Tea Shop. But she obviously approved of what she saw, because she said, "And we're here for an early lunch. If you'll have us, that is."

"Right this way," said Drayton, stepping in. "I have a lovely window table for the two of you."

"Charming!" yipped Scarlette, her voice ratcheting back to Theodosia as Drayton led her and her guest to a table.

"Whew," said Theodosia, when she met Drayton at the counter two minutes later. "There's a lady who likes to make a big entrance."

"She's colorful," agreed Drayton, as he set about measuring scoops of tea and rattling teapots.

"And awfully loud," said Theodosia.

"Then grab your earplugs," said Drayton, his face going slightly grim. "Because the din in here is about to get even louder."

"What are you—?"

Drayton aimed a sharp nod at the door.

Theodosia spun around to find Delaine Dish and her sister, Nadine, standing in the doorway, gazing at the crush of customers, looking nervous and a little unhappy.

"Should we have called for reservations?" Delaine asked. She said it in a petulant, singsong voice that indicated she clearly felt entitled. That she was a regular customer and thus should be accorded the very next table.

Theodosia rushed to greet her. "You're in luck," she told Delaine, "we have one small table left."

"And thank goodness for that!" exclaimed Delaine. "We've been positively *slaving* away all morning, getting ready for our Silk and Syrah event, and we're in dire need of sustenance."

"I never asked," said Theodosia, as she led Delaine and Nadine to their table, "is your fashion and wine event part of the Charleston Food and Wine Festival?"

A cagey look slid across Delaine's face as she took her seat. "We're not *exactly* a sponsored venue. We're more like . . . what would you call it? Casually piggybacking on the event."

"We *know* Silk and Syrah will have huge appeal to women," Nadine added, looking smug.

"I'm sure it will," said Theodosia, focusing on Nadine now. "By the way, have you managed to come up with any answers for the Charleston police?"

"Answers for Detective Tidwell, you mean!" spat out Delaine. "He's the one who's been pestering poor Nadine to death!"

"Better than being stabbed to death," Theodosia remarked. But Nadine was pointedly ignoring her, and Delaine had swung around in her chair to flash a big, cheesy grin at Scarlette.

"Scarlette Berlin!" cried Delaine. "I had no idea we'd end up sitting next to a bona fide celebrity and art entrepreneur!" She popped up from her chair just as Scarlette popped up, too. Then the air kisses began in earnest, along with squeaks, peeps, caws, and giggles.

"I think I'm going to be sick," Theodosia told Drayton, as she leaned across the counter to grab a bowl of sugar cubes. "Delaine and Scarlette are fawning all over each other like a couple of aging starlets who are on the prowl for one more big role."

Drayton's lips puckered as he stifled his own laughter. "They are a bit over the top."

"No," said Theodosia, "Bette Davis was over the top in *What Ever Happened to Baby Jane*. Uma Thurman was over the top in *Kill Bill*. This is just pure, unadulterated craziness."

"Speaking of craziness," said Drayton, "do you still want to arrange that meeting with Professor Muncie?"

"The pirate professor?" said Theodosia. "Heck, yes."

"And you still want me to go along," said Drayton. It was a statement, not a question.

"Obviously," said Theodosia. "Since you're part of the investigation team."

"I wish you wouldn't put it that way."

"Why not?" asked Theodosia.

"Because you know I'd rather not get pulled into this."

"Okay," said Theodosia. "How about this. I want you along because you're the voice of reason in the group."

"The group being . . ."

"You and me."

"Small group," said Drayton.

"With a smaller chance of figuring out who stabbed Rob and snatched that crazy skull."

"Don't sell yourself short," said Drayton. "With you on the case all bets are off."

12

Lunch went off without a hitch, if you didn't count Delaine and Scarlette forming a mutual admiration society, bemoaning the state of contemporary art, then wandering around the Indigo Tea Shop looking at every tea tin, tea strainer, and teacup, but not buying a single thing.

"Everyone's lingering," said Theodosia, gazing out across the tea shop. It had to happen today of all days, when she had so much to do.

"And that's a bad thing?" Drayton inquired.

"It is if we want to work on the cheese pairings," said Theodosia. "And help Haley prep the appetizers for my housewarming party tonight."

"And shoehorn in Professor Muncie."

"There's that," said Theodosia. "Did you call him?" She jiggled a teapot nervously. "Why don't you run back to my office and call him."

"Me?" said Drayton.

"You're on the board of the Heritage Society," said

Theodosia, "so you can make our meeting sound a little more academic."

"Instead of like we're trying to ferret out a murderer?" said Drayton. "Or launch a wild-goose chase over a skull drinking cup?"

"Well . . . yes."

"Oh, Drayton!" called Scarlette, rushing up to the front counter, "I wanted to get a tea recommendation from you."

Drayton gave a solicitous nod. "Of course, dear lady."

"My ex-mother-in-law is coming to visit," said Scarlette, "and I wanted to host a small tea party." She turned slightly to include Theodosia and said, with an eye roll, "Of course, the woman's such a busybody she positively *dominates* every conversation!"

Theodosia couldn't resist. "Then why don't you serve a Darjeeling from India's Namring Garden," she suggested. "It's so brisk it'll keep her puckered up for a good long time!"

"The cheeses have arrived," said Haley. She'd slipped out into the tea room, where three tables of customers were sipping afternoon tea and enjoying her raisin scones.

"Huh?" said Drayton, looking up from a tin of Egyptian chamomile tea. He'd been studying the label and contemplating placing another order.

"Guy just delivered 'em to the back door," said Haley, jerking her thumb backward. "Good thing I heard him pounding or we'd have ended up with a big box of cheese fondue."

Drayton's brows pinched together. "What are you talking about?"

"You know," said Haley, "all the cheese would have melted from the sun."

"Doubtful," said Drayton.

Haley shrugged. "Whatever. It's here."

"Fabulous," said Theodosia, who was eager to get going. Once they'd worked out the cheese and tea pairings she could relax, knowing that tomorrow night's event finally had a bare-bones plan. But that particular thought also prompted a little shiver. Bare bones were not what she had in mind. Obviously, that crazy skull cup was preying heavy on her brain!

"Haley," said Drayton, handing over a hot, steaming teapot, "be a love and do refills, will you? Theo and I need to put our heads together for a few minutes."

"Okay," said Haley. "But you guys are going to give me a hand with the stuff for tonight, right?"

"You know we will," said Theodosia, as she and Drayton headed for her back office.

"Oh, these are really excellent," Drayton enthused. He'd already ripped open the top of the cardboard crate and pulled out two cold gel packs. Now he was gazing in delight at the assortment of cheese. "The cheesemonger sent the exact French Camembert I was hoping for. Perfect. Really perfect."

Theodosia slid into the chair behind her desk, while Drayton perched on the big upholstered chair across from her. The fanciful chair they'd dubbed the tuffet.

"Please tell me you have this pretty much worked out," she told him.

Drayton, who was still pulling out wedges and wheels of cheese, nodded. "You take notes while I mumble a bit, will you?"

"Deal," said Theodosia. She grabbed a pen and a sheet of paper.

"So with this Camembert," said Drayton, "we should serve a full-bodied tea. Probably an Assam."

"Camembert goes with Assam," said Theodosia, writing it down. "Check."

"This goat cheese would be perfect with a Darjeeling."

"Okay," said Theodosia.

"And cheddar will work very well with an oolong."

"Got it," said Theodosia. She was beginning to feel better about the pairings, now that they had the cheese in hand. Likewise, Drayton had obviously put a lot of thought into this.

"Gorgonzola," said Drayton, balancing an enormous wedge in his hand.

"Now we're getting into the stinky cheeses," laughed Theodosia.

"*Strong* cheeses," said Drayton. "Nice and ripe."

"So what does ripe cheese pair best with?" she asked.

"Definitely a Pouchong," said Drayton, reaching into the carton again. "And as for these two hard cheeses, the Asiago and Parmesan, we'll serve them with Keemun tea."

"This all sounds terrific," Theodosia enthused. "But how do you want to work the tastings?"

"I've thought about that," said Drayton, "and I think the best way is to have three or four different tea stations."

"Kind of like a cocktail party," said Theodosia. "Where there's a different appetizer at each table."

"Something like that," said Drayton. "We'll cut the cheese into cubes and wedges, set out our crackers and sliced bread, then have the appropriate teas right there with the cheeses."

"You're thinking the tiny Chinese cups?" They had a couple of boxes of small ceramic cups without handles that they'd used for previous tea tastings.

"The Yi-Xing cups," said Drayton. "Yes. They'll be perfect."

"I think so, too," said Theodosia. She sat back and smiled, then pulled her legs up and tucked them under her, relishing the feeling of finally having a good, workable plan.

Too bad those happy feelings didn't last!

Because not five seconds later, Timothy Neville called.

"Anything?" he demanded. Timothy didn't bother with the niceties of identifying himself or rendering a friendly "Hello, how are you?"

"Not yet," said Theodosia, her feeling of accomplishment

suddenly bursting like so many tiny soap bubbles. "We've been working on the skull cup angle, but so far nothing's jumped out."

"Can you stop by my office late this afternoon?" he asked.

"Just a minute," said Theodosia. She dropped the phone to her chest and said to Drayton, "What time is our meeting with Professor Muncie?"

"Three," said Drayton.

"Timothy wants us to drop by his office."

Drayton pursed his lips. "Going to be tight."

"We'll see you at four," said Theodosia.

"Good enough," said Timothy. Then a faint click sounded in Theodosia's ear.

"You're welcome," she said. "And good-bye." She glanced at Drayton. "Timothy sounded awfully . . . intense."

"I didn't tell you," said Drayton, "but he called me last night. Right after I got home from the concert."

"Did he grill you?"

"Of course," said Drayton, "about what you did or didn't do."

"I wish Timothy were bugging Tidwell as much as he's bugging us," said Theodosia.

"Rest assured," said Drayton. "He is."

"*I've got it* all under control," Haley told them, as she chopped, sliced, and diced like a professional state fair vendor.

"I'm glad somebody does," said Theodosia.

"No," said Haley, "I really do. I didn't think I could do it alone, but I've got most of the appetizers ready to go for your party tonight." Her charm bracelet rattled on her wrist as she worked, a present from Theodosia.

"Are you sure?" asked a skeptical Drayton. He and Theodosia were hunkered in the doorway of the kitchen, torn between staying to help and dashing off to their meeting with Professor Muncie.

"What I did," said Haley, "was ask Miss Dimple to come in and help. In fact, she should be here any minute." Miss Dimple was their freelance bookkeeper, a mature, motherly woman who loved nothing better than helping out in the tea shop.

"An excellent idea," said Theodosia. "So what's on the menu? Or is it going to remain a deep, dark secret?"

"Eggplant crostini," said Haley, as she scooped diced eggplant into a large bowl.

"Yum," said Theodosia.

Haley nodded. "Plus, I'm going to do a tomato and basil dip, some cheesy bruschetta, and, as a wild card, my salmon tartare."

"Raw salmon?" said Drayton. "Seriously?"

Haley grinned. "Think of it as tarted-up sashimi. A tasty little concoction of crème fraîche, chopped salmon, and minced onions served in my special coronets." Haley's coronets were paper-thin, ice cream cone–shaped biscuits. The perfect crunchy container for all manner of pâté or tartare.

"What do you want us to do?" asked Theodosia. The menu was spectacular but sounded like a lot of work.

Haley lifted a hand and made a shooing motion. "Just go. Leave me alone and I'll get everything done faster than if you were breathing down my neck."

"Haley," said Drayton, "we never breathe down your neck."

"Drayton," said Haley, "you always do."

Professor Irwin Muncie had his office in the Middleton Building on the campus of the College of Charleston. Theodosia and Drayton wandered down a long, wood-paneled corridor that smelled of burned coffee and lemon oil, where dozens of professors' names were stenciled on windows of pebbled glass. They took one wrong turn, backtracked, then finally found Professor Muncie's office and the source of the burned coffee.

Muncie must have been a fairly big-shot professor, because he didn't rate just an office; he had a small suite. The outside office, really a cluttered reception room, overflowed with books, tilting bookshelves, and old-fashioned filing cabinets crammed full of paper. There was also a human skeleton dangling in the far corner of the room.

"Is this the office of a history professor or the Grim Reaper?" Drayton muttered, looking askance.

At which point a young man snapped the Off switch on a decades-old Mr. Coffee, frowned, and said, "May I help you?"

"We're here to see Professor Muncie," said Theodosia.

"We have a three o'clock appointment," Drayton added.

The young man inclined his head toward a half-open door that led to an inner office. "Go on in, he's expecting you."

"Don't mind Wilbur," exclaimed a small man with sparkling brown eyes and a slight stoop who suddenly loomed in the doorway. "He's left over from when I used to share an office with an anatomy professor. But Professor Winston has long since retired, while Wilbur continues to entertain my guests."

"It's great to meet you," said Theodosia, shaking Muncie's hand.

"Many thanks for agreeing to see us so quickly," said Drayton.

"Peter," said Muncie, glancing at the young man. "You care to join us?" He aimed a quick, perfunctory smile at Theodosia and Drayton and said, "You don't mind if Peter sits in, do you?" He made an introductory motion. "Peter Grace, my grad student. He's a bit of a pirate aficionado, too."

"Nice to meet you," said Drayton.

"Hello," said Theodosia, as they all crowded into Muncie's office and settled into sagging red leather chairs.

Muncie, obviously used to being quizzed on all things

pirate, jumped right in and grabbed the lead. "You're looking for information on the missing skull cup."

"That's right," said Drayton.

"And your interest is?" asked Muncie. His bright eyes, slightly magnified behind round, horn-rimmed glasses, bounced from Drayton to Theodosia and then back to Drayton.

Drayton glanced sideways at Theodosia, then said, "I'm on the board of directors at the Heritage Society, and Theodosia and I promised Timothy Neville we'd look into things. Privately, of course."

"Privately without the police?" asked Muncie.

"Privately as a favor to Timothy," said Theodosia. "Our mission is fact-finding rather than investigatory." *Ouch, that was a bit of a white lie, wasn't it?*

"As you might imagine," said Drayton, "Timothy is quite upset by this whole thing. The murder, obviously, but the theft is on his mind, too."

Muncie's gnarled fingers tapped against his desk for a few moments, and then he said, "The murder was heinous, yes. But I don't mind telling you I was utterly shocked by the sudden appearance of the Blackbeard skull cup."

"Excuse me?" said Theodosia, leaning forward in her chair.

"You see," said Muncie, "I'd assumed the skull was gone forever. That the Brethren of the Coast had long since hidden it. Or maybe even forgotten about it."

"The Brethren . . . ?" stammered Theodosia. Clearly there was a lot she didn't know about this skull!

"The Brethren of the Coast," said Muncie, "is a secret society. A closed group that's basically primogenitary in nature. That is, membership is handed down from father to son."

"But who are they really?" asked Theodosia.

Professor Muncie glanced at Peter.

"Old families," said Peter, jumping in. "Founding fathers."

"How old?" asked Theodosia.

"Blackbeard was killed in 1718," Peter told them, "so do the math. We're basically talking pre–American Revolution."

"And you believe this secret society had the skull cup in their possession for . . . what?" said Theodosia. "A century or so? And then somehow lost it?"

Muncie leaned forward in his squeaky chair. "That's correct."

"And now these secretive types have stolen the skull back again?" she asked. It was a fantastical tale she wasn't ready to buy into.

"I don't know that for a fact," said Muncie. "Really, the thief could have been anyone."

"Anyone who wanted it in their private collection," said Drayton.

"Or knew the legend," said Peter Grace.

"Legend," said Theodosia.

Muncie gave a nervous smile as he ran a wizened hand through thinning silver hair. Then he leaned forward in his chair and said, "Surely you've heard the legend about Blackbeard's treasure."

13

Seconds passed in which they could have heard the proverbial pin drop. Then Theodosia yelped, "What?"

"Excuse me?" said Drayton.

"You've never heard about Blackbeard's treasure?" asked Muncie.

"Uh . . . no," said Theodosia. Could he not tell by her stunned expression? By her less-than-intelligent retort?

"Tell us," said Drayton.

"There's supposedly an inscription on the underside of the skull cup," said Peter Grace, "that points to the location of the treasure."

Theodosia let loose a sigh. "You're not serious," she said. He couldn't be serious. Inscription on the cup? Blackbeard's treasure? In this century?

"What kind of treasure is it?" Drayton asked in a matter-of-fact tone, as if he were inquiring what variety of peaches the greengrocer was selling today.

"Typical pirate's treasure," Muncie chortled. "Gold, silver, and precious gems thrown in for good measure."

"Gems meaning diamonds?" asked Theodosia.

"That would be the general idea," said Muncie. "With the diamond in the missing skull cup supposedly offering a tantalizing hint of what's to be had in the missing trove."

"Assuming there really is an inscription," said Theodosia, "do you know what it says? Or how it might pinpoint the location of this supposed treasure?"

"No, no, no," said Muncie, shaking his head vigorously. "I said *point* to the treasure, not pinpoint. Blackbeard himself was quoted as saying he'd buried his treasure 'where none but Satan can find it.'"

"So the inscription on the skull cup only *alludes* to a general location," said Theodosia. This was getting more and more complicated!

"Something like that," said Grace, jumping in again. He cleared his throat, then said, "Apparently, the skull is just one of three items that, when read together, reveals the precise location."

"What are the other items?" asked Drayton.

"There's supposedly a cipher stone," said Muncie. "A type of brick with writing carved into it."

"Has this brick been lost to posterity, too?" asked Theodosia.

"That's where it all gets appropriately fuzzy," said Grace. "One account has it buried in a wall somewhere, possibly out on Folly Island, where Blackbeard owned a small cottage."

"Do we know if the place is still standing?" asked Drayton.

"Knocked down a century and a half ago," said Muncie. "Swept away in a monumental hurricane."

"The other account," said Grace, "the one *I* personally subscribe to because there have been multiple historic references, is that the cipher stone ended up as a doorstop in a long-ago Charleston bookbinder's shop."

"Interesting," said Theodosia. "Has anyone ever searched for it? For the bookbinder's shop, I mean?"

"People have," said Muncie, "but no one's ever found it. The shop or the cipher stone."

"These legends and lore are fascinating," said Drayton, "but I don't see how you can put much stock in them."

But Theodosia was still processing this new information. She knew that legends were often based on little bits and pieces of historic flotsam that bobbed and swirled their way through the decades. So there might be something here, the operative word being *might*. Swiveling her head toward Muncie, she asked, "Have you ever searched for the treasure?"

Professor Muncie clapped his hands together, then quickly pulled them apart, as if to indicate that something important was now irretrievably lost forever. "Dear lady," he said in a kind of wheeze, "if I had even an *inkling*, I'd probably be out hunting right now."

They sat there for a moment, silence settling around them. Late-afternoon rays of sunlight shone through the windows, revealing slowly twisting dust motes. Theodosia inhaled sharply and said, "You said there were three items that would help fix the location. What's the third one?"

"It's Blackbeard's actual ship," said Grace. "The *Queen Anne's Revenge*. It's been discovered off the coast of Beaufort Inlet, North Carolina. A bronze bell, a brass blunderbuss, pewter ware, and cannons have already been brought up. Now there's a large-scale recovery being planned to try to salvage the anchor and hull structure."

"Good heavens," said Drayton. He suddenly looked as if he *did* believe the legend. "They're bringing Blackbeard's ship up after more than two hundred years?"

"Trying to," said Grace. "As we all learned with the *Hunley* expedition, underwater archaeology is dicey at best."

Theodosia nodded. The *Hunley* was a Civil War submersible that had been located in 1995. Finally, in 2004 the city of Charleston had staged a funeral for the eight-man crew who'd been lost at sea all these many years. She remembered well the solemn procession of men in replica Confederate uniforms and the stately horse-drawn caissons.

"I hope we've been some help to you," said Muncie, pulling himself to his feet. His knees made sharp popping sounds as a quirky sort of punctuation to indicate the meeting was concluded.

"You've given us an amazing amount of information," said Theodosia. "More than we hoped for."

"But nothing to help you solve the murder of that poor boy," said Muncie. "Or recover Timothy Neville's skull cup."

"Probably not," said Drayton, "but at least we can go back to Timothy and, in all good conscience, tell him we did our best. Thanks to you."

"If you think of anything else . . ." said Theodosia, handing Muncie her business card.

Professor Muncie nodded. "I'll have Peter search our files and see if there's any other data we can pull up for you."

"Happy to," said Peter.

"Anything's appreciated," said Theodosia. "No matter how insignificant you think it might be."

"What do you think?" asked Drayton, as they bounced across town in Theodosia's Jeep, heading for the Heritage Society and their late-afternoon meeting with Timothy.

"Lots to digest," said Theodosia. They were running late, and she was doing her best to maneuver through heavy traffic on Beaufain Street without cutting off too many drivers and alienating everyone in sight. Somewhere, in that part of her brain that clung to the old-fashioned notion of fairness and justice, she knew there had to be a happy medium between politeness and good, offensive driving.

"Muncie's stories could all be a bunch of hooey," said

Drayton. He glanced out the window, focusing on a line of swaying palmettos that stood like the queen's guard against red brick buildings with brilliant white window trim. "Probably are."

"Maybe so. Then again, maybe not."

"You're undecided?" asked Drayton. "Sitting on the fence?"

"The thing is," said Theodosia, "if you buy into all the legends and lore, then factor in the clues and historical facts, it all merges into a kind of . . . what would you call it? A chain of evidence?"

Drayton pursed his lips and picked at a bit of fuzz that had attached itself to his navy blue jacket. "Whatever do you mean?"

"Putting it simply," said Theodosia, "if the skull cup leads to the treasure, then the treasure probably leads to the killer."

"And if there is no treasure?"

"Doesn't matter if there is or isn't," said Theodosia. "What we have to keep in mind is that the killer *believes* there is. And that's why he didn't hesitate to kill."

"Unless he's just some deranged coot who's crazy for skulls."

"There is that," agreed Theodosia.

Timothy Neville wasn't alone in his office when they arrived. An older gentleman, at least Timothy's age or older, was crumped into one of the high-backed leather chairs that faced Timothy's acre of ebony desk.

"You're here," said Timothy, inclining his head to observe Theodosia and Drayton's arrival. "Finally."

"We've just come from a rather interesting meeting," said Drayton.

"Yes, yes," said Timothy, impatiently. "But introductions first. I have someone I want you both to meet."

Theodosia wasn't psychic; she especially didn't believe in horoscopes or tarot cards or lucky numbers. But deep down in the limbic part of her brain, the intuitive part, she felt a quick spark and knew instantly the identity of Timothy's guest.

"Mr. Pruett," said Theodosia, extending a hand to the elderly gentleman.

"How did you know who he was?" Timothy rasped.

Theodosia couldn't tell whether Timothy was pleased or annoyed. Probably the latter. "Took a wild guess," she told him.

The elderly Pruett closed his small hand around hers and shook her hand weakly. "Nice to meet you, Miss . . ."

"It's Theodosia," Timothy snapped, "the woman I was telling you about. The only person who had the presence of mind to rush to the rescue Sunday night."

"Lovely to meet you, my dear," said the old man.

"I take it you *are* Sidney Pruett?" said Theodosia. Timothy still hadn't made a proper introduction, even though she was pretty sure this was the man who'd donated the skull cup some forty years ago.

"I am, indeed," said Pruett. He gazed past Theodosia and said, "And you must be Drayton, of whom I've also heard a great deal."

"Good to meet you, sir," said Drayton, who did everything but click his heels together and bow like a fencing instructor.

"Pull up a chair and sit down, you two," Timothy ordered. "We've just been talking about our missing skull cup."

"I imagine you have," said Theodosia.

"I know this is going to sound strange," said Pruett, once they were all settled around Timothy's desk, "but I'm worried my donation may have brought the Heritage Society a spot of bad luck."

"Why would you think that?" asked Theodosia. *As if it hasn't already brought bad luck. Especially for poor Rob Commers.*

Timothy Neville was also startled by Pruett's words. He canted his small, bony head, waiting for an answer.

Pruett suddenly looked uneasy. His tongue flicked out to lick his lips, and he seemed to be weighing his thoughts. He finally said, "The thing is, that awful skull cup brought my grandfather nothing but bad luck. And we're talking more than one hundred years ago."

"A long time has passed since that skull cup came into his possession," said Drayton. "Time for any number of legends to percolate." He hesitated. "Legends that are probably just ghost stories."

"Still," said Pruett, "right after that skull came into his possession, my grandfather pretty much lost all his investments and land holdings."

"Do you know how your grandfather came to own the skull cup?" asked Theodosia.

"Not really," said Pruett. "Knowing him, he probably won it in a poker game. He had a definite wild streak."

"But you really believe," said Theodosia, "have *always* believed that the skull cup is the genuine article, crafted from Blackbeard's actual skull?"

"Oh my, yes," said Pruett.

"Okay," said Theodosia. "Then you must also believe that Blackbeard's trusted second-in-command buried a large pirate treasure and had a clue to its location engraved on the bottom of that cup?"

"I've never subscribed to that notion," said Pruett. "The engraving's there, of course, but I've never heard of any treasure. Surely, if the engraving pointed to a location, my grandfather would have been off and running." He gave a quick smile. "Off and *digging.*"

"But the treasure is part and parcel of the Blackbeard

story," said Theodosia. "There are supposedly clues on Blackbeard's ship, the skull cup, and the cipher stone."

"Excuse me?" said Timothy, who suddenly looked startled. "Exactly how did you come by all this information? I've never heard about this ship or a . . . what was the term you used . . . cipher stone?"

Theodosia and Drayton quickly recounted their meeting with Professor Muncie and his grad student, Peter Grace, and laid out their newfound information.

"Amazing," breathed Timothy. "I've lived here all my life and never heard these far-fetched tales."

Pruett shook his head. "I only knew about the engraving on the skull cup. And then I still never knew what it *meant*."

"Your Professor Muncie is quite a fountain of knowledge," said Timothy.

"It's too bad," said Drayton, "that no one took the time to read the cup's inscription." He frowned, lifted a hand to scratch his cheek, then said, "Or did they?"

That thought tickled Theodosia's curiosity. "That's a very good question. Did anybody here take a look at the bottom?" And, pray tell, why hadn't she thought to ask this before?

Timothy gave a halfhearted shrug. "I certainly didn't."

"But someone must have seen the inscription," said Theodosia, starting to warm up to the idea. "Who handled the cup? Who set up the display?"

"George Meadow, one of our curators, set up the display," said Timothy.

"Can we get him in here?" asked Theodosia.

"Unfortunately," said Timothy, "George is on his way to a trekking expedition in the Himalayas even as we speak."

"Someone else, then?" said Theodosia.

"Camilla helped," said Timothy. "I distinctly remember her making a comment about tarnished silver, then taking the skull cup and doing a beautiful job polishing it."

"There you go," said Drayton. "We should talk to Camilla. She may have read the inscription!"

"She's still in the hospital," said Timothy.

"Even so," said Drayton, "we may have to get in touch with her. This is important. Practically life and death."

"We can't just call Camilla up and start firing questions," said Theodosia. "It might . . . frighten her. If she's in a fragile state of mind, the murder and the assault could come crashing back at her." She hesitated. "It could all be dangerous to her psyche."

"She's being discharged later today," said Timothy. He glanced at his watch and seemed surprised at the time. "Maybe right now."

"Perhaps she'll be at the funeral tomorrow?" offered Drayton.

"The funeral," Theodosia murmured. "Yes, we should probably attend."

"No telling what Camilla will remember, though," said Drayton. "She got hit awfully hard."

They sat for a while in Timothy's palatial office. Low lighting fell upon the Oriental carpets and mahogany bookshelves as the tick of an old clock kept time with their thoughts.

Finally, the proverbial lightbulb went off over Theodosia's head. "I have an idea." It was a *big* idea, she thought. A *cagey* idea.

"What?" asked Drayton.

"There's a chance we could get a look at that skull cup after all," said Theodosia.

"What are you blathering about?" Timothy snapped. "The skull cup's missing! It didn't suddenly come waltzing back in here of its own accord."

But a slow smile was beginning to spread across Theodosia's face. "The photo and blurb that appeared in last week's

Post and Courier? We need to get in touch with the reporter who wrote that blurb. Nick Van Buren."

"Goodness," said Drayton, "Theo's right."

"And talk to his photographer," said Theodosia. "Because maybe, just maybe, those newspaper guys got a shot of the bottom of that skull cup!"

14

❧

"We're here to see Nick Van Buren," Theodosia told the receptionist. She was slightly out of breath from rushing across town and was feeling more than a little jangled. After all, in less than two hours she was supposed to don a silk blouse and long hostess skirt and play the role of warm and charming new homeowner. She also had her fingers crossed, hoping against hope, that dear, dependable Haley and good-hearted Miss Dimple would schlep all the appetizers to her home and keep them warm and cozy in the oven while they set up wineglasses, small plates, and everything else. Oh, and could they please deal with Earl Grey, too, whose nose or entire muzzle might possibly be out of joint?

"Sign here," said the receptionist. She was an older lady with frizzled gray hair and a no-nonsense black pantsuit. Without glancing up at them, she slid a pen across the counter, followed by a large book that looked a little like an old-fashioned ledger. "Name, company, time of arrival," she told them.

Theodosia signed in, then passed the pen to Drayton. Once they were officially logged in, the receptionist gave them visitor's passes to clip to their clothing and instructed them to wait in the lobby while she phoned for Nick Van Buren to come down and escort them upstairs to the newsroom. They'd called Van Buren on their way over, and he'd graciously agreed to meet with them. Of course, Theodosia knew he wasn't doing this out of the goodness of his heart. Van Buren was doing it because, like a good bluetick coonhound scenting fresh game, he sensed the continuation of a juicy story.

But Van Buren was as good as his word. He appeared before them barely two minutes later and hastily escorted them up to his cubicle in the writer's bullpen on the third floor.

When they were ensconced in uncomfortable director's chairs, their three sets of knees practically touching, Theodosia said, "Were you able to get hold of the photos?"

Van Buren hesitated before he answered. Then he said, "Yes, I did. Sort of."

"You don't have them," said Drayton. "I knew it." He threw his arms up. "Yet another wild-goose chase."

Theodosia lifted a hand to make a calming gesture. "Let him explain, Drayton."

"If I share the photos with you," said Van Buren, "then I need to have some kind of assurance that you'll share your information with me. And I'm talking any and all information about the skull cup and that so-called treasure you mentioned."

"I hear you," said Theodosia. "And I agree." She slid her foot over and nudged Drayton's foot. "We agree."

"I suppose," said Drayton.

"Okay," said Van Buren, leaning back in his chair, looking relaxed now. "Good enough."

"And the photos are . . . ?" asked Drayton.

"The photographer has the ones we didn't print," said Van Buren. "A freelance guy named Sonny Wickes."

"How many are there?" asked Theodosia.

"Fifteen, maybe twenty shots," said Van Buren.

"Some showing the bottom of the cup?" asked Theodosia. After all, this was the biggie; this was why they'd chased over here like crazy people.

"He says yes," said Van Buren. "Anyway, I already spoke with Sonny and he's promised to e-mail you jpegs. We both agree that's the best way."

"Jpegs," said Drayton. "That means photos?"

Theodosia nodded. "When can I get them?"

"Possibly tonight," said Van Buren, "tomorrow at the latest."

Theodosia dug in her purse and pulled out a business card. She twiddled it between her fingers, then handed it to Van Buren. "I'll be home tonight and at the tea shop first thing tomorrow. All my numbers are right there."

"I'll call you first thing tomorrow," said Van Buren. "See what kind of game plan we can work out."

"*You didn't mention* the cipher stone," said Drayton, once they were well outside the building.

"Not yet, I didn't," said Theodosia.

"It's our little secret?" said Drayton.

"I wish," said Theodosia, "but I have the distinct feeling that news of the cipher stone is going to go viral very shortly. Think about it. Professor Muncie and Peter Grace know about it, as do Timothy Neville and Sidney Pruett. Tomorrow, I'll probably have to cut Van Buren in."

"So now it's a race. A competition of sorts," said Drayton, as he climbed into the Jeep. "To see who finds out what first."

"Always is," said Theodosia. She climbed in, pulled her

door shut, and kicked over the engine. A throaty and not-so-subtle vroom burst from the rear pipes.

"When are you going to trade this thing in?" asked Drayton.

She gazed at him. "Never?"

One of his eyebrows pulled up into a quivering arc.

"I love my Jeep," said Theodosia. "What else can take me into the low country so I can gather wild dandelion greens, herbs, and morels?"

"Maybe they'll bring back that Cash for Clunkers program from a couple of years ago," Drayton muttered as he pulled his seatbelt across and fastened it.

"I heard that," said Theodosia. "I'm sitting right here, you know." She put the Jeep into gear and pulled into traffic on Rivers Avenue. "Just for the record, do you have any thoughts on the cipher stone?"

"Such as?"

"Well, do you think it might still be kicking around Charleston?"

"No idea," said Drayton.

"Noodle it around, will you? If the cipher stone was used as a doorstop at an old bookbinder, where's the old book-binder now? Have you thought about that?"

"Not really," said Drayton, "but I could certainly do some research."

"That's a great idea," said Theodosia, hoping her enthusiasm might spark some more spirit on Drayton's part. "Because you're our resident book lover and history guru. So while you're at it, think about where that cipher stone might have disappeared to. Did some antique dealer snap it up? Is it now a stone in somebody's backyard garden? Or, if it was a big enough curiosity, could it be the cornerstone in some old building?"

"All good questions," said Drayton.

"I have another one," said Theodosia.

"What's that?"

"If we're hunting for this cipher stone," said Theodosia, "is our killer hunting for it, too?"

Theodosia could only wish for blessings to rain down upon Haley's and Miss Dimple's heads. Because when she finally arrived home, far later than she'd ever expected, the two of them were bustling about like they owned the joint. Haley was fluffing pillows with a vengeance, lining up wineglasses in tight little rows, and stacking small plates on the highboy. Miss Dimple was humming away as she damp-mopped the entryway.

"How can I ever thank you!" Theodosia cried, dropping her suede jacket and hobo bag in the middle of the living room.

"You can start by picking those things up and stowing them away properly," said Haley, pointing at the jacket and bag. She was a neat freak of the first magnitude: compulsive, order-loving, and probably the perfect person to ensure that Theodosia's home was shipshape for tonight.

Miss Dimple toddled over to greet her. A plump septuagenarian, she was their freelance bookkeeper, pinch-hit waitress, and all-around go-to gal.

"Happy to help out," said Miss Dimple, standing on tiptoes and embracing Theodosia in a motherly bear hug. "You know I love to be needed."

"You're needed," said Haley, her eyes darting around the living room, "there's no doubt about that."

"The food's all prepared?" Theodosia asked.

"Everything's stashed in the kitchen," said Haley, "so we're good to go. I thought I'd wait until about five minutes before the opening bell and then put everything out."

"Opening bell?" said Theodosia.

"You know what I mean," said Haley, as she dashed over to straighten a picture on the wall.

"But you're supposed to be a guest at the party," Theodosia called after Haley. She turned around to smile at Miss Dimple. "You, too. I don't want the two of you working during the party."

"No, no," said Haley, making a beeline for the highboy again. "It's not going to work *unless* we're working." She stopped, scratched her head, and said, "Does that make sense?"

"Yes and no," said Theodosia.

"Anyway," said Haley, "look at you, standing there all casual and slightly bedraggled! You'd better run upstairs and change. I'd say you've got twenty minutes at best!"

"Scoot," said Miss Dimple, falling under the spell of Haley's rush-rush mode. "We'll take care of everything else."

"How can I ever repay you?" Theodosia asked, hurrying up the stairs.

"Not to worry," Haley shouted out, "I'll think of something!"

Theodosia's second floor consisted of three rooms: a nice-sized bedroom with a rounded turret corner that she'd turned into a cozy little reading nook, plus two other smaller rooms. She'd splurged on a jungle gym of aluminum shelves and clothes bars and converted one of the smaller rooms into a walk-in closet. Which was where she now stood, gazing at her reflection in the mirror and wondering if her black silk blouse was too revealing, the long plaid skirt a little too wintry?

No, you look fine. Get on with it. Don't be a paranoid ninny.

She padded barefoot into the bathroom, fluffed out her auburn hair until it swirled around her shoulders, then added a hint of Chanel's Pink Sand lip gloss.

Perfect.

Well, not quite. She still had to decide on shoes. So . . . maybe black mules or, better yet, the shoe booties she'd bought at Delaine's shop? Sure, why not? The booties were cute and kicky and would win points with Delaine, which was always a good thing.

As she got down on her hands and knees, digging the shoe booties out from where they'd somehow been flung under a plastic bag that held a winter coat, her phone began to ring. Theodosia snagged the boots, pulled herself up, rushed into her bedroom, and dug out her cell phone. "Theo here," she answered breathlessly.

It was Parker. And he was calling with bad news.

"I can't make it tonight," he told her.

"What?" she cried. "Oh, no. Seriously?"

"Seriously," said Parker. "I'm not even in town."

"You're still in Savannah?" He was supposed to be back in Charleston this morning at the latest.

"Afraid so. I'm stuck down here for the time being, still wrangling away about money and a bunch of other stuff you wouldn't believe."

"Wow," said Theodosia. She gazed at the top of her dresser, where a half-dozen colorful teacups held random gold chains, strands of pearls, bangle bracelets, and pairs of earrings. And realized she felt bad for a couple of reasons. One, Parker wasn't going to be here tonight when she got to show off her cute little cottage. And, two, she hadn't really thought about Parker all that much in the last couple of days. Of course, she'd been chasing around like a madwoman trying to ferret out information on that crazy skull cup.

Still . . .

"Are you still there?" Parker asked.

"I'm really sorry you can't make it," said Theodosia. "But I understand."

"I knew you would because you're that kind of lady. So, uh, have fun, okay?"

"I will," said Theodosia.

"But not too much fun," said Parker. He gave a merry laugh, but she thought she'd detected a down note in his voice, too.

"Miss you," said Theodosia, just as the downstairs doorbell chimed.

15

❧

It was truly a night to remember. Lovely and perfect and filled with good friends who were more than eager to bestow good wishes upon her.

And stacks of housewarming presents, too.

"You shouldn't have!" Theodosia exclaimed as Delaine thrust an enormous pink-wrapped gift with a yellow froufrou bow into her arms. Interestingly enough, the pink gift matched Delaine's one-shouldered pink sheath dress.

"Don't be silly!" said Delaine. "Of course I should. Max and I want only the best for you in your new home, don't we, dear?" Delaine tilted her head toward Max and made a kiss-kiss motion with her lips. Like a dutiful boyfriend, Max obliged her with a quick peck. "Now run into the kitchen, dearie," she told him, "and see if you can find me a glass of champagne." She held up a finger. "And make sure it's brut and not just extra dry. You know my metabolism can't *tolerate* too much sugar!"

"Is Nadine going to be able to make it, too?" Theodosia

asked, knowing in her heart she'd never have the guts or the heart to treat a man as if he were a Labrador retriever. Certainly not *that* man, anyway.

Delaine gave an airy wave as her sharp eyes roved back and forth, taking in the crush of guests as well as the décor in Theodosia's living room. "She and Bill Glass are probably five minutes behind me," she chirped. "Oh, *that's* new, isn't it?" She pointed toward an antique beveled mirror. "I don't remember seeing it in your old place. Of course, you didn't have a lot of space to work with. And there certainly wasn't as much charm as this little carriage house has. Actually, this place positively *oozes* cuteness and charm. How did you ever manage to *afford* it?"

Two minutes later, Drayton showed up. And five minutes after that, another dozen guests piled in, so the party was definitely launched.

Miss Dimple, relishing her role as official greeter, answered the door and dutifully took coats. Haley, who'd changed into a short black ruffled skirt, black tank, and crisp white apron, circulated with trays of appetizers. Earl Grey padded quietly among the buzz of guests, looking happy and proud that so many people, dog lovers to be sure, had showed up to view his new home.

"Tea," Drayton said to Theodosia. He held up a shiny black and gold tin and gave it a quick shake. "We have to brew a pot of tea, if only to allow the rich scent to waft through your home and work some aromatherapy magic."

"Which tea did you bring?" Haley asked, cutting in and resting her tray against one hip.

"A harmonious new creation," said Drayton. "Something I call Theodosia's Housewarming Blend." He plunked the tea tin into Theodosia's hands. "Created just for you."

"Oh my gosh," said Theodosia, utterly delighted, "I've got my very own blend?"

"You do now," said Drayton, pleased that she was pleased.

"What's in it?" asked Haley.

"Chinese black tea with a hint of citrus and ginger," said Drayton.

Haley narrowed her eyes. "Isn't that the one you were going to call China Bright?"

"For all of eight seconds," said Drayton, grabbing Haley by the shoulders and spinning her around. "Now it's called Theodosia's Housewarming Blend."

"Perfect," grinned Theodosia. She really was thrilled beyond words.

"Still seems fishy to me," muttered Haley, as she ambled off to make the rounds with her appetizers.

"Nice in here," said Drayton, glancing about the little kitchen.

"It needs work," said Theodosia, as she ran water into her teakettle. "As you can see, the cupboards are beyond blah and I'm in dire need of new appliances."

"New appliances are a snap," said Drayton. "You go to Sears or Home Depot and pick them out. Or, if you've got a little extra cash tucked away, you treat yourself to Wolf or Sub-Zero."

"The real problem is the cupboards," said Theodosia, wrinkling her nose at the cheap plywood with the ugly black metal pulls.

"They do exude a certain cheesy fifties-rec-room look," laughed Drayton. "Do you have a particular improvement in mind?"

"Haley has that carpenter friend who works with reclaimed Carolina pine," said Theodosia. "That would be the ticket. Redo pretty much everything. Cupboards, counters, maybe even the back door and window frames."

Drayton nodded. "Pine reclaimed from old barns?"

"Something like that," said Theodosia, setting the teakettle on the stove and turning on the heat. "Anyway, it's what I've got my heart set on. For now."

"Out with the old, in with the new," said Drayton. "By the way, where's your friend Parker?"

"Still stuck in Savannah, dickering over some restaurant deal. Never made it back."

"Pity," said Drayton.

"Knock knock," yelled a brusque voice, and then the swinging door shot inward and smacked so hard against the bad cupboards that Theodosia could hear her cups and glasses rattling from the impact.

"Detective Tidwell!" Theodosia exclaimed, as the oversized detective barged into the room and wedged himself in front of them. "What a surprise!"

"Not at all," said Tidwell. "Imagine *my* surprise when I stopped by the Heritage Society and Timothy Neville regaled me with stories of pirate legends and lore." His beady eyes gazed at Theodosia without emotion. "I felt like I was transported back to the days of my youth, sitting in a tree house and reading hair-raising passages from *Treasure Island*."

"You have to admit," said Theodosia, "that a mysterious inscription on the bottom of the skull cup certainly ups the ante."

Tidwell's unblinking gaze stayed fixed on her. "For whom?"

"For everyone," said Theodosia.

"I was also informed," said Tidwell, finally directing an equal-opportunity disapproving glance at Drayton, "that the two of you enjoyed a rather informative gab session with a certain Professor Irwin Muncie."

"So what if we did?" said Drayton, folding his arms and assuming a somewhat defensive posture.

"Because it tells me that you're once again meddling!" Tidwell barked. "All this running around to dig up information on jolly old Blackbeard and his so-called treasure is mucking things up and getting in the way of my official—need I repeat that word? Oh, yes, I think I will. My *official* police investigation!"

"But we're *not* meddling," said Theodosia. "We're concerned citizens who are trying to uncover useful information."

"Useful to whom?" asked Tidwell. Like a hyperactive teakettle, he seemed to have gone from a mere simmer to a roiling head of steam.

Theodosia fought to keep her cool. "Did Timothy tell you about the other clues?"

"Other clues?" said Tidwell. His jaw seemed to click hard and lock tight in an unhappy grimace.

"There's some sort of cipher stone kicking around Charleston," said Drayton, jumping in, "that helps pinpoint the treasure. And there's something else, a clue, aboard Blackbeard's ship."

"The *Queen Anne's Revenge*," said Theodosia, trying to be helpful.

"Did I just wander onto the *Gilligan's Island* back lot?" Tidwell demanded in a thunderous voice. "Are you seriously trying to solve a murder by searching for a treasure?"

"When you put it that way . . ." Drayton mumbled, gazing down at his shoes.

"We're not trying to solve a murder," Theodosia explained. "That's clearly your jurisdiction. All we're trying to do is shed some light on an impossible situation."

"And you're making a mess of it," said Tidwell. "I understand you even want to interview the Heritage Society's interns."

"Nothing we've done is illegal," Theodosia replied, making up her mind *not* to tell Tidwell about the jpegs that might reveal the actual inscription on the skull cup. At least right now she wasn't going to, since he was in such a butt-kicking, all-fired rage. And to top it off, he was an invited guest in her home. Hah!

A subtle scratch sounded on the other side of the kitchen door.

"Now what?" thundered Tidwell. He spun around, arms akimbo, almost getting stuck between the cupboard and the refrigerator.

The door creaked open and Earl Grey looked up at Tidwell with his solemn, brown-eyed gaze. A steady gaze that said he wasn't intimidated, didn't have a bone to pick, and wasn't remotely interested in the detective's silly affairs.

"You want to lie on your bed?" Theodosia asked her dog. Normally, Earl Grey slept in her room on a big, cushy, over-priced dog bed. But tonight she'd moved that dog bed down to the kitchen so he could sack out early and still be able to share the moment.

Earl Grey eased past Tidwell, accepted a pat from Drayton, and padded over to his bed, which had been positioned beneath the small kitchen table.

"Good boy," said Theodosia. "Just take it easy. In fact, why don't we all try to take it easy."

Lo and behold, just as Theodosia lured Tidwell into the living room with promises of cheesy bruschetta and salmon tartare, Dougan Granville strolled in. He planted his beefy self in the entryway and looked around with an air of quiet confidence and an amused smile on his face.

Theodosia was stunned that Granville had showed up, but pleased at the same time. Since he was a self-proclaimed member of the Jolly Roger Club, maybe she could quiz him on a couple of things. Like . . . treasure?

"That's him," said Theodosia, tapping Drayton's shoulder. "Granville."

"The neighbor?" said Drayton, suddenly interested. "The pirate fan who owns the Kingstree Mansion next door?"

"One and the same," said Theodosia. "Think we should ask him about the cipher stone?"

"Maybe," said Drayton. Then, "What harm could it do? Dollars to doughnuts, he's probably never heard of it."

But when they buttonholed Granville some thirty seconds later, it turned out he had heard of it.

"Oh, absolutely," said Granville, once introductions had been made and the subject of the cipher stone brought up. "Supposed to have some kind of clue engraved on it."

"For the treasure," said Theodosia.

"If there ever was a treasure," growled Granville.

"Where do you suppose the cipher stone is now?" Theodosia asked.

Granville shrugged. "It supposedly ended up in some old printer's shop."

"Bookbinder," said Drayton.

"Whatever," said Granville.

"The thing is," said Theodosia, "have you ever heard any rumors about it turning up *after* its stint at the printer or bookbinder's shop?"

"Can't say as I have," said Granville. "But if you ask my opinion, I'd say that stone probably ended up in the foundation of one of our local shops or mansions." He stuck his hand into his jacket pocket, fumbled around, and said, "Purely as a curiosity, of course."

"Hard to go crawling behind magnolia bushes and peering at everyone's foundation," said Drayton, giving a nervous laugh.

Granville pulled out a slim, elegant-looking cigar. "These days you'd probably get yourself arrested." He chuckled, rocked back on his heels, and stuck the cigar in his mouth.

"You can't smoke in here," said Theodosia.

"Hah?" said Granville. He reached up, took the cigar from his mouth, and twiddled it. "You want me to take this outside?"

"If you would," said Theodosia.

Granville shook his head. "I suppose. These days you can't smoke anywhere." He jabbed his cigar in the direction of Delaine. "Who's that gal over there? The chick in the hot-pink dress?"

"A friend of mine," said Theodosia. "Delaine Dish, the owner of Cotton Duck Boutique. Perhaps you've heard of her shop?"

"Not really," Granville muttered, "but she's a classy-looking broad."

Theodosia managed a slow, reptilian blink. "Yes. Yes, she is."

"You say he's an attorney?" Drayton asked, as Granville did a quick cut-and-run maneuver, then headed straight for Delaine.

"Odd duck, isn't he?" said Theodosia, giving a little shudder. "Would you ever think of putting him on retainer?"

"I'd consider putting him on a leash," said Drayton. "Still, he might just hit it off with Delaine. You never know about relationships and attractions. Pheromones and all of that."

But Theodosia was suddenly focused on the arrival of a couple more guests.

"Theodosia!" exclaimed Nadine, as she pulled Bill Glass after her. "What a lovely party! What a lovely little home!"

"Thank you," said Theodosia. "Glad you two could make it."

Glass lifted his Nikon and aimed it directly at Theodosia and Drayton. Then he squinted at them and said, "Move closer together, will you?"

"You're taking a photo?" asked Drayton, looking startled.

"Sure," said Glass, still squinting. "For a quick little side-bar. *Shooting Star* goes to a housewarming. Man, I like how that sounds. Do you like how that sounds?"

Nadine nodded vigorously. "Brilliant journalism, Bill."

"You know," said Theodosia, holding up a hand, "I really

don't want my party publicized." *And I really don't want anyone to see the inside of my house.*

Glass looked startled. "You don't? Sheesh! Most folks would give their eyeteeth to get their picture in my paper. They're begging for their little turn at celebrity."

"Maybe Mr. Glass could take a few photos tomorrow night," suggested Drayton.

Glass lowered his camera. "Whaddya mean? What's tomorrow night? A better party? An A-list party?"

"We're hosting a tea and cheese tasting," said Theodosia. "The Indigo Tea Shop is one of the Food and Wine Festival venues."

Glass chuckled. "Don't you mean *wine* and cheese?"

"No, we really don't," said Drayton, but Glass was already glancing about, looking bored.

"Still," said Theodosia, trying to get Glass's attention, "the Food and Wine Festival can always use a little publicity."

Suddenly, Glass did a double take and said, "There's that fat detective! The one who kept needling Nadine!"

"Tidwell," said Theodosia. *Oh, no, they're not going to mix it up here, are they?*

"Ooh, I just *hate* him," said Nadine, practically baring her teeth. Which immediately sent Glass careening toward Tidwell.

They are *going to mix it up. Great.*

"I hope you're happy with yourself," Glass said, his voice loud and strident as he railed at Tidwell.

Tidwell tilted his large head and gazed down his nose at Glass. One part of his upper lip curled in abject scorn. "You're talking to me?" he asked, in a voice that could flash-freeze a pan of sizzling bacon.

"You better not pester my girlfriend again," said Glass. He tried to look menacing but was starting to look more and more uncomfortable. He'd started something he didn't quite know how to finish.

"Are you threatening an officer of the law?" Tidwell asked, his voice dripping with disdain. "If that's the case, we can easily resolve this matter." He reached into his jacket and pulled out a cell phone, looking as if he were about to summon cadres of screaming squad cars.

Tidwell's pudgy finger was poised above the Send button when Dougan Granville stepped in with a casual swagger. "Care for a cigar?" He didn't wait for an answer, but stuck a stogie into Tidwell's other hand. "It's a Cohiba. One of Fidel's faves."

Nonplussed, Tidwell stared at the cigar for a few moments, then said, "Seriously?"

"By way of Freeport, Bahamas, by way of Montreal, Quebec," said Granville. He let loose a conspiratorial snicker. "But you don't have to mention *that* to ATF."

Amazingly, Tidwell looked intrigued. "I wouldn't mind trying this," he said, rolling the cigar between his thumb and forefinger, looking like a true cigar aficionado. His harsh words with Bill Glass seemed suddenly forgotten.

Delaine, who hadn't said a word but was watching like a wary cat, suddenly stepped forward and said to Granville, "Would you ever offer a cigar to a lady?"

Granville grinned broadly and said, "For you, babe. Absolutely."

"*That's one way* to defuse a sticky situation," Max remarked.

"And clear out a room," said Theodosia. She turned to face him, grinned, and said, "You don't have a party drink."

"Probably because I don't party," said Max. "Or drink."

"Not even wine? Or champagne?" She'd laid in a large supply of both.

Max shrugged. "Alcohol just never interested me that much."

"Well . . . I have other things to drink."

"Such as?" said Max.

"What about tea?"

"When I'm eating moo goo gai pan at the local greasy chopstick," said Max, "I've been know to amuse myself with a cup or two of oolong."

"But restaurant tea's not always the best or the freshest," said Theodosia. "Most of the time they use tea bags."

"Bags aren't good?" asked Max.

"They're generally just the dregs of what's left over after the leaves have been processed and packaged. Bits of leaves and stems. Why not let me brew a cup of something that's really top quality?" Theodosia offered.

"Sure," said Max. "I'm up for pretty much anything."

Theodosia glanced out the window and saw the glowing red tips of three cigars. "Then I'll fix you up," she told him. "Be right back." Turning, she pushed open the door to the kitchen and slid inside.

"Nice kitchen," Max said, directly behind her.

Theodosia spun around, startled. She hadn't realized that Max had followed so closely on her heels. "Please go back and join the party," Theodosia urged. "I'll bring the tea out to you. It'll only take a minute."

"It's okay," said Max. "It's nice in here. Nice and quiet."

Nice and intriguing. And maybe a little dangerous if Delaine decides to abandon her cigar and saunter back in.

"So," said Theodosia, as she waited for her teakettle to boil, "as the new PR director for the Gibbes Museum, I'm guessing you have a degree in journalism or mass media?"

Max shook his head. "Unh-uh. Museology."

"No kidding. Where'd you go to school?"

"Right after I returned from the Gulf War, I did a double major in Greek art and journalism at NYU. Then I got a master's in museology at the University of Chicago."

Theodosia did a little mental arithmetic. Max was a little older than she'd first thought.

"So you've worked in other museums, too?" Theodosia

asked. She stared at the kettle. Nothing seemed to be happening. No rattle, no bubbles. Except, of course, she was fidgeting like crazy. Such an attractive man, such a small kitchen.

"I've worked here and there," Max told her. "Did some contract archaeology for the state of Washington, worked in salvage archaeology for a while near Boston, and then did publicity and event planning at the de Young Museum in San Francisco."

"An eclectic career," Theodosia remarked, measuring scoops of tea into a Brown Betty teapot, keenly aware that Max seemed to be inching his way closer to her.

"I know a little about a lot of things," said Max.

"A Renaissance man," Theodosia remarked. "We need more of those in this day and age."

Max smiled at her.

"Is the Gibbes Museum involved in the Food and Wine Festival?" she asked. It was another neutral subject and all she could come up with at the moment.

Max leaned in closer. "No, but I'd like to take in a few of the food venues. Got any suggestions?"

The words slipped like butter off Theodosia's tongue. "We're having a cheese and tea pairing at my tea shop tomorrow night." She regretted her casual invitation the minute she said it.

But Max was appropriately intrigued. "Sounds like fun."

Toenails scratched against fabric, and then Earl Grey pulled himself up from his dog bed and emerged from his temporary cave. He stretched languidly, then gave a good shake that started at the tip of his nose and ended with his whip tail.

"My dog," she said. "Earl Grey."

Earl Grey wagged his tail and clicked his way slowly across the tile floor toward Max. When the dog was a few inches away, he gazed at Max intently. Then, very slowly, Earl Grey nudged his muzzle into Max's hand.

"He likes you," said Theodosia.

Max cupped his hand gently around Earl Grey's muzzle,

then reached out with his other arm and pulled Theodosia close to him. He was tall, strong, smelled of something spicy, and was infinitely hard to resist. "And I like you," he said, his breath tickly and hot against her bare neck. Then his lips touched her neck and, as Theodosia gasped, traveled upward. His mouth lingered a millimeter from hers, then closed gently over it.

Theodosia put her hands on his shoulders and tried to push him away. She couldn't, she shouldn't . . .

But when Max didn't budge, when their kiss continued, warmer and more intense, Theodosia felt her knees begin to buckle and, like ladies of yore, definitely felt a swoon coming on.

That was when Theodosia reversed her efforts. Grasping the lapels of Max's jacket, she used all her strength to pull him closer.

16

❧

Jasmine Cemetery was a place of indescribable beauty and infinite sadness. Elegant live oak trees, swathed in gray-green strands of Spanish moss, stood like sentinels amid graves that dated back two hundred years. Down in a dip, a small pond shimmered with dappled sunlight. And up the rolling hills of the ancient cemetery, statuary and graves, monuments and mausoleums littered every square meter. Here heroic brigadier generals and common citizens were entombed side by side, Jasmine Cemetery being the great equalizer for those souls who'd crossed over to the other side.

Theodosia and Drayton arrived at the cemetery some ten minutes before the memorial service for Rob Commers was supposed to begin. After stopping at the gatehouse to locate the appropriate section of graves, they reached the rather large graveside conclave and found they had to settle for seats in the last row of wobbly black metal folding chairs.

"Uncomfortable," murmured Drayton, as he settled gingerly on his tippy chair.

Theodosia didn't know if Drayton meant the chair or this final graveside service. Either way, she pretty much had to agree with him. They weren't exactly close friends of Rob Commers. In fact, they'd met him only once, for about five minutes, right before he was murdered. Theodosia didn't know if that counted for anything, but she hoped it legitimized their presence here today.

Drayton balanced precariously on his chair as Theodosia fidgeted with her skirt and worried about ruining her Bruno Magli shoes in the damp grass. Finally, she allowed her thoughts to drift back to last night.

The housewarming party had been grand, of course. All her friends (and some not so friendly) dropping by to celebrate her lovely new home.

And that stolen kiss in her kitchen? Unforgettable.

The big problem, of course, was Delaine.

No, that isn't quite right. There's another problem, too. Parker Scully.

Because, oh my goodness and double oops, she'd almost forgotten about Parker! Had almost relegated him to the back burner of her harvest gold seventies-style stove.

So that gave Theodosia one more thing to worry about and a nice sack of guilt to tote around.

And what should she do to relieve her guilty conscience? Confess all to Parker and try to start over? Dump Parker for Max? Or simply do nothing at all?

Theodosia knew that the thing to do, of course, was to carefully sift through her feelings. Figure out exactly what conclusion she *wanted* to take place, before she did anything extremely crazy or rash.

Putting a hand to her mouth, Theodosia stifled a nervous hiccup. Truth be told, she pretty much knew she'd *already* done something rash. She'd returned Max's kiss. His insistent, all-enveloping kiss that had left her dazed, dreamy, and craving more.

And when was the last time she'd felt like that!

Honestly? Not for a long time.

Because Max's kiss had been good. No. She checked herself. It had been better than good. It had been shooting-stars-and-pinwheels great.

Drayton leaned toward her and pressed his shoulder against hers.

"Camilla," he said, in a low voice.

Theodosia slowly drifted back to the here and now. She lifted her head, looked around, and spotted Camilla. Limping slowly across the grass, using a cane, Camilla was being guided by a solicitous-looking Timothy Neville. Camilla wore a black dress that hung well past her knees and large, oval sunglasses to shield her eyes. A white bandage still covered part of her forehead. Almost moving in slow motion, the two of them headed for the front row where two more chairs had magically materialized, thanks to an attentive funeral director.

Then a salt-and-pepper-haired minister in his requisite black suit appeared, and the service was under way.

There were songs, prayers, and fine tributes given, but Theodosia didn't hear a word of it. She was pretty much fixated on scanning the mourners' faces looking for something, anything, that didn't feel right. And she wasn't the only one. Out of the corner of her left eye, she could see Detective Tidwell doing the very same thing.

Great minds think alike? More like suspicious minds in sync.

At the end of the service all the mourners raised their voices in an a cappella version of "Amazing Grace." But without a trained choir, without any musical accompaniment, their song just sounded sad and lonely, drifting away on the morning breeze like so many scattered ashes.

"We should go talk to Camilla," Drayton whispered.

Theodosia was already clambering to her feet. "Let's do it."

Negotiating an end run around the other mourners, they were the first to reach Camilla.

"How are you doing?" Theodosia asked Camilla, putting an arm around her. Camilla seemed to slump against her, then steeled herself and gracefully pulled it back together.

"My head may be on the mend," said Camilla, "but my heart is still broken."

"You poor dear," said Drayton, his eyes sad and sparkling.

"It's been a difficult couple of days," Camilla admitted. She touched a hand to the bandage on her head. "But I'll be okay . . . eventually." She dug into her black handbag, found a white hanky, and pressed it to her mouth. "But poor Rob," she whispered. "He was such a good boy."

"Timothy spoke very highly of him," said Drayton, trying to offer some comfort.

"I know he did," said Camilla. "Timothy doesn't always show it, but he can be quite caring."

"And we've been . . ." Theodosia glanced around to make sure nobody was listening in, especially Tidwell. "Drayton and I have been looking into things. Unofficially, of course, but at Timothy's express request."

"Aren't you a dear," said Camilla, daubing at her red-rimmed eyes. Then she reached a hand out, grasping for Drayton. "You, too, Drayton, you're a love. You sometimes play at being a curmudgeon, but you're really a great big sweetie."

"Nice of you," said Drayton, his voice catching in his throat.

"I realize this is awkward," Theodosia continued, "and I truly hate to impose . . ." She fidgeted for a few moments. "But I wanted to ask you a couple of questions. Questions that pertain to . . ."

"It's okay," Camilla replied in a whisper. "Ask."

"The skull cup," said Theodosia. "Timothy said you were the one who polished it up?"

Camilla nodded.

"The cup had some words engraved on the underside," said Theodosia. She paused once again. "Do you remember what they were?"

"The bottom was quite corroded," said Camilla, struggling to remember, "but I saw the engraving. I know what you're asking. Unfortunately, nothing really registered with me at the time." She blinked against bright morning sunlight that streamed through tendrils of Spanish moss, creating moving, illusory patterns on white marble tombstones. "You know what I mean?"

"Kind of," said Theodosia, unwilling to let it go. She hated to push Camilla, but if the poor dear could remember anything at all . . .

"I mean, there were letters there," said Camilla, "but I didn't pay particular attention to them." She looked both sad and perplexed. "I'm not much help, am I?"

"Just take your time and think back," Theodosia urged. "Because anything you remember might be useful." Theodosia knew she'd find out about the inscription when the jpegs arrived. Still, she wanted to prod Camilla a bit and see what her recollection was.

Camilla thought again, then said, "I can't say for sure, but I don't think the words were in English."

"What language do you think?" asked Theodosia. "Maybe French?"

Camilla bit her lower lip as tears sprang to her eyes. "It's awfully hard to recall."

Theodosia put both arms around Camilla. "I know it is, and I apologize for getting you all upset."

"You're very brave," Drayton told Camilla.

"One more thing," said Theodosia, releasing Camilla. "Do you know if anybody else at the Heritage Society might have looked at the words on the skull cup?"

"A few people, yes," said Camilla.

*   *   *

Twenty minutes later Theodosia and Drayton arrived back at the Indigo Tea Shop.

"How was the memorial service?" asked Haley, leaning over the counter to greet them. Dressed in a long filmy skirt and a pink cotton crop-top sweater, she was the perfect image of a bubbly, friendly hostess—a distinct contrast to Theodosia's sedate black suit and her equally sedate mood.

"A sad event," said Theodosia.

"Sobering," agreed Drayton. "Funerals always drive home a keen sense of one's own mortality." He grimaced. "We have to remember we're only on this earth for a finite period of time."

Haley put a hand on one hip and turned a circumspect gaze on Theodosia. "Drayton's doing it again. He's talking old."

"He does that sometimes," said Theodosia. She slipped off her jacket and replaced it with a long, black Parisian waiter's apron. Then she glanced quickly about the tea room. Almost every table was filled, but capable, pinch-hitting Miss Dimple seemed to be handing things with ease. Theodosia decided she'd have to do something extra special to thank Miss Dimple for all her help. Especially for her able assistance last night, today, and probably again tonight.

"I for one wish Drayton wouldn't toss out the 'oldster' card," Haley said to Theodosia. "Because I don't think of him as being old. Seems to me he's got some good years left in him."

"You're talking about me like I'm an eighty-six Pontiac Fiero," said Drayton. "My engine's still reliable, but I'm pebbled and pocked and my tires are worn clear through."

"That wasn't much of a car," remarked Haley.

"Has the shop been busy?" Theodosia asked, deftly changing the subject.

"Not so bad," said Haley, grabbing a red-and-yellow paisley teapot. "I've been brewing tea and schlepping food to

Miss Dimple, and she's been skittering between tables, delivering orders. Our customers are quite in love with her, you realize." She wrinkled her nose and flashed a lopsided grin at Drayton. "Almost as much as they love you."

"Be still my heart," said Drayton, one eyebrow raised and slightly quivering.

"And I made those tea cakes everyone seems to like," said Haley. "Although I think Miss Dimple has eaten as many as she's served."

"Then they must be tasty," said Theodosia.

"Oh, hey," said Haley. She checked herself as she headed back to her kitchen. "I almost forgot to tell you, Theo. There's some guy here to see you. Peter Grace? He said you'd know who he was."

Theodosia gazed out across the tea room, inspecting the tables more carefully this time. Sure enough, there was Peter Grace, sitting at one of the smaller tables, reading a book while he sipped a cup of tea and nibbled a scone.

"He's a real cutie," said Haley, in a conspiratorial purr. "Where'd you find him?"

"He's Professor Muncie's grad student," said Drayton. "And it looks as though he's brought us some additional pirate data."

"Well, he can scuttle my schooner anytime," laughed Haley. "I was chatting with him earlier and I thought he was pretty cool. For an earnest young man, that is."

"Pretty cool and dateable, you mean," said Theodosia.

"That, too," said Haley. "Of course, it helps that he's got that attractiveness quotient and is well educated."

"You know what, Haley?" said Theodosia. "You're turning out to be a fine judge of character."

"Peter," said Theodosia, sliding into a chair across from him.

Peter Grace looked up from his book in surprise, then

quickly swiped a hand across his mouth, making short work of a couple of crumbs. "Hey," he said, sounding pleased.

"Nice to see you again," said Theodosia. "How's that scone?"

"Delicious," said Grace. "Not like the usual scones you get at those take-out coffee places. Those are always so hard and crumbly." He paused. "Yours are loads better. Moist and kind of cakey."

"You can thank Haley for that," said Theodosia.

A wide grin lit his face. "I already did."

"Next you'll be wanting the recipe," Theodosia joked.

"Think she'd give it to me?" asked Grace, then grinned. He knew that Theodosia knew he was interested in Haley.

"You brought us some more information?" Theodosia asked. She lifted a finger to indicate a stack of papers on the table.

"I did," said Grace. "I dug through our files and pulled up some extra stuff for you."

"Whatcha got?" asked Theodosia, reaching for the papers.

"A couple of things we didn't really touch on in the meeting yesterday," said Grace. "You know that three different museums claim to own an original Blackbeard skull cup?"

Theodosia nodded. "I'm thinking skull cups must be a standard souvenir item."

"Yeah," said Grace, fanning out some of the papers "Apparently, taking a human skull and making a drinking cup out of it is not exactly a unique idea." He shoved two papers at her. "Here's a list of the museums that have skull cups in their collections, as well as recent references to skull cups in general."

Theodosia studied the papers. "They're not exactly big-time museums, are they?" One was a small museum in Bend, North Carolina; another was a historical society outside Lynn, Massachusetts.

"No," said Grace, "and I don't think the Metropolitan

Museum in New York will be knocking down their doors to make offers on any of those skull cups. But the interesting thing is that none of the three known skull cups are engraved."

Theodosia's eyes met his. "But ours is."

Grace shook his head slowly. "You can't prove that, of course . . ."

"No," said Theodosia, "we can. There are several people at the Heritage Society who saw the engraving with their own eyes." She glanced at her watch. "In fact, I'm supposed to be receiving some jpegs from one of the *Post and Courier* photographers so we can hopefully make out the exact words."

"They have photos?" asked Grace. He seemed surprised.

"So they say."

Grace sat back in his chair, thinking, then seemed to warm to the idea.

"Well . . . good. Excellent, in fact. When you're done with the photos, when all this is just a memory and the killer is apprehended . . ."

"Then I'll be happy to turn the photos over to you and Professor Muncie," said Theodosia. "To add to your pirate database."

"I was hoping you'd say that," said Grace, giving a broad smile. "In fact, that's extremely kind of you." He glanced around. "Is . . . is Haley terribly busy right now? Do you think I could pop in and say good-bye to her?"

"They're here!" Theodosia sang out. She was sitting at her desk, sipping a nice brisk cup of gunpowder green tea and scrolling through her e-mails.

"What's here?" asked Drayton, poking his head into her office.

"The jpegs," said Theodosia. Her hands flew across the keyboard, opening the jpegs and watching photo images bloom on her screen.

"Ho ho!" said Drayton. He scurried around her desk, dodging cases of teacups and jellies, and positioned himself directly behind Theodosia. The better to peer over her shoulder, of course.

"Here's one that shows the full frontal skull face," said Theodosia.

"Nasty-looking thing," commented Drayton.

"Just remember," said Theodosia, "that underneath our skin and flesh we all look like that. We all have the same . . . what would you call it? Internal architecture."

"You make the concept sound far more poetic than the actuality," said Drayton.

"Here's an angled shot," said Theodosia, clicking open another jpeg.

Drayton cocked his head. "That one makes the skull cup look snarly."

"I'm guessing that was the whole idea."

"But what about the inscription? Any shots of that?"

"Hold on," said Theodosia, "and kindly keep your fingers crossed." She opened two more jpegs, but still didn't find what she was looking for. Could Van Buren have been mistaken? Maybe the photographer hadn't taken shots of the so-called inscription after all.

She opened the last jpeg, mentally crossing her fingers, hoping for the best. And there, finally, was a shot that captured the corroded bottom of the skull cup. Along with a rather blurred inscription.

They stared at it for a few moments, then Drayton said, "Why do you think the photographer took this particular shot?"

"Not sure," said Theodosia, "maybe the Everest principle?"

"Translation, please?"

"Because it's there."

"Ah," said Drayton, adjusting his reading glasses, "but now that we have this mysterious inscription in front of us,

what exactly does it say? Can you make that photo larger?"
Drayton was non-techy, bordering on Luddite.

"I can make it larger and print it out," said Theodosia.

"Please do so."

But when the photo came whooshing out of Theodosia's
laser printer, she was still stumped. And keenly disappointed.

"It's just letters," said Theodosia, staring at it. "Nonsensi-
cal letters." Not only that, the inscription was so worn from
age it was barely readable. Theodosia put her hands to her
head and massaged her temples in slow circles. That they'd
gone to so much trouble just to discover ancient gibberish
was positively headache-inducing!

"Let me take a closer look," said Drayton. He picked up
the paper and studied it. His normally placid face pulled into
a frown, his eyes closed to mere slits. "Mmm. It *is* difficult
to read."

"The inscription's completely worn," agreed Theodosia.

"I half expected that," said Drayton. "Face it, the skull
cup is a very ancient piece."

"Can you make out anything at all?" asked Theodosia. "I
mean, do you think it could be some foreign language?"

"That doesn't seem quite right."

"Maybe it's written in Greek?"

"No, it's just . . . strange," murmured Drayton. "Random."

"Could we try running a computer search? On the parts
we *can* make out?"

"Not sure," said Drayton.

"You don't know what to make of it, do you?" asked
Theodosia, looking deflated. Then again, neither did she.

"No, not offhand," said Drayton.

"Then it's the end of the line," said Theodosia, letting
loose a deep sigh. She felt depressed and a little foolish at the
same time. She'd been positive they were hot on the trail of
a major clue, and now it all seemed to have dead-ended. And

who liked to admit defeat, after all? Who wanted to throw in the towel?

"Maybe . . ." Drayton mumbled, pulling his shoulders back into a stiff posture.

"What?" asked Theodosia.

Drayton didn't answer her. Just studied the photo with a bland, unreadable expression on his face. His lips moved slowly, as if he were reading some sort of ancient text, and his fingers clenched and unclenched the paper. Then, slowly, very slowly, a puzzled, almost cagey expression crept across his lined face.

"What?" Theodosia asked again. She could feel the tiny hairs on the back of her neck beginning to stir.

"I'm not positive," Drayton said, in a hushed tone. "But this could be a Caesar cipher."

17

❧

For some reason, Theodosia's mind immediately fixed on a tasty Caesar salad complete with anchovies, garlic, and croutons. Then, just as quickly, she skipped on to Augustus Caesar.

Drayton, a crooked, wary expression on his face, said, "If I'm correct, and it's possible that I am, this is written in a code invented by Julius Caesar."

"Which is why it's called a Caesar cipher." *Duh. Of course, that's why.*

Drayton gave an absent nod. "Caesar used his own coded invention to transmit important communiqués to his generals. To go undetected by enemies, of course."

"So it's an old Roman code," said Theodosia. "And probably very tricky."

"No, not so difficult," said Drayton, gaining a little more enthusiasm as he went along. "The Caesar cipher is a fairly basic encryption technique. A single alphabet cipher where each plaintext letter is replaced with another letter that's a fixed number of spaces down the alphabet."

Huh? Theodosia put a hand above her head and made a zooming gesture.

Seeing Theodosia's puzzlement, Drayton said, "You know . . . like shifting down three spaces, so *A* is really *D*."

"Ooooh," breathed Theodosia. "Now I get it. Like a secret decoder ring."

"Er . . . something along that line," said Drayton.

"Then . . . can you decode it?" Things were suddenly looking way more hopeful, thanks to clever Drayton!

Drayton glanced at his watch. "I promise to give it my very best shot once I have a little more time to spend on it."

"Okay," said Theodosia, glancing at the clock on her desk. "After lunch, then."

"Shepherd's pie," said Drayton, with obvious relish. "Haley, how did you know that's one of my absolute favorites? What magical intuition do you possess?"

Haley placed a wedge of shepherd's pie on a salad plate, added a generous mound of citrus salad, and said, with guileless blue eyes turned upon Drayton, "Gosh, I hope I made enough. I hope there'll be a piece left over for you."

"Don't tease him," Theodosia laughed. "When it comes to his food faves, Drayton's never in a joking mood."

"Oh, Drayton," said Haley, serving up yet another piece, then arranging five completed luncheon plates on a large silver platter, "you know I'll save you a piece."

"I don't know that at all," said Drayton, as Haley picked up the platter and handed it to him.

"Well, I will," said Haley. "I am."

"In that case, I thank you," said Drayton, as he negotiated the doorway and headed for the tea room to deliver his orders.

"You tease him unmercifully," said Theodosia. She stood at the butcher block counter, munching a blueberry scone that Haley had deemed too lumpy and shapeless, and thus unworthy of being served to paying customers.

"Tit for tat," said Haley. "Makes up for all the times he teased me about boyfriends."

"Speaking of such," said Theodosia, "you and Peter Grace seem to have hit it off."

"Isn't he a nice package?" Haley bubbled. "Tall, attractive, and smart, too."

"I know exactly what you mean," said Theodosia, letting her thoughts wander in Max's direction. And back to last night's big kiss, a world-class smackeroo if she did say so herself.

"I hope you don't mind," said Haley, "but I invited Peter to drop by tonight for our tea and cheese tasting." She spun quickly as a buzzer sounded, then grabbed an oven mitt and pulled a pan of apricot bars out of the oven. They were golden brown and bubbling with sticky goodness. "So, that's okay, isn't it?"

"Of course it is," said Theodosia. "We're glad to have him. He's been a great help to us."

Haley set the tray of bars on the counter and poked gingerly at them with a finger. "So . . . did you invite that Max guy?"

"What?" said Theodosia, startled.

"Why not?" asked Haley. "You like him, don't you?"

Theodosia caved immediately. "It's that obvious?"

Haley nodded. "Oh, yeah, sure. And he likes you. I could tell by the way he was staring at you all last night. All moon-eyed and goofy."

"Holy cats," said Theodosia. "Do you think anybody else noticed?" This wasn't good. Well, it was good for her, just not good for her reputation. If that made any sense.

"Not sure," said Haley. "Everybody was pretty much drinking and whooping it up, so they may not have noticed. But I saw how Delaine treated that guy Max, and you could tell by his body language that he's not having it. She's ancient history."

"You really think so?" asked Theodosia. She hoped that might be the case. But in a good way. Did *that* make any sense?

"Absolutely," said Haley, with a young person's typical assuredness of the world and all its permutations. "Delaine's gonna get kicked to the curb—and quick. You know, when it comes to matters of the heart? Stuff like that?" Haley gave a slow wink. "I can always tell."

"*How are you* doing?" asked Theodosia. Drayton was sitting on the tuffet, scribbling on a notebook page and mumbling to himself.

"Mmm," said Drayton. He had a task-oriented personality and didn't like to be disturbed.

"Getting anywhere?"

Drayton scribbled for a few more seconds, then finally glanced up. "If I had a piece of that lovely shepherd's pie, it would probably help improve brain cell function."

"Coming right up!"

Theodosia swung by the kitchen, picked up a slice of shepherd's pie for Drayton, then hit the front counter, where Miss Dimple had just brewed a nice, steaming pot of tea.

"What's fresh?" Theodosia asked.

"Orange pekoe," said Miss Dimple. "Per a customer's request." She lowered her voice. "Although I've never been completely sure what orange pekoe tea really is."

Theodosia checked the back of the tea tin. "This one's a classic blend of strong Assam tea blended with fine black Ceylon tea," said Theodosia. "Smooth with lots of body."

"You folks really know your tea," remarked Miss Dimple. "Then again, you're the tea lady."

"Supposedly I am," said Theodosia. "But just when I think I've got it all figured out, Drayton springs something new on me. A Russian blend that combines Lapsang souchong with a bit of Assam. Or a Japanese Bancha tea blended with rosebuds."

"The whole tea-blending process reminds me a little of the perfume-making process," exclaimed Miss Dimple. "A drib of this, a drab of that."

"But so much tastier," said Theodosia.

"Delicious," Drayton proclaimed as he set down his fork. "One of the finest shepherd's pies I've tasted in memory."

"I'll be sure to tell Haley," said Theodosia.

"And you even brought me an apricot bar."

"Served with a dollop of Devonshire cream," said Theodosia. "Haley's idea."

With a small spoon, Drayton daubed a bit of Devonshire cream onto his bar and took a bite. "Excellent," he said, chewing with relish. "Really wonderful."

"I ask you," said Theodosia, "what food isn't improved by a dollop of Devonshire cream?"

"Not sure," said Drayton, taking another generous bite. "Maybe . . . turnips?"

"No," said Theodosia, "I'm sure that would taste good, too."

Drayton made short work of his dessert, then pushed his plate aside and picked up his notebook. "I've made some progress," he announced.

"I knew you would."

"Taking a wild guess and basing this on what I think might be a four-letter shift," said Drayton, "I've come up with two possible words."

"Okay."

"First word," said Drayton, as if they were playing a game of charades, "is *ealon*."

"What?" said Theodosia, her voice rising in a squawk.

She'd been expecting a genuine word, not another puzzle. "What on earth does *ealon* mean?"

Drayton thought for a minute. "I'm thinking that it's possibly a surname?"

"Maybe," said Theodosia, sitting down at her computer. "So let's run a quick search." She typed "ealon" into the Google search engine and waited for a few moments. "Okay, here's something. There was a Major Josiah Ealon from South Carolina who was in the Revolutionary War."

"That could be a possibility," said Drayton.

"What about the second word?"

Drayton made a face. "It's hard to make out, but it looks like *faesten*. Does that mean anything to you?"

"You're sure that's what it says?" She glanced at the printout she'd made earlier. "Mmm, the engraving is difficult to read."

Drayton scrunched up his face, thinking.

"Sorry to put so much pressure on you," said Theodosia. "I guess you didn't sign on to be a master tea blender *and* cryptographer."

Drayton made a few more jottings, then stared at them for a few moments.

"Nothing jumps out, huh?" said Theodosia.

"Maybe . . ." Drayton began in a whisper.

"What?" asked Theodosia, pouncing on him like a hungry duck on a skittering bug.

"It could be Old English," Drayton said, in almost a monotone.

"What could?" asked Theodosia.

"The two words," said Drayton. "I told you I've been rereading *Beowulf* . . ."

"Talk to me!" urged Theodosia.

Drayton pushed his glasses up onto the bridge of his nose and hunched over his notes. "What if this word *ealon* is really *ealond*?" said Drayton.

"Okay," said Theodosia, thinking that still didn't help clarify things.

Drayton gazed at her with a studious almost professorial look. "Then, in Old English, the word would mean 'island.'"

"Island," said Theodosia. "Referencing one of our nearby islands?" Her thoughts began to race. "But which one? There are hundreds of islands around Charleston as well as up and down the coast!"

"Perhaps the key lies with the second word," said Drayton. He peered at it with a mixture of speculation and fascination. *"Faesten."*

"Fasten?" with Theodosia. "Like fastening a zipper?"

"No," said Drayton. "In Old English, *faesten* means 'fortress.' So if I'm right—and I think I might be—this clue means 'island fortress.'"

"Holy magoomba!" Theodosia cried. She jumped up from her desk and raced over to Drayton. "You cracked the code!" she exclaimed, as she threw her arms around him, locking him in a super tight squeeze.

"But what island fortress?" came Drayton's muffled response.

Theodosia relaxed her grip. "What one could there be?"

"Probably several dozen," said Drayton. "Most of which have been lost through the ages."

"Doggone," said Theodosia. "But . . . we have to try." Just offhand she could think of a few island fortresses. Old Fort Moultrie, Castle Pinckney, even Fort Sumter. "So now what?" asked Theodosia.

Drayton looked thoughtful. "We'll have to do some research."

"Excellent," said Theodosia. She patted Drayton on the shoulder and said, "You did good."

Drayton wasn't quite convinced. "This search of ours is making me nervous."

"How so?"

"Now we're engaged in a treasure hunt as well as a hunt for the killer," said Drayton.

"The thing is," said Theodosia, "the treasure was obviously the motive. So if we can come anywhere near that treasure, we might also find the killer."

Drayton gazed at her, worry pinching his face.

"The only problem," Theodosia added, "is that we don't want to get too close!"

Thursday afternoon's repast at the Indigo Tea Shop consisted of apricot bars, chocolate chip scones, and lemon poppy seed tea bread. Guests trickled in, but it wasn't the usual busy flurry. Probably, Theodosia decided, folks were holding out for the start of the Food and Wine Festival tonight. There were something like a dozen different venues to help kick off the festivities. And, as planned, the Indigo Tea Shop was one of them.

"Haley?" Theodosia popped into the kitchen where Haley was studying a recipe book and Miss Dimple was slicing lemon tea bread. "Are you going to be ready with your appetizers?"

"We're way cool," Haley assured her. "As soon as four o'clock rolls around, we'll put out the CLOSED sign. Then Miss Dimple's gonna pitch in and help me with the final preparations. Aren't you?" She grinned at Miss Dimple, who grinned back.

"I still can't believe you people are serving tea and cheese," said Miss Dimple. "But the whole thing sounds so creative I can't wait to taste a few of your crazy pairings."

"You're a real sport," Haley told her. She looked up at Theodosia. "Isn't she a sport?"

"That's why we love to have her around," Theodosia agreed.

"Oh, you two!" exclaimed Miss Dimple, turning a lovely shade of embarrassed pink.

Delivering a plate of scones to a table of four, then heading back to the front counter, Theodosia found Drayton brewing up a pot of Assam golden tips.

"You realize," she told him in a low voice, "we also need to do research on bookbinding shops."

Drayton measured out a third spoonful of tea leaves, then said, "You still think we should do that?"

"Yes, I do."

"Just because it's *called* a cipher stone," said Drayton, "doesn't mean it's going to jump out and hand us a clue. The doggone thing's been lost for ages."

"You're probably right," said Theodosia.

"And my best guess," said Drayton, "is that it's really just a common old brick or stone with some writing or a few symbols scratched into it. Really architectural salvage."

Theodosia stared at him. "Say that last part again."

"It could be a brick or a stone . . ."

"No, the very last part," she said, waggling her fingers.

"Architectural salvage?" he said.

"Drayton, you tea blender extraordinaire, you just said a mouthful!"

"Max," said Theodosia, once she had her newfound friend (or was he more than that? Of course, he was!) on the phone. "This is Theodosia. Do you remember last night when you . . . ?"

"I have absolute perfect recall," Max purred into the phone. "Your lips . . . our kiss . . ."

"Whoa!" said Theodosia. That wasn't what she was calling about.

So . . . better tell him. Better be up front about this. "That's not exactly why I'm calling."

"It's not?" said Max, a hint of disappointment creeping into his voice.

Maybe we can chat about that kiss in the future, but just not right now.

"Last night," said Theodosia, "you mentioned that you'd had experience with salvage archaeology."

"Right," he said, with a slight hesitation.

"I need your advice on something."

"You want to do salvage archaeology?" asked Max. Now he just sounded amused.

"Something close to it," said Theodosia. "Anyway, I guess what I'm really asking is if you have any contacts here in Charleston? Companies that salvage pieces from old buildings or antique dealers who handle that type of thing?"

"Mmm . . . I know a couple," said Max. "What have you got up your sleeve? Wait, don't tell me. You're planning to tear the friezes and pediments off the front of the Gibbes Museum of Art and sell them on eBay."

"Not quite," said Theodosia, deciding it might be better to chat with Max in person. "Actually, I think I need to run this by you in person."

"Great. You want to get together tonight?"

"I'm hosting my tea and cheese event tonight," Theodosia told him.

"That reminds me," said Max. "I never did get my cup of tea last night."

"Whose fault was that?" Now she was being coy and enjoying it.

"Mmm," said Max, "then I do expect to get some tonight."

"You mean tea?" asked Theodosia.

But Max only chuckled.

18

❧

The night was dark and warm with a languid breeze wafting in from the Cooper and Ashley rivers. It riffled the flames on the tall, white pillar candles and swooshed the aromas of a dozen different teas into a mingled blend that was at once sweet, pungent, malty, and citrusy.

"A perfect evening," Drayton proclaimed. He and Theodosia stood at the front door, welcoming guests and shepherding them toward the various tea and cheese stations. Just like at a cocktail party, the stations were set apart from each other, encouraging guests to wander, mingle, sample freely, and chat with each other.

Theodosia had the bright idea to pull most of the tables and chairs out of the tea shop and arrange them on the sidewalk. So now the early arrivals, the ones who'd already grabbed their tea and cheese samplings, were sitting outside enjoying the night air and the electrical buzz that ran up and down Church Street.

A half block down, the Chowder Hound was serving blue

crab chowder and she-crab soup. A nearby Italian restaurant was offering a five-course tasting menu. A small French restaurant was doing wine tasting and handing out samples of French onion soup.

"I never dreamed we'd draw such a large crowd," said Theodosia. "I hope the food holds out." She'd gone from fretting about no one showing up to concern about having enough food. Wasn't it always something?

"We'll be fine," Drayton assured her.

Besides the tea and cheese pairings, Haley had whipped up some additional appetizers for their guests. Tiny grilled shrimp on cheesy crostini. Parmesan bread twists. And tasty goat cheese truffles, which were essentially melon ball scoops of goat cheese that had been rolled in mixtures of chopped almonds, chopped dates, and fresh basil.

"Ah," said Drayton, "here's Timothy."

But Timothy wasn't alone. Chugging up the street with him was Sidney Pruett, the man whose family's donation had triggered the unfortunate chain of events at the Heritage Society.

"Good evening, Timothy," said Theodosia. "Nice to see you again, Mr. Pruett."

"How are you doing?" Drayton asked Timothy. It was a polite, almost rhetorical question, but Timothy chose to grab it and run with it like a crazed dog with a bone.

"Terrible!" Timothy cried, his facial muscles tensing. "My board of directors has been all over me—calling nonstop! Not you, Drayton, but the others. They're positively apoplectic over this skull cup business." He turned toward Theodosia and dropped his voice. "Have you found out anything more? Anything that might help calm the board members, get them to stop rattling their proverbial sabers?"

"We're, um, working on a sort of translation," Theodosia told him.

Timothy cocked a rheumy eye at her and said, "You are? Translation on what?"

"The inscription on the bottom of the skull cup," Theodosia told him. "Lucky for us, the photographer at *Post and Courier* got a fairly decent shot of it."

"Nothing lucky about it," Timothy snapped. He turned toward Sidney Pruett. "I'm beginning to believe that cock-and-bull bad luck story you told us might even be true!"

"Mr. Pruett," said Theodosia, trying to work her way past Timothy's anger and peevishness, "have you ever heard of an organization called the Brethren of the Coast?"

Pruett screwed up his face, looking thoughtful. "Not that I can recall."

"Think hard," said Theodosia.

"He already said he didn't know!" said Timothy.

Now Pruett looked embarrassed. "Perhaps I could check through some of my grandfather's old papers? Maybe there's something there?"

"That would be very helpful," said Theodosia.

And still guests continued to arrive. Miss Dimple poured tea into outstretched cups so rapidly that Drayton was kept permanently busy behind the counter.

"You doing okay?" Theodosia asked him. She had one eye on the frantic Drayton and another on the four different tea and cheese stations they had to restock constantly.

"My head's above water," he told her, "but barely."

"What's the concoction in the pitcher over there?" Theodosia asked. She'd spotted Haley hurrying from one guest to another, offering an iced drink from a tinkling glass pitcher.

"Oh, that," said Drayton. "Just a recipe I threw together. Black tea and ice wine. Since the weather turned so nice and warm, I thought we could use a kind of cooler."

"Sounds wonderful," said Theodosia. "You've made it before?"

Drayton shook his head as he popped the top off a tea tin. "No."

"But you taste-tested it."

Another head shake. "Not really." *Plop-plop* went the tea leaves into the teapot. They swirled for a moment, then sank to the bottom.

"Then how do you know it's fit to serve?" Theodosia trusted Drayton implicitly, but she was curious.

Drayton straightened up, tugged at his impeccable cream-colored linen jacket, adjusted his bow tie, and said, with a crooked smile, "It's what I do." He looked amused rather than insulted by her question.

Theodosia threw both hands in the air and grinned. "Forgive me. I forgot you're the arbiter of taste when it comes to *l'mode* tea."

"Speaking of arbiters of taste," murmured Drayton, casting a glance into the crowd.

Theodosia swiveled her head and saw Delaine Dish steam-rolling toward them.

"Theodosia!" Delaine cried out. "*Lovely* event. I never thought you'd pull this strange cheese event off and actually attract customers, but you sweet dear . . . you've made a believer out of me." She glanced quickly at Drayton. "You, too, Drayton. Tea and cheese! What a quirky combo! Who would have *thought* it!"

"Perhaps . . . a gourmet?" said Drayton.

Delaine fanned herself with one hand and said, "Well, I'm just a little old Charleston gal who prefers her shrimp perloo, country barbecue, and she-crab soup. If you two don't *mind*."

"Of course," muttered Drayton, reaching for a tin of spicy, aromatic Yunnan tea.

Delaine suddenly lasered her attention back on Theodosia. "Nadine was supposed to meet me here and I haven't run into her yet. *Très* strange?"

"I haven't seen her all night," said Theodosia, hastily arranging another two dozen small ceramic cups on a tray. "Although we've been crazy busy, so I could have missed her." Then again, Nadine was awfully hard to miss.

"I can't imagine where my dear sister could be," Delaine fretted.

"Maybe with Bill Glass? Have you called him?"

"You're right," Delaine agreed, glancing around. "She'll probably show up any moment."

"On the other hand," said Theodosia, a mischievous grin creeping onto her face, "maybe the two of them sneaked off and eloped!"

"They wouldn't dare!" screeched Delaine. "If my sister robs me of the chance to plan her wedding, I'll . . . I'll *kill* her!"

"Let's hear it for sisterly love," remarked Drayton.

"It *is* a strong bond," agreed Delaine. She reached into her glittery clutch purse, pulled out a hot-pink lipstick, and applied it without taking her eyes off the crowd. "Theo, dear, do you know if that lovely, refined neighbor of yours is going to show up tonight?" Delaine's eyes glittered, as if she were gearing up for a good chase.

Theodosia's first reaction was, *I have a lovely, refined neighbor?* Then she realized, with a weird jolt, that Delaine was referring to Dougan Granville.

"I'm not sure this event is even on his radar," said Theodosia. "He's . . . well, we're not exactly close." *Now there's an understatement.* "Besides, I though you were, um, in a semicommitted relationship with that PR fellow, Max." She fought to keep her voice cool and casual. *Can't let her see me sweat,* Theodosia thought to herself. *If Delaine sees me sweat, I'll never ever hear the end of it. Plus, she might get all snippy and imperious and keep Max in her clutches just for sheer sport.*

But Delaine assumed a slightly bored expression at the mention of Max's name. "Max is *nice* enough," she said with a dramatic sigh. "And he definitely scores a ten in the looks department. But a girl—me being that girl, tee-hee—craves a man who's a trifle more . . . how shall I put it? Worldly? Urbane?" Delaine narrowed her eyes and languidly thrust out a hip, almost mimicking the gesture of a sleek, predatory cat. "*My* personal preference? I prefer a more rugged man."

And still guests continued to arrive. Thomas Hassel, the art dealer, cruised in with one of his antiques expo boosters, a man by the name of Chaz Poor who owned a shop over in the French Quarter.

And Haley's new friend Peter Grace wandered in.

"Is Haley around?" Grace asked Theodosia, his eyes darting about the tea room, obviously searching for Haley.

"Right over there," said Theodosia, with a quick gesture. "She's putting out yet another wheel of cheddar." Theodosia was keeping her fingers crossed that they wouldn't run out of cheese, since the guests seemed to be munching their way through the food like a pack of famished rodents.

"Looks like she could use some help," said Grace. "Think she'd mind if I gave her a hand?"

"Peter," said Theodosia, "this is just a wild guess on my part, but I think Haley would be thrilled."

When Theodosia had a spare moment, she grabbed a cup of Assam and took a fortifying sip. And because it was warm in the tea shop and growing warmer from the ever-increasing crush of bodies, she headed for the front door to enjoy a quick break and a cool breeze.

"Theo!" a male voice called, just as she stepped out the door.

Theodosia blinked as her eyes slowly became accustomed to the inky darkness that had descended upon Church Street. Then she was able to put a face to the voice and broke into a big smile. "Parker? You made it back!"

Parker Scully opened his arms, and Theodosia automatically slipped into them. He was comfortable, infinitely huggable, and very, very sweet. She clung to him tightly as he bent down and kissed the top of her head.

"I leave you alone for one second," said a deeper male voice, "and I find you in another man's arms."

Theodosia stiffened. Oh, no! A fear she hadn't realized she had was a fear that had suddenly been realized. Parker and Max together. Super big oops!

"Hi, Max," she said, deftly escaping Parker's arms. "Great to see you again. Do you know Parker Scully? He's the owner of Solstice Restaurant." Theodosia continued her introductions, babbling away, aware she was babbling away and feeling trapped and embarrassed at the same time.

The two men shook hands and mumbled casual hellos, and then each took a step back, leaving Theodosia in the middle. When nobody said anything for a few moments, both men seemed to take stock of each other and slowly acknowledge that each of them was interested in her.

Like a low rumble of thunder that foretells a major storm, Theodosia saw this happening and worried about a possible confrontation. Better still, she tried to head it off at the pass.

"Delaine's inside," she briskly told Max. "And would probably love to see you." Then she smiled brightly at Parker and said, "Could you help me with something?" She turned quickly, without waiting for an answer, and headed back inside her crowded tea shop. What she fervently wished, of course, was that she could get lost in the crowd.

No such luck.

Parker followed on Theodosia's heels as she slipped behind the counter, searching wildly for something to task him with.

"How can I help?" he asked.

She smiled at him. A smile that probably came across as sweet but felt false. "How about . . ." Theodosia reached up, grabbed a large tin of Nilgiri tea, and handed it to him. "Open this for me?"

Parker snapped the lid off with ease and tilted the tin toward her. So much for the helpless-female ploy.

"And measure it out?" she asked, handing him a wooden scoop.

"How much?"

Theodosia plucked a large, yellow ceramic teapot from the opposite shelf and pushed it at him. "Three or four good scoops."

As he measured out tea, Parker said, "You're acting awfully fidgety. Is everything okay?"

"I'm sorry," said Theodosia. "It's just that we're frantically busy." And they were. Guests milled all around them, clutching small plates filled with chunks of Brie and triangles of cheddar, all the while balancing small cups of tea.

"I hope I'm this busy tomorrow night," said Parker. He was hosting a tapas bar and red wine tasting, another of the official Food and Wine Festival events.

"Oh, but you will be," said Theodosia. "I have it on good authority that this year's Food and Wine Festival is going to be a roaring success."

"Who told you that?"

She dimpled prettily. "The Food and Wine Festival committee."

They shared a chuckle, and then Parker said, "You're coming tomorrow, right?" He looked at her hopefully, his eyes inquisitive and searching.

"I'll try to," said Theodosia. "But Drayton kind of committed us to a gallery opening."

Parker frowned. "What do you mean, *us*? I thought *us* was you and me?"

She wanted to say it was, but her mouth felt dry and cobwebby.

Parker shifted from one foot to the other, as if sorting through his thoughts. Finally he said, "And who's that guy you introduced me to?" He clutched the teapot tight against himself, waiting for an explanation.

"Max is the new PR director at the Gibbes Museum," Theodosia told him.

"No," said Parker, "I mean who is he to you?"

"Um . . . a friend?" Theodosia cringed inwardly, knowing it was a clumsy answer and instantly regretting it. Parker meant too much to her to be so dodgy. Besides, dishonesty was something she'd always loathed.

Parker set down the teapot, stared at her for a few long moments, then turned and walked away.

"Where's he off to?" asked Drayton, sliding in next to her and grabbing two more teapots. "I thought he just got here."

"Parker just met Max."

Drayton's brows shot up. "Awkward," he said, approximating Valley Girl–speak with a cultured accent.

"No kidding."

Drayton gave a discreet snort. An I-told-you-so snort. "That's what you get for being adorable and undecided."

"That's what I get?" said Theodosia. Drayton's humor or wit or whatever scenario he was implying was completely lost on her. "Then what's my payoff for trying to be nice to everyone? For trying, at all costs, not to trample people's feelings?"

"I don't know," said Drayton, "but I wouldn't hold out for a reserved box seat in heaven."

19

By nine o'clock, the event was winding down. Crumbles of cheese littered the tables and floor, as if so many cadres of crazed mice had staged a mighty raid. Teapots sat everywhere, their contents now just soggy dregs. And a dozen or so people hung around the Indigo Tea Shop, chatting and mingling, not wanting the night to end.

Delaine had exited stage left a long time ago. Max, who'd been cordial but newly cool to her, still lingered. And Peter Grace continued to schlep dishes and follow in Haley's wake like a big, friendly puppy.

"She's going to wear that young man out," observed Drayton. He was lounging at the front counter with Theodosia and Max, drinking tea and watching the whole shebang come to a fine conclusion.

"Young love," commented Max.

"I should say so," said Drayton. He cast a quick sideways glance at Theodosia, then turned his attention back on Haley.

"So," Max said to Theodosia, "you wanted information on architectural salvage dealers."

"I did," she said. "I do."

"And you were going to explain why . . . in person," said Max.

"Because of the cipher stone," Theodosia told him.

Max looked puzzled. "The what?"

"It's this crazy old stone," said Drayton, "that supposedly has a clue written on it."

"I'll bite," said Max, good naturedly. "A clue for what?"

"Blackbeard's treasure?" Theodosia told him in a small voice.

Max stared at Theodosia, then turned his attention to Drayton. Then he focused once again on Theodosia. Moments spun by before he said, "This has something to do with the murder at the Heritage Society?"

Theodosia nodded.

"And you're involved?" said Max, squinting at her.

"Only peripherally," said Drayton.

"Actually, we're quite involved," said Theodosia. Better Max should know about her amateur sleuthing right up front. Just in case their relationship . . . um . . . progressed.

"Delaine did mention to me that you were a bit of an amateur detective," said Max. "I thought she was kidding around."

"She wasn't," said Drayton.

Max stared at Theodosia, and then a smile appeared on his face. "You're really something," he murmured.

"Not really," said Theodosia, embarrassed now. "We don't have anything figured out yet."

"*Yet* being the operative word," said Drayton.

"So checking out architectural salvage places is somehow related to this murder?"

"No," said Theodosia.

"Yes," said Drayton.

"We're just sort of stumbling around," Theodosia told him. "Testing various theories and such. And you having experience in salvage archaeology . . . well, I thought . . ." Theodosia knew it might be wishful thinking, but she was hoping Max had pulled a name or two out of a hat.

Max reached into his pocket and grabbed a small spiral notebook. He flipped it open, tore off a sheet, and handed it to her. "There are a couple of places here in Charleston you could check out."

"Two places," said Theodosia, studying the sheet. She knew it wasn't much to go on.

"Short list," said Max. "Still, it might be a start."

"Let me see," said Drayton, sliding his glasses on.

Max gazed at Theodosia, the expression on his face a blend of amusement and fascination. "And you think this— what did you call it? Cipher stone? You think it's still kicking around?"

Theodosia shrugged. "You never know. Stranger things have happened." Stranger things *had* happened.

Max wasn't convinced. "Such as?"

"Oh," said Theodosia, "a month or so ago a bone from a Civil War–era soldier turned up in my tulip bed."

"Seriously?" said Max. "You're sure it wasn't sheep or cattle bones or something?"

"Oh, no," said Theodosia. "It was a genuine human femur." Who would make that up? Who would want to?

Max peered at her, and then the corners of his mouth twitched upward. "And you were speaking metaphorically, of course. You don't really grow tulips, do you?"

"I don't grow anything," said Theodosia, "since I'm pretty much possessed of a black thumb. But luckily for me, previous owners were more talented and inclined than I, so they planted scads of crepe myrtle, dogwood, and magnolias. And, of course, one previous visitor gifted us with that bone."

"A human bone," said Max, as if he still didn't believe her.

"Human," said Drayton, confirming her story.

"Apparently," said Theodosia, "because Charleston dates back to the early seventeen hundreds, artifacts are turning up all the time. Both the human and nonhuman variety. In fact, one of the state archaeologists informed me that people have actually found unexploded ordnance from the Civil War in their gardens."

"Minié balls and mimosa," observed Drayton.

"But right now you're hot on the trail of this so-called cipher stone?" asked Max.

"A picture's worth a thousand words," said Drayton. "Best to show your friend the computer printout."

Theodosia crooked an index finger. Drayton was quite correct, time to reveal all. "Come with me," Theodosia said, as she led Max through the party debris and back to her office.

"This is cozy," said Max, stepping into her little fiefdom and looking around. "Messy, but cozy." He studied the wall above the tuffet chair that held framed opera programs, photos of Theodosia on her dad's old sailboat, some exotic tea labels.

"We just received a shipment of T-Bath Feet Treat," Theodosia told him, waving at a stack of cardboard boxes that pressed in close to her desk, as well as a stack of wild grapevine wreaths and a tippy stack of summer straw hats. "So I'm a little cramped for space."

"Feet what?" Max seemed amused.

"I created my own T-Bath line," Theodosia told him. "That I sell here in the shop and online. They're lotions and potions infused with healing teas. We've got Feet Treat, Green Tea Lotion, Chamomile Calming Cream . . ." She ticked off the names of a few products.

"You're quite the entrepreneur," said Max. "I mean beyond the tea shop and the catering business." He seemed duly impressed.

"Thank you," said Theodosia, handing him the stack of

printouts she'd made from the *Post and Courier* jpegs. "But this is what I really want you to see."

Max studied each printout, lingering over the last one that showed the bottom of the cup, then finally turning back to the first one. The straight-on shot of the skull cup. The head shot.

"Interesting," he said.

"What's interesting?"

"Well, besides your little cryptoquip or whatever it is, this particular skull motif is awfully reminiscent of some of the stone carvings on the graves in Jasmine Cemetery."

"Strange you would say that," said Theodosia, "since I was just there this morning."

Max stared at her. "That so?"

"Drayton and I attended the memorial service for Rob Commers, the intern who was killed."

"Ah, of course you would. You're that kind of thoughtful person."

"Take another look at that last printout," said Theodosia. "The one showing the underside of the skull cup." She was eager to pick Max's brain. He was a smart guy, after all, who'd worked with all sorts of art and artifacts. "What do you think?"

"Letters in what's probably a meaningful arrangement. In other words, not random."

"Drayton thinks it's a Caesar cipher," said Theodosia.

"Could be." Max tapped the sheet with his index finger. "You're sure these are meant to be words?"

"What else would they be?" asked Theodosia. To her the Caesar cipher explanation and the Old English words Drayton had extrapolated seemed awfully solid.

Max tilted his head back, thinking, and then he said, "Sometimes letters translate into numbers. There was a cipher used by Mary, Queen of Scots, that was basically just letters to numbers."

"Okay," said Theodosia, though she was still dubious. Truth be told, she was still pretty much wedded to Drayton's theory. On the other hand, Max's idea of letters corresponding to numbers wasn't all that far-fetched, either.

"I'm just saying," said Max. "It's something to consider." He set the papers down on her desk and moved closer to her. "You're a regular Sherlock Holmes, aren't you? Trying to solve a real-life murder mystery."

She ducked her head, a little shy now at being alone with him. "You don't think I'm more of a snoopy Miss Marple?"

"Mmm, no. Miss Marple was fairly well along in years. And you're . . ." His eyes roved over her, and then he took another step closer.

"I'm what?" she asked. Once again, she could feel his energy or chemistry or whatever magical thing it was.

Max's arms reached out to circle her, and then his lips brushed her forehead and traveled downward. "You, my dear," he said, his voice husky and low, "are in your prime."

Theodosia stopped her Jeep directly in front of Drayton's house and put it into park before she said, "What if it's really a numbers code?"

"Excuse me?" Drayton's hand rested on the passenger-side door. He'd shifted his weight, ready to jump out.

"On the bottom of the skull cup," said Theodosia. "I showed the printout to Max and he suggested that the letters might correlate with numbers. Said he's seen it before on some kind of Mary, Queen of Scots, code."

Drayton settled back into the seat with a certain reluctance. "Let me get this straight. You're proposing that *A* equals 1, *B* equals 2, and so on?"

"Something like that." She hesitated. "You know as well as I do that's the most rudimentary of ciphers."

"True. Pirates weren't exactly known for being mathematically inclined."

"The other thing," said Theodosia, "is that Max thought the design of the skull cup eerily similar to the décor on the graves in Jasmine Cemetery."

Drayton peered at her in the dim of the car. "Perhaps because each is related to death and dying?"

"Or perhaps because they hail from the same era," said Theodosia. "Here's the thing . . . did you notice that all the really old graves we walked past this morning had numbers on them?"

"From the cemetery's antiquated numbering system, to be sure," said Drayton. "Set up back in the seventeen hundreds."

"Exactly," said Theodosia. "The seventeen hundreds."

"You're not implying . . ."

Seconds ticked by, and then Theodosia said, "Is it possible that the letters, transcribed to numbers, might match the numbers on a certain gravestone?"

"I don't know," said Drayton. He fidgeted in his seat, scratched his head, and looked thoughtful. "If there *is* a correlation and it matches up with a gravestone, are you thinking that leads to another clue?"

"I don't know."

They sat in the car as another car, something low and sleek, whooshed by, fast, faint music trailing in its wake. Finally Dayton said, "Did you bring the printout?"

"I just happen to have it," Theodosia told him. "Care to make some quick calculations?"

Drayton's shoulders slumped. "And here I was, just inches from a clean getaway."

"C'mon, Drayton, it's not just a job, it's an adventure!"

"I was hoping for a respite from dashing around, snooping on suspects. And my tired old body was hoping for a good night's rest."

"Just a quick look-see?" Theodosia pulled the printout from her purse and handed it to him.

"You're wheedling," said Drayton, pursing his lips. "Putting on the pressure."

"Gently cajoling," said Theodosia. "But if you'd rather not . . ."

Thirty seconds drifted by, then a full minute. Finally Drayton lifted a hand and flapped airily at the dark street ahead. "Let's get on with it then. Let's go take a look."

Jasmine Cemetery at ten o'clock at night was a place of shadows and fog. White filmy tendrils of mist snaked between ancient tombstones that tilted and canted crazily, looking all the world like rows of broken, misshapen, yellowed teeth. Live oaks, gnarled with age, waved banners of dank Spanish moss that whispered and swayed in the night breeze. Down a long slope, in what became a boggy, swampy area each spring, the mournful hoot of a barred owl rose up from a thick copse of trees.

Rustlings of small animals were muted by the fog and nary a light shone anywhere in this city of the dead, save the small flashlight Theodosia carried in her unsteady hand.

"You still think this is a good idea?" asked Drayton. They stepped across dew-laden grass that felt springy and eerily spongy.

"Just a quick peek in the oldest part of the cemetery," said Theodosia, flashing her beam across a large tomb adorned with four moldering Greek columns, "then we're out of here." She was fervently wishing they'd gone back to her home and picked up Earl Grey. A large guard dog would have at least lent some moral support!

"The oldest part," muttered Drayton. "It would have to be the oldest part. My shoes are squishing and my socks are wicking dampness."

"Mine, too," said Theodosia as they trudged down the grassy incline. She figured that, besides Drayton's wet feet, he might also have a case of cold feet.

"And whatever you do," Drayton warned, "don't you dare drop that flashlight. I don't fancy stumbling around here in the pitch black. At my age I could tumble and break a hip!"

They walked another thirty paces, their feet continuing to squish in the damp, soggy ground.

"There's the obelisk," Theodosia said, under her breath. She ran her beam up the thirty-foot-high structure, then down again. The white marble gleamed like bones picked clean. "Spooky," she added.

"We're at the burial section for Civil War soldiers," Drayton murmured. "The war dead from both the Confederate and the Union." He grimaced as he said, "We want the next section over. The next *century* over."

As their breathing quickened, their pace exponentially slowed.

"Getting closer," said Drayton. He was in good shape for his age, but certainly no spring chicken.

"We're close to the oldest part," said Theodosia, still keeping her voice whisper low. "The section they filmed for *Haunted Places* on the Travel Channel."

"No such thing as ghosts," said Drayton, as if suddenly settling upon a suitable mantra.

"What about the orb you saw in St. Phillip's Graveyard?" Drayton, on a late-night walk through Gateway Walk, had sworn he'd seen a glowing blue orb in the old burial ground behind St. Phillip's Church.

"Orbs are a completely different thing," said Drayton.

"Not an entity?"

"No, more like . . . energy," said Drayton.

As they scuffled down the final hill, Theodosia's foot sank deep into wet, muddy earth, sucking her down and causing her to stumble. Arms flailing, she caught herself at the last moment, then righted herself thanks to a quick hand from Drayton. Shining her flashlight downward, she said, "What just happened?"

Drayton made a sour face. "The ground's just terribly uneven here. I suppose, after so many years, the wooden coffins simply . . ." His voice trailed off.

"Collapsed," said Theodosia. It was a grisly, jarring thought. And the notion that they were tromping across rows of Charleston citizens who'd been dead for more than two hundred years gave her pause.

"Okay," said Drayton, "this has to be it." His voice was sharp, his excitement ratcheted to a fever pitch.

"Should I look over there while you—"

"No," said Drayton, "we stay together. There's only the one flashlight, after all."

"Right. Okay." Theodosia didn't exactly relish the idea of wandering around by herself, either. Ghosts didn't scare her, but real people did. People such as the killer who'd attacked Rob and Camilla at the Heritage Society.

"Let's take a look at the number we came up with," said Drayton. On the ride over, he'd studied the printout, done his *A*-equals-1 calculation, and ended up with a thirteen-digit number. He'd told Theodosia it was too many digits, but she'd convinced him to take a wait and see attitude.

Theodosia flashed her light on the nearest tombstone. A gasping skull gaped back at her. "Cute," she said, her flashlight beam wavering slightly.

"The thing is," said Drayton, "two or three hundred years ago, death was a part of life. The dead were washed and clothed at home; coffins were handmade. Burial was almost a family affair. And these icons . . ." He pointed at one of the skull heads. "They were simply grim reminders of how we all end up eventually."

"A lovely thought," muttered Theodosia.

"Still," said Drayton, "it took the mystery out of death. It made a sort of logical connection from cradle to grave, so to speak."

Theodosia moved to the next grave. "Let's look at that number again."

Drayton glanced at the paper, then held it out to her. Theodosia shone her light on it and frowned. "An awful lot of digits."

"That's right. That's what I've been telling you."

Glancing at the gravestone, Theodosia noted the number and the date. "Even taking into consideration the date and the number of a grave . . ."

"We're still left with too many digits."

"Let's try another one," said Theodosia, moving on.

"As you wish," said Drayton.

But their search still didn't turn up a single grave that in any way corresponded to the number they'd figured.

"You were right," said Theodosia. "A dead end." She paused, wishing she hadn't phrased it quite so morbidly.

"A dead end, literally," agreed Drayton.

"Back to the island fortress theory?"

"Maybe so. But, again, which island fortress?" asked Drayton. "Just in the Charleston vicinity alone we've got Castle Pinckney, old Fort Moultrie, and Fort Sumter. Plus there are heaven knows how many old fortresses that have been leveled by hurricanes or just vanished over the past two hundred years . . . like Fort Johnson or the infamous Battery Wagner on Morris Island."

"Lost through time," murmured Theodosia. She opened her handbag and pulled out a piece of paper.

"Now what?" asked Drayton, as she handed him the flashlight.

"I'm going to take a rubbing of this number and date." She searched around inside her shoulder bag. "Got a pencil, by any chance?"

Drayton gave a cursory pat to his pockets. "No. Sorry."

"Never mind," Theodosia said, digging into her small makeup bag. "I've got an eyebrow pencil." She snapped off the top. "Sienna Brown." Positioning the paper over the number, Theodosia flattened it carefully and began to rub. "Hold that light steady." She moved the pencil in long, gentle strokes, gradually capturing the image.

"Looks good," said Drayton, studying her almost-finished work. "But why? What do you want it for?"

"Just to . . . I don't know . . . analyze it," said Theodosia. "Or in case we think of something later. Okay, almost done." The fog had turned damp and cold, wrapping around them like a wet rag.

A few ticks of silence drifted by, and then Drayton said, "I saw you talking with both those fellows tonight."

Theodosia blew a stray tendril of auburn hair off her forehead. "You mean Parker and Max?"

"That's right," said Drayton. He let loose a low chuckle. "Two fellows. So the plot thickens."

Theodosia peeled back the paper. "Or the fog does. Whichever comes first."

20

❧

Azaleas, camellias, and daffodils lent a riot of color to the backyard garden at the elegant Redcliffe House. A large three-tiered fountain pattered merrily into a small pond where tiny, golden fish darted into dark, murky depths. Yellow-and-black swallowtail butterflies flitted from flower to flower, sipping tasty nectar. And a dozen or so tea tour guests sat at white wrought-iron tables on a large flagstone patio sipping Ceylonese black tea and eating jumbo, cat-head-sized maraschino cherry scones drizzled with a powdered sugar glaze.

Theodosia and Drayton were back at it again, kicking off their ten o'clock tea tour with a quick morning repast. And, luckily for them, they were also enjoying abundant sunshine, flora and fauna, and genial company this Friday morning. A far cry from last night's gloomy romp in the cemetery.

"Ladies," said Drayton, "might I specifically direct your gaze to the multiple beds of pink camellias, which are enclosed by low boxwood hedges." He stood, ramrod stiff, like a ballet instructor, in front of the group, all eyes upon him. "This is a fine illustration of a classic, formal English garden."

A tentative hand was raised at one of the tables.

"But this isn't an English-style home?"

"This lovely home, Redcliffe House," said Drayton, "through which we shall stroll in a matter of mere minutes, was fashioned in the Italianate style." Drayton cast an eye toward Theodosia, then continued. "As some of you who live in this area may know, this magnificent home was constructed back in 1820 by Daniel Redcliffe, the wealthy owner of a large rice plantation."

After pouring her last refill, Theodosia hurried to join Drayton at the tail end of his lecture. "As a footnote," she said, "the orangerie you see extending out into the garden was added in 1912 and is a miniature model of the orangerie at the Palace of Versailles."

"And now that you've all been properly fortified," said Drayton, extending both arms and gently motioning for everyone to rise, "we shall begin our tour."

A woman in a robin's-egg-blue suit with matching hat raised her hand and asked, "What are we going to see again?"

Drayton gave a perfunctory smile. "After we explore the first floor of the Redcliffe House, we'll take a quick tour of the nearby Verner House. From there we shall meander over to the Charleston Library Association for a visit, then wander down historic Gateway Walk. At which point we shall jog—and I use that term loosely, dear ladies—down Church Street, where we'll end up at the Indigo Tea Shop for a tasty luncheon."

Theodosia waited until all the women filed into the back door of the Redcliffe House, then drew up the rear of the column. Inside, they wandered through two elegant parlors and a library, while Drayton pointed out particular items of interest: a set of French *vernis Martin* chairs, a Hepplewhite sideboard, and a gilded Chippendale mirror. He also called attention to a fine hand-painted mural of a Tuscan villa and a dark, moody oil painting done by the well-known American portrait painter Edward Savage.

Then they were outside again, this time Theodosia and Drayton leading the women down a walkway under verdant canopies of live oaks. Horse-drawn jitneys with dancing fringe jingle-jangled in the street as they strolled past elegant, immense homes that hunkered together, shoulder to shoulder, like grand old dowagers.

In no time at all, they were climbing the wide, stone steps of the Verner House.

The current owner, a woman by the name of Lenora Perry, met them at the front door and led their group on a short tour. Here was a valuable bombé Louis XV commode, classic stucco fireplace, and silver candlesticks à la Paul Revere, as well as a magnificent free-flying staircase above which hung a spectacular crystal chandelier.

Back outside again, they cut over to the Charleston Library Association. There the group tiptoed into the dark depths of the old building and paid a short visit to the manuscript room. A docent wearing white cotton gloves allowed them to view framed letters handwritten by George Washington and Francis Marion, the heroic Swamp Fox.

Then their merry group was underway again and wandering down Gateway Walk, through the Governor Aiken Gates, and passing directly by the Gibbes Museum of Art.

Theodosia had a wild, giggly moment when she wondered if Max might be sitting inside at his desk, composing a press release. Or maybe he was in a meeting, jotting notes about an upcoming show. The notion tickled her fancy and she was suddenly gripped with a mad urge to dash away from the tour group and pop in to surprise him.

Then reality set in and she began to wonder if the two of them would ever really connect. And, if that might be in the cards, what exactly was she going to do about Parker Scully?

Maybe (and now her anxieties were kicking in big-time) any real, meaningful relationship with Max was doomed. Because of Parker. Because of Delaine. Maybe they were both destined to be in exceedingly pleasant boyfriend-girlfriend relationships with people they really, really liked, but weren't rapturously in love with.

Whoa. Wait a minute, dearie. Aren't we getting ahead of ourselves? Oh, yes, I think so. Because seriously, how do I really feel about Max? Do I love him? No, no, no. It's way too early for that kind of declaration, isn't it? Isn't it? Hmm, I definitely need to give this more time to percolate.

"Theodosia? Theodosia?"

Shaking her head to clear it, Theodosia was suddenly aware that Drayton was calling her name. "Yes?" she called pleasantly, raising a hand.

"If you don't mind," said Drayton, "would you like to enlighten everyone about this lovely statue of Persephone?"

"Of course," said Theodosia, as they all clustered around the white marble statue that graced the back patio of the Gibbes Museum. "Our dear Persephone, as you probably know, is a goddess in Greek mythology. In fact, she was deemed so beautiful that she was kidnapped by Hades and spirited down to the underworld, where the weather was almost as warm and humid as our own Charleston summers." That remark garnered a good amount of laughter, and then Theodosia continued. "Persephone eventually won her release, but she was still compelled to return to the underworld for one-third of the year." She paused. "Much like our own heat that runs June through September." More laughter ensued as they crossed Meeting Street and walked around the Circular Congregational Church with its spectacular Romanesque style of architecture.

From here on, Gateway Walk evolved into a lovely mix of gardens, ghosts, and gravestones. Eerie slate markers from the sixteen hundreds, many with skull-and-bones motifs, mingled with tablets that sported some very *Miami Ink*–looking skulls with angel's wings.

As they walked along, Drayton doled out tidbits of information about the sundial, the concrete tree trunk twisted with ivy, the obelisk, and the many stone markers and plaques that detailed special stories and legends.

And as they wandered deeper into this hidden core of garden and graves, Theodosia couldn't help but wonder about the many stones, monuments, markers, tablets, and plaques.

And cipher stones?

What was a cipher stone, after all? she wondered. A brick? A round cobble rock like the ones that still paved historic Gillon Street?

Or could a cipher stone be any type of stone that had a cipher engraved on it?

As Theodosia passed a large tomb carved with Old English script, she glanced at it with speculation. Moss had grown up one side of the tomb almost covering an inscription that read, TWOUD GRIEVE YOU TENDER READER TO RELATE, THE HASTY STRIDES OF UNRELENTING FATE.

Prophetic lines, she decided. And a little frightening, too.

"And now," said Drayton, as he threw open the front door of their cozy little tea shop, "we bid you welcome to the Indigo Tea Shop."

There were oohs and ahhs as the ladies stepped inside. And when Theodosia finally entered, even she was charmed. Because Haley and Miss Dimple had outdone themselves once again. The three tables set aside for their tour group sparkled with dishes from the Shelley yellow and green Primrose pattern. Crisp white linen napkins were folded in tricky fleur-de-lis arrangements. And yellow silk fabric was tied to the backs of all the chairs and embellished with large poufy bows.

As Drayton seated their guests at the elegantly set tables, Theodosia snapped into hostess mode.

"We'll be serving a luncheon tea today," she told them. "So we'll begin with couscous salad and zucchini bread, then move on to a chilled cucumber soup. Our entrées include bacon and red pepper quiche as well as homemade crumpets spread with chicken salad and cranberry jam, then topped with cheddar cheese and popped under the broiler."

"And tea," said Drayton, as if she'd forget about that.

"Drayton will be brewing several different teas," said Theodosia, "so you can indulge your taste buds and sample several different varieties. In fact, last I heard, he'd selected Darjeeling, a Chinese oolong, and a vanilla chai."

Then Theodosia was off in a whirl, greeting her other guests, seeing to the tea tour ladies, and helping Miss Dimple ferry out the various courses while Drayton focused strictly on brewing tea.

By the time entrées were finished, Drayton was extolling the merits of so many varieties of tea they had to pull the little teacups out again for sampling all around.

"Don't forget about dessert," Theodosia cautioned her guests. "We have bread pudding with brandy sauce, our own creamy dreamy parfait, and lemon chess pie."

"Excuse me," said one of the ladies. "I keep hearing about lemon chess pie, but what exactly is it?"

"According to Haley, our resident baker," said Theodosia, "it's an original farm pie. One that's basically made with whatever's on hand."

"Nothing fancy or expensive," said Drayton, "just put together with love."

Just as Theodosia was busily jotting down orders for take-out scones, Max strolled in. He looked around with a faint smile, and his nose raised ever so slightly.

Sniffing tea aromas? Theodosia wondered.

She hustled over to meet Max with a friendly but inquisitive, "What on earth are you doing here?" She was surprised and pleased that Max had popped in unexpectedly. Or maybe he was . . . psychic? Maybe he'd felt a twinkle when she walked past the Gibbes Museum earlier this morning?

"I came to grab a scone," Max told her. "I understand they're moist, not crumbly, and probably the best in town."

"Who told you that?" she asked. *Delaine?*

Max smiled lazily. "People." He paused. "Any luck last night?"

Theodosia momentarily froze. "How did you know about last night?" He hadn't followed her, had he?

"Took a not-so-wild guess," said Max. "I'm beginning to get a fairly good idea of how your mind operates."

"No," said Theodosia, "you really don't know me at all." She didn't mean it in a snarky or nasty way, she just . . . meant it.

"But I'm *getting* to know you," said Max. "And enjoying every single moment."

Okay, Theodosia decided, *I can easily go along with that.*

"So," said Max, "*did* you discover anything?"

"No," said Theodosia. "Not a thing."

"Apologies then," said Max, "for sending you on such a wild-goose chase."

"Don't worry about it," said Theodosia. "Because you really didn't send me. I made the decision all by myself."

"I don't know what she's saying," said Haley, handing the phone to Theodosia. "She's in hysterics."

"Now what?" Theodosia asked. Max, along with most of their luncheon guests, had departed and she was packing up a final scone order in one of their indigo-blue takeout boxes. "Who's in hysterics, Haley?"

Haley wrinkled her nose and shook back her fine curtain of hair. "I think it's Delaine. Then again, it could be a scalded cat who dialed our number by mistake."

"Delaine?" said Theodosia, into the phone. "What's wrong? What's going on?"

"Theo!" Delaine let out a loud, distressed wail that sounded like a banshee's shriek. "Nadine hasn't shown up to help with the Silk and Syrah show! In fact, I *still* haven't been able to reach her!"

"I'm sure she's fine," said Theodosia. "Like I said last night, she's probably all cozy and hanging out with Bill Glass." *Although I can't imagine why. Gag.*

"I know, I know," chattered Delaine, "but it's still so contrary to her nature. My sister was looking forward to Silk and Syrah almost as much as I am. Or I should say *was*!"

"I'm sure Nadine will turn up," Theodosia offered, in her most solicitous tone.

"Maybe," Delaine whimpered, "but if she doesn't there's no way I can pull this off by myself!"

"Surely Janine can help," said Theodosia. Janine was Delaine's overworked, underpaid assistant. The poor woman always looked perpetually stressed and in dire need of a Xanax. Then again, who wouldn't be stressed, working for Delaine?

"Oh, no," Delaine scolded. "I need someone with far more finesse than Janine."

No, no, no. Delaine's not angling to ask me to help, is she? She wouldn't dare impose on me, would she?

Oh, yes, she would.

"Theodosia!" Delaine cried in a pleading, helpless bleat. "Can you *please* come over and lend a hand?"

"You're not serious!"

"I've got at least fifty women who have RSVPed to this event!" Delaine shrilled. "With dozens of possible walk-ins!"

"I'm awfully busy . . ." Theodosia said, stalling. It was

typical of Delaine to try to impose, and Theodosia was fighting her natural urge to jump in and help.

"And the hideous thing is," said Delaine, sniffling like crazy now, "is that I went *way* out on a limb. Spent *tons* of money and invited two upscale designers with their finest silk collections. I even hired models, a hot new DJ, and a bartender. And now Silk and Syrah is going to be a disaster! It's all going to come crashing down around me and I'll be a complete laughingstock!"

Her heart softening, Theodosia dropped the phone to her chest and glanced about the tea shop. They weren't exactly crazy busy. So Drayton and Haley could probably manage. And didn't she feel a tiny bit guilty about stealing (or at least cajoling?) Max away from Delaine? Even though he wasn't quite away from her yet?

Of course, she did. Sort of.

"I'll come over and help," Theodosia told Delaine. After this morning's successful tea tour, she was feeling magnanimous.

"Oh, Theo!" Delaine squealed, "you're a peach and an absolute lifesaver! I'll never forget this kindness! And I'll make it up to you somehow! I'll do anything, just name it!"

His name is Max. Ha-ha.

"See you in half an hour, Delaine," said Theodosia, hanging up the phone.

"What crisis is spinning her little world off its axis now?" asked Drayton. He was balancing a tin of Fujian black tea in one hand and a tin of Golden Monkey in another. Undoubtedly weighing the merits of each tea before he actually committed to brewing a pot.

"Delaine's having a hissy fit over her Silk and Syrah event," Theodosia told him, rolling her eyes, pretending it was all a big joke.

"When isn't she having a hissy fit?" asked Drayton.

"I can see why she's a little crazed," Theodosia explained.

"Her sister didn't bother showing up to help, and Delaine has a herd of silk-loving women about to beat a path to her door."

"I take it this is another one of Delaine's trunk shows?" asked Drayton. "Which, in reality, is simply a clever ploy to write orders on merchandise she hasn't laid out money for."

Theodosia chuckled. "Drayton, I love that you never let people's ulterior motives sway you from your own quirky spin on things."

"Such as it is," said Drayton.

"So you don't mind if I take off and give Delaine a hand?"

"Go," said Drayton, finally selecting the Fujian. "Scuttle on out of here. I have Miss Dimple to help, and she and I can easily handle the tea room for the rest of this afternoon."

21

"*You're a love,* love, love!" Delaine chirped as Theodosia strolled through the front door of Cotton Duck.

"What do you want me to do?" asked Theodosia. She glanced around and saw that the myriad racks of filmy dresses, cotton slacks, and T-shirts had been pushed aside to yield floor space for the two visiting designers. A pair of white Parsons tables stood like altars, holding look books and promotional materials while racks filled with colorful silk clothing stood nearby.

Delaine's shop, on a normal day, featured elegant, airy cotton clothing perfectly suited to Charleston's climate of heat and humidity. She also stocked filmy tops, long evening gowns, scarves the weight of butterfly wings, strands of pearls, swishy skirts, and even a few racks of vintage clothes. Delaine's latest boutique addition included several high-end lingerie lines, including La Perla, Cosabella, and the brand Guia La Bruna from Italy.

"Where to start?" Delaine screeched back. Her eyes darted

about, looking frantic, then eventually slid back to Theodosia. Delaine's perfectly waxed brows pinched together, and she said, in an acerbic tone, "I know, we'll work on you first. Change your outfit, such as it is."

"What!" exclaimed Theodosia. What in hail, holy heaven was wrong with the summer dress she was wearing?

"A *chic* event such as Silk and Syrah requires we maintain a certain degree of *alta moda*," Delaine simpered.

Theodosia did a quick flash back to her high school language classes. "High fashion?" she guessed.

Delaine gave a curt nod. "After all, Theo, I'll have *society* ladies in attendance today—the crème de la crème of Charleston. Our own *Post and Courier* has even promised to send a photographer from the Style section! Now, dear girl, if you could just slip out of that *thing* and into a silk blouse and slacks . . . created by one of today's designers, of course."

"What's wrong with the dress I have on?" asked Theodosia, even though she knew Delaine wasn't about to be swayed.

Delaine wrinkled her nose and picked her words delicately. "A trifle shopgirlish?"

"Fine," said Theodosia. "Have it your way." What was that quirky phrase W. H. Auden had penned? *I know what every schoolboy knows, no kind act goes unrevenged.* Yes, perfect. Because here she was, volunteering time and energy while Delaine launched criticism in return. Laced with a few barbs at that! Then again, this little scenario was very much in keeping with Delaine's basic nature.

"Indigo blue or sea green?" Delaine asked. She grabbed two silk outfits from a nearby rack, held them up, and shook them until the fabric shimmied, the better to entice Theodosia. Both were elegant tunic tops with matching tapered slacks.

"Indigo blue," said Theodosia. She knew it was better to accept defeat than continue arguing. "How many silkworms died for this?" She'd seen a show on PBS about China's silk

industry and how the poor, hardworking worms got cooked
in their own cocoons.

"Does it matter?"

"Obviously not to you," said Theodosia.

Delaine shoved the blue outfit into Theodosia's hands and
hissed, "Please do hurry!"

By the time Theodosia strolled out of the changing room,
the bartender had arrived and was setting up bottles of Syrah
on a wooden counter that had been swept clear of pearls,
brooches, and scarves. On the other side of the shop, the DJ,
a young kid with shaved head, silver piercings, and black
leather jacket, was doing sound checks.

"She made you change, too?" asked Janine. With her large,
watery brown eyes and brown silk shirt and slacks, Delaine's
longtime assistant resembled a sad basset hound. Her frizzled brown hair hung flat against her head and she looked
as if she hadn't gotten any sleep for days. With Delaine as a
taskmaster, she probably hadn't.

"This outfit's actually kind of cute," said Theodosia, doing
a quick pirouette and studying herself in the three-way mirror. She decided she looked boho-chic. She wasn't completely
sure what boho-chic really meant, but she'd seen the term
bandied about in *Vogue*, the fashionista's bible of all things
stylish.

"That outfit's twenty-one hundred," intoned Janine.

"Dollars?" said Theodosia, suddenly being dropped back
to terra firma. Maybe twenty-one hundred lira or twenty-one
hundred drachma, but dollars? Seriously?

Janine nodded in her typical sad fashion. "Both the top and
slacks are from the Diane Seifert collection. Apparently she
uses only cultivated silk spun from silkworms that are fed a
special diet of chopped mulberry leaves every half hour."

"What insect eats that well?" asked Theodosia. "Or that
often?"

"Silkworms," Janine answered, in a solemn voice.

"Diane . . . she's one of the designers here today?" She looked across the shop and saw a tall, stylish blond woman and a man in a tight blazer with a scarf wrapped around his neck multiple times.

"Along with Neville Bailey," said Janine. "Bailey . . . that's him over there . . . is a crazy British designer who creates the most exquisite dresses and blouses using slubbed and distressed silk."

"So they're probably cheaper," Theodosia reasoned.

"Oh, no," said Janine. "The pieces in Bailey's collection are even more expensive."

"Here you two are!" exclaimed Delaine. "Just chatting away when there's so much work to be done." She had changed outfits and was now dolled up in a black silk sheath dress tied with a red silk obi belt. With her long dark hair pulled up in a twist to accent her heart-shaped face, Delaine looked both dangerous and exotic.

"What do you want me to do?" asked Theodosia. "Just name it."

"Mmm," said Delaine, considering. "I think perhaps greet people at the door?"

"I can do that," said Theodosia. Inwardly, she heaved a sigh of relief. Greeting people was easy. A few *Hi, how are yous* and she'd be out of here. Free as a bird once again.

"And after that," Delaine cooed, "you can circulate through the crowd and help me write up orders."

"Orders on clothes?" Theodosia sputtered. "I'm really not qualified to do that."

"Nonsense," said Delaine, "the process is so simple a child could manage. You simply guide the customers through the decision-making process, then jot down sizes, colors, and quantities."

Theodosia was suspicious. "That sounds more like sales." And would she receive a twenty percent commission for all her guiding and coaxing of customers? Doubtful. More and more, Theodosia wanted to rush to no-show Nadine's apartment, grab her by the ear, and march her over here in lockstep.

"We have a host of wealthy and trend-conscious women coming in today," Delaine reiterated, "so they *expect* to place orders. They *expect* you to be solicitous."

"I don't know . . ." said Theodosia. But Delaine had already dashed off.

"You'll be fine," Janine said, with a baleful look.

Theodosia nodded. She was beginning to understand why Janine always looked so sad.

Theodosia decided that the trunk show, once underway, was your basic nightmare event. First off, she had to stand at the front door and greet a thundering herd of overdressed, super skinny women who not only shrieked greetings to each other, but shrieked nonstop into their cell phones, too. Then she had to gently shuttle them in the direction of the two fashion designers and their well-stocked racks of merchandise. Which turned out to be like herding cats. If a customer so much as noticed a shiny bauble in another part of the store or veered toward the wine bar, Delaine threw her a nasty, disappointed look.

In the end, Theodosia had to pretty much strong-arm all the guests. Which left her feeling like a bouncer in a tough waterfront saloon. Or, worse yet, a Vegas bottle hostess.

When Theodosia was finally able to abandon her post at the front door, Delaine stuck a fat order book in her hand and nudged her toward a rugby scrum of women who were busy quaffing wine, squeezing into sample sizes, and text messaging furiously.

"Excuse me, excuse me," said Theodosia, easing into the

fray. But not a single woman paid one whit of attention to her. She renewed her efforts and tried again. "If any of you are ready to place an order . . ." This time someone jabbed her with a sharp elbow.

Theodosia, who was polite to a fault and fairly easygoing, suddenly hit her zero-tolerance level. Just as she was about to slap her empty order book down on the counter and call it quits, a woman chirped, "Theodosia, is that you?"

It was Scarlette Berlin, the art dealer she'd met at the Gibbes Museum. Scarlette wore an expansive grin on her face and a half-dozen skull rings on her fingers, and she had a silk tunic top clutched in her hands.

"Fancy seeing you here," said Scarlette. She gave a little simper, then added, "Are you picking up something special to wear to my gallery opening tonight?" Looking more than hopeful, she added, "You're still coming, aren't you? You and that adorable Drayton."

"We're still planning to," Theodosia told her. But as the words spilled out of her mouth, she was suddenly wondering why. Why on earth were they going to this crazy lady's gallery? Because, in Theodosia's mind, Scarlette had pretty much slipped to the back of the pack as far as suspects went.

"Excellent," Scarlette bubbled. "The event starts at seven, but you're welcome to come a little early if you'd like. It would give us a chance to get to know each other better."

"Fun," said Theodosia, even though the prospect of making chitchat with Scarlette didn't sound fun at all.

"Taking orders, I hope?" inquired Delaine, as she suddenly slipped up behind them.

"I for one intend to place an order," said Scarlette. "And . . ." She held up the tunic top and dangled it. "Are the samples for sale, too?"

"Everything's for sale," said Theodosia. At which point three more women rushed up to her and asked to place orders.

Theodosia did the best she could, writing down item numbers, sizes, colors, and customer information. When she'd collected the basic details, she turned the orders over to Janine so she could tally up the final dollar amounts and tactfully extract a fifty percent deposit.

"You did fairly well," Delaine told Theodosia some forty minutes later, as they both sipped a glass of Syrah. "Not as many orders as I'd hoped, but you were a great help anyway."

"Thanks," said Theodosia, knowing it was a left-handed compliment and not really caring. When all was said and done, the order taking hadn't been all that painful. In fact, she'd almost felt a part of the design process, since she'd made suggestions as to which pieces to order.

"Still," said Delaine, chewing the tip of her pencil, "I'm still disappointed that Nadine never bothered to show up."

"Do you think she could have gone back to New York?" Theodosia asked. "Maybe some kind of business emergency?"

Delaine was adamant. "My sister would *never* just take off without telling me."

"You've called her apartment?"

"Of course, I've called her apartment. About a jillion times and she's still not answering." Her harsh mask suddenly crumbled and she let loose a choked sob. "Something must be wrong! I *feel* it."

"Take it easy," said Theodosia, trying to dispense a modicum of calm and reason. "Is it possible Nadine had a fight with Bill Glass? Maybe they had some sort of lovers' quarrel and Nadine's just awfully upset? Or, worse yet, she's embarrassed."

Now Delaine looked puzzled. "What could she possibly have to be embarrassed about?"

Duh and double duh. Theodosia wanted to say, *Maybe she's embarrassed about dating a world-class clod like Bill Glass?* But she didn't.

Delaine squared her shoulders and swallowed hard. "I'm sure Nadine will turn up. She *has* to."

"She could wander in at any moment," Theodosia agreed.

"You know," said Delaine, grasping Theodosia's hand in a firm grip and giving a conspiratorial squeeze, "Nadine has always been the ditz in the family."

Though it just about killed her, Theodosia managed to once again hold her tongue.

"I was just about to leave," said Drayton, as Theodosia strolled through the front door of the Indigo Tea Shop. "Haley and Miss Dimple left a half hour ago." The tea shop was empty and Drayton had just finished rinsing out a small Yi-Xing teapot.

"Glad I caught you," said Theodosia.

Drayton reached up, removed his half-glasses, and peered expectantly at her. "You look a little frazzled. I take it an afternoon spent with Delaine was not all fun and games?"

"Delaine ran me ragged with customer meet-and-greets," said Theodosia. "Then I got roped into helping her write up orders. No wonder poor Janine always looks like she just came off a cattle drive."

"So why aren't you home?" asked Drayton. "Listening to a relaxing CD while you luxuriate in a tub filled with your own T-Bath Bubble Tea?"

"Because I was hoping we still had time to hit a couple of those salvage archaeology places."

"Oh, no," said Drayton, fingering his bow tie. "You don't really want to do that, do you?"

"We'll make it quick," said Theodosia.

"You know they're both going to be hopeless dead ends," said Drayton. He shook his head. "I don't understand why you have such a bee in your bonnet about visiting these places."

"Excuse me," said Theodosia, "But this entire wild-goose

chase began when Timothy pleaded with me to look into Rob's murder. And, as I recall, you were standing squarely behind him, egging me on."

Drayton made a small grimace. "I suppose I did."

"Then grab your jacket and let's go."

22

❧

Carolina Roads Architectural Salvage was the first place they hit. It was a small shop on Society Street, a few blocks over from where the cruise ships docked along the Cooper River.

"This doesn't exactly look promising," Drayton commented, as they entered a small building covered with shingles that had once been brown and were now a weather-beaten gray. But once inside, they found themselves instantly transported back to the eighteenth and nineteenth centuries. Antique brass light fixtures dangled from the ceiling; old wooden doors, fireplace mantels, and ironwork leaned against interior walls. There were also church pews, decorative windows, old moldings, and stacks of heart pine flooring occupying almost every square foot of floor space.

The owner, Gene Fritz, seemed happy enough to see them.

"We're interested in antique stones and such," said Theodosia, being a bit circumspect.

Fritz peered at her. "Like for a garden?"

"Sure," said Theodosia. "Perfect."

"Out back," said Fritz, leading them on a winding path through the crowded shop and indicating the back door. "That's where we keep all our stoneware and larger pieces. My assistant Jimmy's out there now, so he can help you."

"Jimmy," Drayton repeated. They pushed through the back door and emerged into a gravel yard heaped with stones, fanciful columns, monuments, marble statuary, pieces of curlicue ironwork, and stacks of old bricks. The yard measured maybe twenty by thirty feet and was surrounded by an eight-foot-high mesh fence with gray plastic strips woven through the wire for privacy.

At first, Theodosia didn't even see the assistant. Dressed in dusty gray overalls and long gray apron, Jimmy looked like one of the stone pieces that stood guard here. His face and hands were dusty, and even his hair looked dusty.

"Hello there," Theodosia called, stopping in her tracks to inspect a large stone sundial. She didn't want to get too close to Jimmy because then she might have to shake hands with him and she didn't have a spare bottle of Purell in her car. "Are you Jimmy?"

The man, who was actually a little younger than he'd first appeared, gave an affable nod. "That's me. What can I do for you folks?"

"Among your inventory," said Drayton, "do you have any old stones or cornerstones?"

"Sure," said Jimmy. "We get those all the time. You folks looking for anything in particular? Something for your garden?"

Theodosia and Drayton exchanged glances.

"That's right," said Theodosia. "A garden. Stones for a garden."

"But something distinctive," added Drayton.

"Do you ever come across old stones with engravings on them?" Theodosia asked.

Jimmy looked thoughtful as he reached up to scratch his face. When he took his hand away, Theodosia swore she could see a clean streak. "You mean like Native American—type stuff?" Jimmy asked. "'Cause when we get those kinds of artifacts, we're supposed to turn 'em over to the State Archaeology Office."

"Do you always?" asked Theodosia.

Jimmy hesitated. "I'm no art historian, so I can't always make an exact determination on the provenance of a piece."

Artifacts. The provenance of a piece. Theodosia decided Jimmy was plenty smart when it came to art history.

"We're just looking for something with a little touch of history," Theodosia told him.

"And you want some kind of engraved stone," Jimmy murmured, casting his eyes downward as he walked, searching his inventory. He poked a piece of granite with his dusty boot. "Got a cornerstone here from an old bank. Dates back to 1877."

"Lovely," said Drayton.

"Anything in a foreign language?" asked Theodosia. "Or Old English?"

"Probably nothing that specific," said Jimmy. He pointed toward a large stack of bricks. "We got a ton of antique Charleston brown bricks."

"Where are they from?" asked Drayton.

"Here and there," said Jimmy. "A lot of these pieces are relics from antebellum mansions; some are from old buildings that have been torn down." Jimmy gave a quick grimace. "That gets the preservationists up in arms."

"I can imagine," said Drayton, a touch of chill in his voice.

"It's funny," said Jimmy, "old statuary and columns are suddenly popular again. There was a time you couldn't give that stuff away. People even chunked it up and used it as landfill. Now, it's the hot new thing for backyard gardens."

"But no engraved stones or cornerstones?" asked Theodosia.

"I've had things like that," said Jimmy, "in the past. But local dealers pretty much cleaned us out. They stop by periodically and pick through this stuff." He grinned. "Most ordinary folks don't realize there's valuable stuff here, but they got the eye."

"Can you give us some names?" Theodosia asked. "Of the dealers who've shopped here recently?"

They followed Jimmy into the shop, where he scrawled a couple of names on a sheet of paper.

"Thanks," said Theodosia. "You've been a big help."

"Come back next week," urged Jimmy. "We're getting a truckload of stuff from an old church."

"Anything?" Drayton asked, once they were in the car.

Theodosia unfolded the list, scanned it, then passed it over to him.

Drayton read the list quickly, then frowned and said, "The Silver Plume is on this list."

"Thomas Hassel's shop," said Theodosia, quickly cranking over the engine.

"You think we should go over there now?" asked Drayton. "Take a look around?"

"Time's a-wastin'," said Theodosia.

But when they got to Thomas Hassel's shop, a good-sized brick building located in a more upscale part of town, the lights were off. A wrought-iron door, inlaid with glass, had a neatly lettered CLOSED sign hanging inside, but they tried it anyway. No luck; the place was locked up tight. They peered in the windows, where old silverware, Baroque pearl necklaces, and antique music boxes sat alongside silver frames and old cameos. But still no shadows moved or lights glimmered in the back offices.

"Just missed him," said Drayton. "Our tough luck."

But Theodosia had spotted a side alley—a narrow corridor that snaked between Hassel's brick building and a red sandstone building. An ancient wrought-iron arch hung invitingly over a passageway that looked dark, cool, and inviting and was paved with old-fashioned cobblestones. "Why don't we take a look around?" she suggested, pointing to the corridor.

Drayton looked uncomfortable. "You mean back there?"

"Sure. Just take a minute."

He shrugged. "No harm in looking, I suppose." As he followed her down the cobblestone walk, he added, "That's all we're going to do, right. Just look?"

"Of course," said Theodosia. She emerged in a kind of backyard, not dissimilar to Carolina Roads, but was stopped by a large metal gate. She put a hand on the lever and jiggled the closure. Almost as if she'd chanted *Open Sesame*, the gate swung magically open.

"You probably shouldn't go in there," said Drayton.

"Probably not," said Theodosia, stepping into the backyard.

"Come now," said Drayton, sounding a trifle perturbed, "you don't really think you're going to find a cipher stone just lying around, do you?"

"There's no telling what we'll find," said Theodosia. She stepped over to a large stone eagle that looked like it might have been chipped off the cornice of an old bank. "From a bank, I think."

"Back when banks still looked like banks," said Drayton, "instead of video stores."

They shuffled around looking at more stone cornices, a trio of querulous-looking gargoyles, a stone Buddha with a large rounded belly, and several stone columns.

"Doric," said Drayton, running a hand down one.

"And this one's Ionic," said Theodosia.

"You've been hanging around the museum," Drayton commented.

Not as much as I'd like to hang around the museum's PR director, thought Theodosia.

"I'm actually quite surprised by all this," said Drayton. "I had no idea Thomas Hassel dealt in architectural artifacts."

"If he's been handling these things for years, maybe he knows about the cipher stone. Or at least about the legend."

"Possible," said Drayton.

"On the other hand," said Theodosia, "if it was Hassel who stole the skull cup, maybe it was the missing link he needed. Maybe Hassel's already got the cipher stone and he needed the skull cup to correlate a location."

"Maybe," said Drayton, not convinced. "And maybe we're spinning a story that has absolutely no credence."

"Wishful thinking," said Theodosia.

"Magical thinking," said Drayton.

"There's that," admitted Theodosia. "Still . . . it might be worthwhile, asking Hassel a few more questions."

They walked back out to the sidewalk and climbed into Theodosia's car.

"I suppose the other places are locked up nice and tight," she said.

"No doubt," said Drayton. He glanced at his watch. "Even with this thing running slow," said Drayton, "we're going to be late for that gallery opening."

"I ran into Scarlette Berlin at Delaine's," said Theodosia. "She wanted to know if we were still coming."

"What did you tell her?"

"I said we were." Theodosia waited a few seconds. "Are we?"

"I suppose."

"It's not like it's an opening at the Met or anything," said Theodosia. "And there'll probably be a gaggle of art lovers there, so we wouldn't be missed."

"You're the one who was so interested in her," said Drayton. "Because of the skulls and things. So maybe . . . a quick howdy-do and then we take our leave. Still, you did have that . . . vibe."

"I did," said Theodosia. "So let's go."

23

❧

Crystal glasses clinked and techno-industrial rock lent a pulsing backbeat as a glamorous coterie of artists, art collectors, art critics, and art wannabes jockeyed for position to view the newest brand of postmodern paintings at Berlin Fine Arts.

"You dressed artsy," Drayton observed, as they pushed their way through the throng.

Theodosia wore a black knit tunic top over a pair of black leggings and long jet-black earrings that swayed hypnotically and matched her beaded bag. Drayton was dressed as Drayton. Tweed jacket, khaki slacks, slip-on loafers.

"You'd have been artsy yourself if you skipped the socks," Theodosia told him.

Drayton snorted in disdain. "No socks? Please. A gentleman always wears socks."

Theodosia gazed around the gallery, which was basically a converted warehouse with highly polished wood floors and de rigueur white walls. "It's so crowded in here I can barely see the paintings," she complained. All she could make out were the very tops of gigantic, colorful canvases.

"Then let's hit the bar," suggested Drayton.

They hunched their way toward the bar, offering the kind of smiles you give to people you don't really know but are going to become physically acquainted with as you slide by.

"Good grief," said Drayton, when they finally reached the bar. "If it isn't Thomas Hassel."

Hassel slid a handful of dollars across the bar, picked up his martini, and turned toward them, a perfunctory smile on his narrow face.

"We stopped by your shop earlier today," Theodosia told him. *Why not jump right in?* she decided.

Hassel bent his head forward and touched his lips to his way-too-full martini glass. "Oh?" he said, finally.

"We even poked around in your back lot," Theodosia told him. "I've got my heart set on a few pieces of architectural salvage." She stared at Hassel, looking for any sort of reaction. There wasn't a ripple.

"For her new backyard garden," said Drayton, jumping in. "Theodosia recently purchased that adorable little carriage house next to the Kingstree Mansion."

"I'm familiar with it," said Hassel. "Charming place. Looks like Hansel and Gretel might have lived there." He took another sip of martini. "Excuse me," he murmured, then slipped away.

"What do you think?" Theodosia asked Drayton.

"No idea," said Drayton. "I got nothing from him. No vibes, no angst, no interest."

Theodosia shook her head. "Me neither." She was feeling more than a little perplexed. She prided herself on having a fairly well functioning truth-o-meter. But she'd detected nothing from Hassel's answers. Of course, many killers and sociopaths possessed the unique ability to remain ice-cool under pressure. Which is why so many of them were able to scoot by standard polygraph tests.

They gazed at each other.

"As long as we're here," said Drayton, inclining his head toward the bartender, who waited patiently to take their order.

"White wine," said Theodosia.

"Dirty martini," Drayton told the bartender. "With a blue cheese–stuffed olive if you have one."

"When did you start drinking martinis?" Theodosia asked him. "I thought you were strictly a sherry or Cabernet guy."

"It's good to change things up once in a while," said Drayton.

Change? Good? thought Theodosia. This from a man who still listened to vinyl records on an actual stereo and shunned computers, cell phones, and all things that were remotely techy?

"Maybe Haley *is* a bad influence on you after all," Theodosia remarked. Then, in the same breath, she exclaimed, "Oh, there's Scarlette!"

Scarlette Berlin was traveling with her posse tonight. Dressed in a bright red dress with a mandarin collar, she swept through the ultra contemporary gallery, murmuring greetings, accepting accolades, and generally looking quite pleased with herself.

"Let's go talk to her," suggested Theodosia, "since she was so hot to have us show up here tonight."

They grabbed their drinks, pushed back through the crowd again, and stood in a makeshift receiving line to greet Scarlette.

"It's Theo and Drayton!" Scarlette whooped when she saw them. "How wonderful to see you. Glad you could make it!"

"A lovely show," said Drayton, even though he hadn't really glanced at any of the paintings.

"We're very proud of Damian," said Scarlette, smiling maternally at a scruffy young man who stood next to her, a cigarette dangling from the side of his mouth. "Damian is from Uzbekistan. He doesn't speak any English, but that doesn't mean he's not basking in all the praise." She smiled broadly at him. "Right, darling? You *are* a star!"

"*Spasiba,*" said Damian. *Thank you.*

"*Spasiba,*" giggled Scarlette. "You're welcome."

Damian turned a leering gaze on Theodosia. "*Ti takaya krasivaya.*"

"He thinks you're very beautiful," said Scarlette. "Maybe you and Damian would like to . . ." said Scarlette, giving a wink.

"Thanks anyway," said Theodosia, "but my dance card is full right now."

"Dance card," said Scarlette, frowning. "I'm not sure I can translate . . ."

"Our Theodosia's a busy woman," said Drayton, interrupting. He flashed a look at Damian that clearly conveyed, *Back off.*

"You're wearing a new ring," Theodosia said to Scarlette. The woman had yet another skull ring, this one in gleaming gold.

Scarlette extended her hand and fluttered her fingers. "Just a little bauble I picked up last time I was in Switzerland," she told them. "Fun, isn't it?"

"Lovely," muttered Drayton.

Theodosia remained mum. To her it looked nasty and reminded her a little too much of a *Totenkopf.*

Scarlette leaned toward Theodosia. "A little bird told me you were investigating that theft at the Heritage Society."

"Which little bird was that?" asked Theodosia. Delaine? Had to be.

"I'll never tell," laughed Scarlette, as Damian chuckled along with her. Then she suddenly turned serious. "But be careful. You never know what could happen."

"You think?" said Theodosia. Was Scarlette taunting her, or was the woman just way too precious for words?

"But enough about skulls and murder," said Scarlette. "We're all here to enjoy the par-*tay*!"

"Gosh," said Theodosia, as Scarlette tottered off, "maybe we should call our next event a tea par-*tay*."

"You're vibrating," observed Drayton. "Or at least your beaded bag is."

Theodosia reached for her clutch purse, pulled out her cell phone, and thumbed the On button. "Theodosia." Who could be calling? Haley? Parker? Or maybe even . . . Max?

"Oh my Lord, Theodosia!" Delaine suddenly wailed in her ear. "I desperately need your help!"

"Now what's wrong?" asked Theodosia. Delaine crying for help twice in one day? Truly a new land speed record. And oh so tedious.

"You'll never guess who just showed up at my front door!" cried Delaine.

Max?

"Nadine!"

"That's great," said Theodosia. She had her eyes focused on Scarlette, who was touching someone on the head, as if administering a blessing.

"No, it isn't!" cried Delaine. "Nadine's in a terrible state! Poor dear was abducted!"

"What?" said Theodosia.

"And somehow, with a little luck, she managed to escape!" A sob rent from Delaine's throat. "But from the shape she's in, I'd say she's been bound and gagged and dragged through the swamp!"

"What are you *talking* about?" Theodosia demanded. What kind of wacky story was this, anyway?

"Theo, I know my sister's made up stories before," said

Delaine, the words tumbling out hastily. "But this time I'm *positive* Nadine's telling the truth! In fact, I *swear* she is! And we need you to . . ."

"She was kidnapped?" Theodosia repeated in a nervous whisper. She was still in a state of disbelief.

"Who's been kidnapped?" asked Drayton, leaning in, interested now.

A thousand thoughts zapped through Theodosia's brain, but she tried her best to prioritize them. "You're positive?"

"Of course, I'm positive!" Delaine snapped.

"What's Nadine's condition right now?" Theodosia wondered if, besides the police, they might need an ambulance.

"Her hair's an absolute wreck and her clothes are filthy!" Delaine sobbed. "And she's got that rotten-egg smell . . . like she crawled through a sewer pipe!"

"But your sister's not badly injured?" Theodosia asked.

There was mumbling and rumbling on the end other, and then Theodosia heard Nadine say, "My legs are covered in scratches and my nails are completely broken off!"

Back on the phone, Delaine said, "Every fingernail is ragged and her legs look like she's been *flayed*. Honestly, I've never seen such . . ."

"I'm calling Detective Tidwell," said Theodosia. "Right now. You two stay put."

"You'll come over?" Delaine pleaded. "You're always such a . . . a calming influence."

"We'll be there in ten minutes," Theodosia promised. "Just hold tight and don't do anything, um, stupid."

"Stupid!" screeched Delaine. "Who do you think you're talking to?"

Tidwell was sitting in his Crown Victoria, waiting for them, when they pulled up in front of Delaine's home. When he saw Theodosia swing into the parking space ahead of him, he slowly hauled his bulk out of the car, like a lethargic brown bear emerging from its den.

"I'll have you know," said Tidwell, looking greatly put upon, "I was watching the director's cut of *Madadayo* when your call came in."

"Ah," said Drayton, "you're a Kurosawa fan."

Tidwell ignored Drayton's comment. "You know I abhor any kind of disturbance during my off-hours," he muttered, then shook his head and let loose an indignant rumble.

"My deepest apologies," Theodosia told him as they hurried up the walk. "But there's been a kidnapping and you're the only officer of the law that I actually know. And trust," she added.

"Lucky me," Tidwell grumbled, as the door banged open and Delaine hustled them all inside, like a mother hen herding chicks.

Nadine was curled up on a brocade couch, huddled under a blue cashmere afghan and drinking what looked to be a large tumbler of straight Scotch. Tidwell heaved his bulk into the floral club chair across from her, while Theodosia, Drayton, and Delaine took seats close by.

Nadine didn't bother waiting for the formalities. "I was kidnapped!" she blurted, her eyes rolling and wide with terror.

"When? How?" Theodosia demanded, as Tidwell took his own sweet time about opening his notepad and removing the top of his shiny Montblanc pen.

"Yesterday," said Nadine. "I'd just come out of Scanlon's Grocery." She took a quick gulp of Scotch. "You know, that darling little place over on Cumberland that carries the nice fresh morels and truffle oil?"

Theodosia nodded. She knew it.

"Just as I was about to open my car . . . this man grabbed me from behind!" Nadine said, in a hoarse whisper, her face filled with dramatic tension. "Believe me, I fought him off like a wildcat, but he overpowered me and shoved me inside his truck!" As if retelling the experience were too much for her, a few tears leaked down Nadine's face. "Then he closed the door and locked me in!"

"Pickup truck? Panel truck?" inquired Tidwell.

"Um," said Nadine. "Panel truck?"

"No," said Tidwell, "the question was intended for you."

Nadine's lower lip quivered, and she began crying in earnest. "I don't know! It all happened so fast!"

"Just tell the nice man what you *do* remember," Delaine coached. To Theodosia she said, "Poor dear must be suffering from posttraumatic stress syndrome."

Nadine blew out a glut of air and hiccupped. "The next thing I knew, I was trussed up like a Thanksgiving turkey and we were driving for what seemed like *hours*." She touched the back of her hand to the side of her head. "I think either I was in deep shock or I blacked out for a while." She made a pitiful mewling sound, then took another good gulp of Scotch.

"Were there windows in this truck and/or van?" asked Tidwell. "Could you see where you were going?"

"Not really," said Nadine.

"How about a description?" asked Tidwell.

Nadine made jerky hand motions in front of her face. "He was wearing a ski mask!"

"Then what happened?" Theodosia asked, fearing the worst.

Nadine ducked her head like a sorrowful puppy. "He dragged me into some kind of shack out in the boonies and started firing questions at me."

"Questions about what?" asked Drayton, suddenly jumping in.

"About what I saw Sunday night!" Nadine shrilled. "At the Heritage Society!"

Oh, no, thought Theodosia, as she felt a knot tighten in the pit of her stomach. *Had Nadine been in the clutches of the actual killer?*

"What did you tell this person?" asked Delaine.

"That I didn't see anything!" Nadine wailed. "Nothing at all! But he kept asking me over and over, practically brow-beating me!" She took another hit of Scotch. "It was awful! Terrifying!"

"Hold on," said Tidwell, putting up a big paw. He leaned forward, focusing hard on Nadine, and said, "Can you give me a general description?"

"I told you!" Nadine cried, "the man wore a ski mask!"

"But surely you gleaned an overall impression," said Tidwell. "Young? Old?"

"I don't know!" Nadine wailed. "I didn't exactly *ask* to see his ID."

"Wait a minute," said Theodosia, "you say this guy held you overnight?"

Nadine nodded.

"How on earth did you manage to escape?" Theodosia asked.

"I chewed the ropes," said Nadine. She was making tiny little sobs that shook her entire body like a bad case of hiccups. "I have very strong teeth."

"She does," Delaine cooed, as she patted her sister's back. "When she was little we used to joke that she was part rodent."

"You didn't have to bring *that* up!" snarled Nadine.

"Nadine . . ." said Theodosia.

"What? What?" cried Nadine. Her head snapped from side to side, her hair swirling furiously. "I did the only thing I could think of . . . when he left me there, I kicked out a window and ran away!"

"Try to focus," said Theodosia. "Once you escaped . . . once you escaped from this shack, where did you think you were? What part of Charleston? Somewhere in the city? Out in the country? Where?"

"I was in the middle of *nowhere*," Nadine wailed. As she blinked furiously, eye makeup streamed down both sides of her face, giving her the look of a sad raccoon. "I stumbled through this horrible swamp full of dank, dirty water and finally ended up on a highway."

"Do you know which highway?" Drayton asked.

Nadine's lower lip quivered. "Um . . . I think the Maybank?"

"So you might have been held somewhere out near Wadmalaw Island?" said Drayton. He shot a sideways glance at Theodosia. Wadmalaw was where the Charleston Tea Plantation was located, where they bought a lot of their bulk tea.

"How'd you get back here?" Theodosia asked. Clearly some key pieces were missing from her story.

"I hitchhiked," said Nadine. This news she delivered in a matter-of-fact tone.

"How enterprising," said Tidwell. Clearly he wasn't taking Nadine's disappearance all that seriously.

"No," said Nadine, "that whole experience was ghastly as well! First nobody would pick me up because I was so filthy and disheveled; then I finally flagged down this rattly old pickup truck. The guy driving it gave me a ride, but I had to sit beside a mangy old yellow hunting dog that was probably infested with wood ticks! The whole experience was totally traumatic, like something out of that movie *Deliverance!*"

"Somehow I doubt that," said Tidwell.

"Poor dear," cooed Delaine. "Those ticks can give you Lyme disease."

"Lymmmmmmmme!" wailed Nadine, just as a furious pounding started up on the front door.

Then a man's voice screamed, "Nadine!" and Bill Glass suddenly flew into the living room.

"Bill!" Nadine half-rose and threw open her arms. One hand flew to her forehead, giving the impression of a modern-day Camille.

"My dear, my darling, my buttercup!" cried Bill.

"Poopsie!" cried Nadine, as he bent over and hugged her.

Tidwell rose from his chair. "It's quite clear you don't need me to help play out the rest of this little scenario."

"Please!" begged Delaine, "can't you treat this seriously? We're dealing with a serious crime here!"

"Doubtful," said Tidwell.

"Then I'm going to call an attorney!" Delaine huffed. "In fact, I'm going to phone that lovely Mr. Granville."

Tidwell had his hand on the doorknob, ready to leave, when Theodosia grabbed him. She pinched his jacket sleeve and yanked him out onto Delaine's front porch.

"Can't you open a case on this?" Theodosia asked.

Tidwell's eyebrows rose like a pair of furry caterpillars. "A case concerning what?" he asked.

Theodosia glared at him. Was he that obtuse? "Kidnapping!"

"But she's here," said Tidwell. "Safe and sound." They heard a strangled cry, glanced through the front window, and saw Nadine explaining her plight to Glass, pretty much throwing another hissy fit. "Well, she's safe, anyway," said Tidwell, amending his words. "Crazy as a bedbug, but safe."

"What about a missing-person case?" Theodosia prodded.

"Clearly," said Tidwell, "the woman is no longer missing."

"But she *was*!" said Theodosia.

"And now she's back!" countered Tidwell. "Case closed."

"But it was never open!" cried Theodosia.

A soothing Sarah McLachlan CD on the car stereo did nothing to assuage Theodosia's frustration and anger as she drove Drayton home.

"I'd like to throttle Tidwell," Theodosia raged. "I call him out on an emergency and he doesn't even bother to take it seriously!"

Sitting beside her in the dim of the car, the dashboard lights glowing green, Drayton was also grim. "He did seem awfully callous about the whole thing."

"You can say that again," said Theodosia, still fuming.

"But you believe Nadine was kidnapped?"

I absolutely do," said Theodosia. "Much as I think Nadine is totally fruit loops, I still believe her story."

"But what was the basic motive?" asked Drayton. "Who would abduct her and why would they do it?"

"Only one thing I can think of," said Theodosia. "Because Nadine lied."

Drayton did a sort of double take. "Excuse me? Lied to who?"

Theodosia goosed her car around a slow-moving truck, then said, "Nadine lied about seeing the killer at the Heritage Society. She lied to Nick Van Buren when he wrote the newspaper article, and then she weaseled around with the police."

"But the only story the killer knew," said Drayton, quickly connecting the dots, "was the one he read in the *Post and Courier.*"

"Bingo," said Theodosia.

"You think that's the sole reason Nadine was kidnapped? Because she told a fib?"

"A fib that the killer believed!" said Theodosia.

"I'm still having trouble wrapping my brain around this whole thing," said Drayton.

"You think Nadine set it up? Fabricated the whole thing?"

"Noooo," said Drayton, slowly. "For one thing, she's too prissy to actually drag herself through mud."

"You got that right," said Theodosia.

They drove for a while in silence, down Church Street, past the Indigo Tea Shop, then turned onto Tradd, heading for Drayton's house. They slipped past an Italianate mansion, a Victorian, and a Charleston single home, all lit by antique streetlamps and flashing by like images on an old-fashioned stereopticon.

Finally Theodosia pulled in front of Drayton's small

two-hundred-year-old home and rolled to a quiet stop. They sat there, darkness surrounding them like a black cushy pillow, the sound of the engine slowly ticking down.

Now what are we going to do?" Theodosia wondered out loud.

"About . . . ?" said Drayton.

"Flushing out this killer."

"I don't think we should attempt that at all," said Drayton.

"But if there were a way," mused Theodosia.

"It would have to be a very safe way," reasoned Drayton.

They sat there for a good five minutes, both of them thinking.

Finally Theodosia said, "What time is it?"

Drayton brought his wrist close to his face. "Almost nine thirty. Why?"

The wheels were suddenly turning in Theodosia's head, along with a rising tide of panic in knowing she might be facing a time crunch.

"I need to call that reporter, Nick Van Buren," said Theodosia. "To see if I can get something planted in tomorrow's newspaper."

Drayton looked hesitant. "You mean an article about Nadine being kidnapped?"

"No," said Theodosia. "A brand-new story concerning the Blackbeard skull cup. A special story about the *genuine* skull cup."

24

❧

It was a small, hand-picked group that convened in the basement storage vault of the Heritage Society this Saturday morning.

Theodosia and Drayton. Timothy Neville. And Brooke Carter Crockett.

"You're convinced this will work?" Timothy asked, his inner tension magnified by the angles and deep creases in his face. They were gathered around a small metal table with a large shop light dangling above it. In the middle of the table sat a human skull.

"It's the best idea I've had yet," Theodosia told him. "But, ultimately, it's up to you, Timothy. You're the one with the skull, and you're the one who's hosting the party tonight."

Timothy's small front teeth ground together as he gave her idea final consideration. Finally he said, "Yes, let's do it. That is, if we *can* do it."

"Brooke?" said Theodosia, turning her attention to her friend.

"Worth a try," said Brooke.

"Okay, then," said Theodosia. She reached out and gingerly picked up the skull. Tilting it one way, then another, she gazed at Timothy and said, "One of your ancestors?"

Timothy blanched. "Someone's ancestor."

"And you just happened to have it here," said Drayton.

A mousy smile played at Timothy's lips. "It's amazing what strange and bizarre artifacts one finds hidden in the storage vaults of this old institution."

Theodosia turned to Brooke and said, "The timing's the stickler. You're sure you can work something up before tonight?"

Brooke reached a finger out and touched the skull gently, almost reverently. "I think so. Whatever I come up with is going to be awfully . . . um . . . fragile. You won't be able to handle it or anything, but I think I can create a fairly good approximation of the skull cup."

"Fabulous," said Theodosia. With Brooke's help they were going to set a fine trap. A trap that would hopefully snare a murderer.

Timothy nervously patted his jacket pockets and fished out his glasses. When he put them on, Theodosia noticed that they magnified his eyes. "Show me the article, please?" said Timothy.

Drayton laid the morning edition of the *Post and Courier* on the table. On the front page, just below the fold, was the article Theodosia had cajoled Nick Van Buren into writing.

And, truth be told, Van Buren had come through like a champ. He'd written a breezy, shivery article about the stolen skull cup and how it had actually been a fake. Couched in among this information was high praise for the Charleston Police as well as an implication that they were ready to make an arrest in last Sunday's murder of Rob Commers.

But the real clincher was Van Buren's phonied-up revelation about the *authentic* skull cup. He hinted that the

Heritage Society viewed it as a priceless artifact, which was the reason a *copy* had actually been on display. The last line of Van Buren's article, the real kicker, mentioned that the genuine Blackbeard's skull would be on display tonight at Timothy Neville's private party.

"You certainly put a bug in that reporter's ear," remarked Brooke.

"Nick was incredibly cooperative," said Theodosia. "Although I had to promise him full access to the party tonight as well as an exclusive story in case we flush out the murderer."

"Goodness," said Drayton, looking wary, "that trips off your tongue as if it's a *fait accompli*."

"Let's hope it is," said Timothy.

"Getting back to the skull," said Theodosia, addressing Brooke, "you'll set it with the requisite diamond?"

Brooke nodded. "Sure."

"An actual diamond?" asked Drayton.

"No," said Brooke, smiling, "I wish I owned a nice big juicy ten-karat rock, but I don't. However, I can use a large cubic zirconia. If we arrange our dummied-up skull cup in a display case just so, and light it carefully, nobody will be the wiser."

"Except us," said Drayton.

"And you all believe this will work?" asked Timothy. He was looking even more haggard and drawn than when they'd started this morning. "You think this will trick the killer into . . ." He shook his head, reluctant or too nervous to finish his question.

"Into revealing himself?" said Theodosia, who was more jittery than worried. But good jittery. "Yes, yes I do."

"We're going to need police cooperation," said Timothy.

"I'm going to handle that," said Theodosia.

Drayton nodded. "And we're sending special e-mail invitations to all the members of the Jolly Roger Club, Pirates and Plunder attendees, folks we've deemed as possible suspects, and a hand-selected group of art and antique dealers." He paused. "Well, *I'm* not going to do the e-mails, but Haley will."

"Understood," said Timothy.

"The gist of the invitation," continued Drayton, "is two-fold. Invite folks to take a peek at the *authentic* Blackbeard skull and attend my surprise birthday party."

"I'm sorry it won't be a surprise anymore," said Theodosia, patting his arm.

Drayton coughed and cleared this throat. "I'm not."

"Okay, then," said Theodosia. "We all know what to do."

Drayton frowned, then said, "Did we put Professor Muncie's name on the list? I can't remember."

"Invite him, too," snapped Timothy. "We need to smoke out this culprit!"

"Remember," Theodosia cautioned, "we're talking about a murderer. A stone-cold killer."

They wandered upstairs then, each lost in thought. Drayton headed for the Heritage Society's small archives while Theodosia wandered into one of the galleries.

It was funny, she thought, how fast the Pirates and Plunder show had been disbanded and a new show put up in its place. Here now was a display that celebrated the old rice plantations of the low country. There were photos of plantation homes and mills, maps of plantation locations, and some great shots of the Santee River. Memorabilia included antique wooden pestles for pounding the rice as well as flat fanner baskets woven from palmetto leaves. These fanner baskets had been used in the early years to flip the pounded rice up and allow the husks to detach and float away.

Theodosia was well aware of rice plantation culture. Her Aunt Libby lived at Cane Ridge Plantation, which had been an old rice plantation. Many of the ancient ditches, banks, and sluiceways were still visible, though most were buried beneath layers of kudzu.

"Carolina gold," she murmured to herself, as her cell phone jangled. She grabbed it and said, "Hello?"

"You never made it to my tapas and wine tasting last night," said Parker. He sounded both disappointed and accusing.

"Sorry," said Theodosia. "We went to that opening at Berlin Fine Arts, and then one thing led to another."

"Problems?"

"Fireworks. Delaine called and claimed her sister was kidnapped."

"And let me guess," said Parker, "you rushed to be at her side."

"Well . . . yes. Delaine and her sister were naturally upset."

"Sometimes I wish something terrible would happen to me," said Parker, "so you'd rush to my defense."

"That's an awful thing to say," said Theodosia.

"But it's legit," said Parker, "it's how I feel. So . . . what about tonight? Can we get together and talk?"

Theodosia hesitated for a few seconds. With the dummy skull cup being set up for Timothy's party, was this the best time to have a relationship talk with Parker?

"Never mind," he said, before she was able to answer. "I'm sure you've got something else going on. So, okay . . . good-bye." There was a click and the line went dead.

Theodosia stared at her phone. Should she call him back? Make nice and apologize? Then again, what was she apologizing for? She hadn't been rude, she'd been honest. She hadn't led him on anymore than he'd led her on. She'd always been frank with him. There were feelings, yes. But they were nice feelings, not the all-out head-over-heels passion that she suddenly craved.

So what now? Theodosia heaved a mighty sigh, trying to

figure out the right thing, the proper thing to do. And realized there really wasn't a *proper* thing per se.

She tapped her index finger against her phone, wondering what was the emotionally honest thing to do?

She surprised herself by dialing Max's number.

He wasn't there, but she left a voice mail. Maybe, hopefully, they could connect tonight. After this whole skull thing was finished. After the trap had been sprung.

She turned as she heard footsteps nearby.

"I did a little research on island fortresses," said Drayton. He stood at the end of the corridor, backlit by sunshine that streamed in from one of the clerestory windows.

Rice plantations suddenly forgotten, Theodosia quickly caught up with him and asked, "Find anything interesting? Something to follow up on?"

"I'd say so," said Drayton, switching into studious mode. "For one thing, I found several old maps that are quite helpful."

"Showing locations of old fortresses?"

"Yes, indeed," said Drayton. "Here, take a look at this one." He unfurled a crackly old map and handed it to her.

"This is a map of Wadmalaw Island," said Theodosia.

"That's right." Drayton tapped a location with his index finger. "And it just so happens that an old fortress was located right here. A place known as Fort Dandridge. Dates back almost as far as the Revolutionary War."

Something blipped in Theodosia's memory. "That location seems awfully close to where Nadine was picked up."

"My thought exactly," said Drayton.

"So if there really was an old fortress there," Theodosia murmured, "do you suppose Nadine was held nearby? In some old shack out where it's still wooded and swampy?"

"It's possible," said Drayton.

"But you have an inkling," said Theodosia. Truth be known, the moment she'd looked at the old map, she'd felt an inkling, too.

Drayton twiddled his bow tie. "Mmm."

"I think," said Theodosia, "we should make an executive decision and drive out to Wadmalaw Island. Do a little exploring."

Concern flickered on Drayton's face. "You think we should tell Tidwell what we're doing?"

"Visiting Wadmalaw Island, no," said Theodosia. "About tonight, yes, of course. After all, Tidwell's assistance is going to be integral to our plan. In fact, he's probably going to figure out the setup as soon as he sees the front page of today's paper."

"Perhaps he's already seen it."

"Then the phone is ringing off the hook over at the tea shop."

"Or he's sitting at a table with steam coming out of his ears."

"Fuming and stuffing his face with scones," said Theodosia. "In any event, I intend to give him a wake-up call around six o'clock tonight. Extend a sort of personal invitation to the fireworks."

"If they happen," said Drayton.

"And we hope they do."

"So that's your plan for police protection?" said Drayton. "You're going to goad Tidwell into showing up at Timothy's party?"

Theodosia shrugged. "Can you think of a better plan?"

Wandering out into the reception area of the Heritage Society, they ran into Camilla. She was walking slowly, still using a cane, but her eyes seemed clear and focused.

"Camilla!" Theodosia cried. "It's great to see you here!"

"Back at it," enthused Drayton.

"Easing back into it, anyway," she replied. Then she seemed to adjust her internal attitude and turned speculative eyes on Theodosia and Drayton. "Timothy told me about your plan for tonight."

"He did?" said Drayton, trying to look innocent.

"About creating a fake skull cup," said Theodosia. "Yes. It's a long shot, but we think it's worth a try."

"It sounds like a decent enough scheme," said Camilla. "Dangerous, but better than anything the police have come up with."

"We think so," said Theodosia. "We *hope* so."

"You know," said Camilla, reaching out to clutch Theodosia's arm, "Rob was like a son to me. I don't know if either of you know this, but I was never married, so I never had the pleasure of children. But for whatever reason, Rob and I absolutely clicked. Bonded," she added.

"I hear what you're saying," said Theodosia, blinking back tears.

"When a person you love becomes a memory," Camilla murmured, "that memory becomes a treasure." Tears sparkled in her eyes as she gripped Theodosia's arm even tighter. Then she said, in a low, tight voice, "You catch him, girl. You find that killer and drag him to hell!"

"*What are we* looking for?" Drayton asked. They'd sped out on the Maybank Highway, passed the turnoff for the Charleston Tea Plantation, then turned onto Bears Bluff Road. Now they were pretty much in the heart of Wadmalaw Island. They passed Angel Oak Antiques, a bait shop selling thoroughbred crickets, and a small white church with a Gothic steeple and a neon sign that said LOVE. They sailed past the Irvin House Vineyard, where four varieties of Muscadine grapes were being cultivated on forty-eight acres of rich, fertile land, and continued along the winding, two-lane road.

"It's out here somewhere," Theodosia murmured, slowing down as she scanned both sides of the road. She hadn't driven this road in a few years. Still, the area hadn't changed that much. There were farmsteads and small clusters of homes, as well as hundreds of acres of wild, tangled woods and swampland where alligator eyes still peeked up from beneath briny waters and tupelo trees stood like sentinels in purple-dark groves.

"Buzzard Bar and Oyster House," Drayton announced, as they zoomed past a small restaurant. The wooden exterior had once been painted yellow but had faded to weather-beaten gray. Tin Coca-Cola, Palmetto Brewing, and Thomas Creek Brewery signs were nailed to the front. Perched above the door was a black wrought-iron buzzard, its wings extended, its mouth gaping wide.

"That's a great little joint," Theodosia told him. "I ate there a few years ago. The oysters were May River Selects from Bluffton and the shrimp were fresh-caught off Georgetown."

"Maybe we'll give it a try," said Drayton. "Although I'll feel naked without my T-shirt and trucker cap."

"By the way," said Theodosia, "what *is* that jacket you're wearing?" Drayton had on a khaki-colored jacket that pretty much resembled a bush jacket.

He touched the front of it. "My Orvis Bandera jacket."

"Looks like you're all geared up to excavate the pyramids at Cheops. Or look for some lost city in the Congo."

Drayton pursed his lips. "Just call me bwana."

They drove for another couple of miles. "It's along here *somewhere*," Theodosia murmured, then suddenly let out an excited yip. "Oh yeah, oh yeah, here we go." She cranked the steering wheel hard, her wheels spitting white gravel, and then they rocked to a stop in a small parking lot.

Drayton blinked when he saw the tidy, white clapboard building that stood before them. "The Wadmalaw Historical Center?"

"That's it," said Theodosia. "That's what I was looking for."

"And pray tell," said Drayton, "what do they have to offer that the Heritage Society does not?"

"Local history," said Theodosia, unsnapping her seat belt. "And, hopefully, local gossip."

The Wadmalaw Historical Center was pretty much a single room. Framed black-and-white photos hung on the whitewashed walls, and three glass cases stood in the center of the room. Parked against the back wall were a row of beige file cabinets, two green metal desks, and a buzzing Coke machine. An older woman with white hair sat at one of the desks, hand-lettering names onto name tags. A second woman, almost her twin, but with blue-tinted hair, came forward to greet them. She was small and birdlike, with bright blue eyes and wore a name tag that said BERNICE. "Help you?" she said, with an eager docent's smile.

"We just stopped to look around," said Theodosia. "I've been here before, but it's been . . . years."

"If I can be of help . . ." Bernice told her, lifting a tiny hand.

Theodosia and Drayton shuffled to one of the cases, where a brass lamp and ship's log was on display.

"You have some nice maritime pieces," Drayton remarked.

Bernice nodded, pleased. "Old ones, too. Dating back to the early eighteen hundreds."

"And I see you have an original sketch by Audubon," said Drayton, moving to the next case. Charles Audubon had done many sketches in the swamps and woods surrounding Charleston.

"That piece is only on loan," said Bernice. "Of course, we're thrilled to have it, even if only for a short time."

"I was wondering," said Theodosia, "if you ever run across any pirate memorabilia?"

"We did a pirate show here a couple of years back," said

Bernice. She turned and called back to the woman at the desk, "When was that pirate show, Letty? Back in oh-eight?"

"More like oh-six," answered Letty.

Bernice nodded. "You get to be my age, the years just slip by faster and faster like some kind of crazy, speeded-up movie." She smiled at Theodosia, a little shyly. "I'll be eighty-seven next month."

"Congratulations," said Theodosia. "And you've lived out here all your life?"

"Pretty much," Bernice admitted.

"Then let me ask you this," said Theodosia, "have you ever heard any legends or lore about Blackbeard? I mean, concerning this area?"

Bernice peered at her. "You mean about the treasure?"

"What do you know about a treasure?" Drayton asked, practically pouncing on her words.

Bernice assumed a serious look. "Just that one of Blackbeard's stashes is reputed to be buried out this way."

"Oh, it's out here all right," Letty called from the back. "We all believe it's buried out here."

"Why do you think that?" asked Theodosia. Could there be some special, time-worn clue these residents were privy to?

Bernice's eyes crinkled knowingly, and she said in a stage whisper, "The treasure's supposed to be buried close to Teach's Kettle, don't you know."

25

❧

Time stood still for Theodosia for a few moments, and the air seemed to leave the room. Then she said, "Did I hear you right? You said . . . Teach's Kettle?" She held her breath, almost afraid to say anything more. There it was. A link to Edward Teach, that fearsome English gentleman known as Blackbeard.

"What is Teach's Kettle?" asked Drayton. "Some kind of historical marker?"

"Ah," said Bernice, pleased to offer up her historical know-how. "It's an old stone kettle built by Blackbeard. For heating tar to repair his ships. There's one kettle located up in North Carolina, and we've got one here."

"No kidding," said an astounded Drayton. "First I've heard of these things."

Now Letty rose from her desk in back and walked toward them. "They heated the tar then poked it into the gaps to keep their ships watertight."

"I think *we* need to fill in some gaps," said Theodosia.

"You're hunting for the treasure?" asked Bernice. She wore a patient, knowing look. Probably, more than a few would-be treasure hunters had dropped by the Historical Center looking for information, hoping to get a leg up, anything.

"Um . . . we're looking indirectly," said Theodosia.

"We're more interested in the historical aspect of Blackbeard," said Drayton.

"Then you should haul yourselves down to Bone Beach," instructed Letty.

"Excuse me," said Drayton, pulling out his map to quickly study it. "But wasn't there an old fortress there?"

"That's right," said Bernice, "Fort Dandridge. Completely destroyed in the hurricane of forty-two. *Eighteen* forty-two." She chuckled. "Of course, that was long before I was born."

"Nothing left of the fort at all?" asked Theodosia.

"Nary a brick," said Letty. "Just a beach strewn with driftwood that's been picked clean. Tides come surging in and tumble and deposit all sorts of odd things. It's like some kind of graveyard for the Atlantic down there. But if you search inland, you might be lucky enough to stumble on the ruins of that old tar cauldron. Last I heard there were maybe a third of the stones still standing."

"Interesting," said Drayton. He glanced sideways at Theodosia.

"How do we find this Bone Beach?" asked Theodosia.

Bernice waved a hand. "Keep on driving down this road until you come to the end. Then head left, that's east, through the dunes until you hit woods."

"I hope you have one of those off-road vehicles," said Letty. She pronounced it *ve-hi-cle*, hitting three distinct syllables, like the police often did. "It's awfully tough going."

"One more question," said Theodosia, "why do they call it Bone Beach?"

Bernice's eyes twinkled. "You don't want to know."

* * *

"*So continue down* this road," said Drayton, as they jounced along.

"Not much of a road," said Theodosia. "Looks like the blacktop ends up ahead."

It did, turning into a narrow, twisty dirt road.

"This is lovely," said Drayton, rolling up the window to escape the billowing dust.

"This is your adventure, bwana," said Theodosia. They came flying up over a sharp rise, and suddenly the road dropped away to nothing but twenty feet of wet sand and then an open stretch of brackish water. Theodosia jammed on the brakes, slaloming the Jeep into a quarter turn.

"Looks like quicksand up ahead," said Drayton.

"Maybe is," said Theodosia. "But, lucky us, this is where we head left."

"There's a path off here to the right."

"But Bernice said go left."

"Okay, then," said Drayton. "Got it in four-wheel drive?"

"Oh, yeah," said Theodosia. She revved her engine, cranked the steering wheel hard, and headed directly into the low brush.

"Yipes!" said Drayton. Tall trees whipped at their windows, and brush tickled the undercarriage.

"Just like a ride at Disneyland," laughed Theodosia. "The Jungle Cruise."

"Let's hope it's not Pirates of the Caribbean!"

"C'mon, Drayton, have a little spunk."

"I have spunk, I just don't care to break my neck."

But ten minutes later, the going got much tougher. The dirt shifted to sand, causing Theodosia's Jeep to grind and slip sideways.

"This is as far as we can go," said Theodosia. "Now we have to hop out and walk."

*   *   *

"This is awful," Drayton complained. They'd been slogging through sand for a good ten minutes. Tall reeds whipped their faces, and sharp sand burrs prickled their ankles. "Good thing I wore socks."

"Good thing you wore that jacket," said Theodosia.

"Do you think we're on track?"

"Not sure," said Theodosia. "With all the reeds and underbrush, we could have passed within ten feet of Teach's Kettle and not even noticed it."

"Do you think any bears live on Bears Bluff Road?" asked Drayton.

"I don't know," said Theodosia. "But if I were a bear, I'd confine my ramblings and rootings to the forests and swamp where there's lots more shade." It was past midday, and the sun was beating down on them mercilessly. Air stirred the very tips of the reeds but did nothing in the way of cooling them.

Drayton stopped suddenly. "I think I'm ready to throw in the towel on this."

"I think I might be, too," said Theodosia. They stood there for a few minutes, red-faced and huffing tiredly.

"Listen," said Theodosia. She'd detected a faint sound coming toward them on the faint breeze.

"What?" said Drayton. "Birds?"

"No," said Theodosia, pressing forward up the dune. "I hear waves lapping on shore."

As they came up over a rise, the great expanse of Bone Beach spread before them. It was a white sand beach strewn with bleached driftwood as far as the eye could see. Huge, twisted shapes rose up like primordial creatures, logs that had been tossed and tumbled and had possibly even ridden the waves all the way over from Africa.

"Amazing," said Drayton. "I've lived here practically thirty years and I never knew any of this existed."

"I've heard of it," said Theodosia, "but never seen it."

"This place has a sort of beauty," said Drayton, gazing around, "in an oddly primitive way."

"Just think," said Theodosia, "Blackbeard brought his ships in here, through one of the channels. They probably came riding in at high tide. Then when the tide went out, the ships were beached just enough so they could manage repairs."

"In a secret spot not many people knew about," said Drayton.

"Or could even find," added Theodosia. She was starting to enjoy the lap-lap-lap of the water and the whirr of cicadas in marsh grass that, a few months earlier, had been winter green and now was turning summer gold.

Drayton gave a measured glance back over his shoulder. "So Teach's Kettle must be just inland from here."

"Probably."

Drayton narrowed his eyes. "You think Nadine was held captive out here?"

Theodosia shrugged. It was a theory. "Not sure. There don't seem to be any structures around." She peered down the stretch of beach. "In fact, I don't see a darned thing."

"Maybe she was completely off on her directions," said Drayton.

"Maybe so," replied Theodosia. "Still . . . it could be right."

Late Saturday afternoon and the big fish fry at White Point Gardens was in full swing. A country band cranked out a rousing version of "Green Grass and High Tides," driving hard with twanging guitars, while dozens of deep-fryers bubbled and sizzled and spat out crispy, golden brown fillets of redfish and grouper. Red-and-white-striped tents looked like billowing sails, tables were lined end to end, and people were jostling about, talking, dancing, and eating, while some stretched out lazily on blankets.

Theodosia and Drayton had come directly from their jaunt to Wadmalaw Island and were eager to chow down.

"Where's Haley?" worried Drayton, as they pushed their way through the crowd. "She was supposed to save a table for us."

Theodosia grabbed two tall glasses of sweet tea from a vendor and handed one to Drayton. "Chill, Drayton, we'll find her."

"She said she'd be with Angie Congdon and Teddy Vickers from the Featherbed House. They were going to save a couple of places for us."

"Then they will." Theodosia put a hand above her eyes, scanned the raft of picnic tables, and finally saw Haley waving at them. "There she is. There's Angie, too."

"Are there chairs?" worried Drayton. "Are there places?"

"You know," said Theodosia, "that's probably the last thing you should be concerned about right now." She dug in her bag, clicked on her phone—she'd had it turned off for most of the day—and saw she'd received a raft of calls, most from the same number. As she scanned the log, knowing the bulk of them had come from Tidwell, the phone jangled right there in her hand. She pushed the Receive button. "Hello?"

"You're incredibly foolish, you know that?" Tidwell screeched in her ear. There was no *Hi, how are you*, no *Howdy-do*. Just a full-on assault.

"I'm guessing you saw the front page of this morning's *Post and Courier*," said Theodosia. How could he miss it?

"I saw it and I think what you did is utterly moronic!"

"And here I thought I'd devised a rather clever plan," Theodosia told him. She moved away from the crowd, over to a copse of dogwood, the better to survive his verbal bombardment.

"You're so clever you're going to get yourself killed!" Tidwell roared.

"That's exactly why we need *you* at Timothy's party tonight," Theodosia told him. "When we hopefully snare the killer. And if you could kindly bring along a couple of your finest officers, that would be great. Undercover officers for Timothy's sake, otherwise he'll probably blow a gasket."

"You realize this is tantamount to blackmail!" Tidwell raged. "Setting up this ridiculous booby trap of yours!"

"I view it as a few civic-minded citizens trying to assist our very capable and beloved police department."

"That's poppycock and you know it!"

"Care to give your own version to the *Post and Courier*?" Theodosia asked. "Better yet, if our killer *is* lured in and apprehended, we'll let you assume full credit. For the skull cup ploy, the arrest, everything. We'll stay in the background and you can hog all the glory!"

Tidwell fumed. He growled, gnashed his teeth, and raged like an angry bull elephant. But in the end there wasn't much he could do except go along with the plan. Fact was, Theodosia's plan had already been set in motion and he was, unwittingly, one of the players.

"You're going to owe me big-time," Tidwell growled.

"And I'll be happy to pay you back big time," Theodosia acknowledged. "Perhaps you could even take it out in trade at the tea shop." She chuckled. "Hand over all your baked goods in small, unmarked scones."

"Ridiculous," grumbled Tidwell. "You're playing with fire. There's a desperate man out there who'll stop at nothing to get his hands on that skull cup!"

"And that," said Theodosia, "is exactly what I'm counting on."

26

❧

Timothy Neville loved nothing better than throwing parties, and the bigger the bash, the better. Garden parties, post-opera fetes, symphony soirees, holiday galas, you name it—Timothy was one of the most congenial hosts in all of Charleston.

Not only that, Timothy's enormous Italianate mansion on Archdale Street was a glittering showpiece filled with antiques, artwork, and fine design. It gave guests the opportunity to peek into the kind of gilded lifestyle most could only dream about.

Standing on his expansive piazza, dressed in an impeccable white dinner jacket, Timothy welcomed all his guests with just the right amount of effusiveness and sly Southern charm.

"Timothy's always in a good mood when he entertains," said Theodosia, as she and Drayton strolled up the walk to Timothy's home. "But when he's on a tear at the Heritage Society . . . watch out!"

"Timothy suffers from Jekyll and Hyde syndrome," laughed

Drayton. "But you of all people know his heart is generally in the right place."

"Tucked in a safe-deposit box down at First National," Theodosia quipped, as they climbed the stairway to greet Timothy.

"Hah," Drayton chuckled. "Good one."

Timothy caught sight of Theodosia and Drayton and beamed from ear to ear until his face practically cracked. "It's all set up," he told them in a hoarse whisper. "Tidwell's here and the skull cup is displayed in the back garden under the watchful eye of a plainclothes policeman." Then he exclaimed, in a loud, crackling voice, "Theodosia, my dear, you're looking lovely tonight. That pale green silk reminds me of a beautiful Luna moth flitting about the garden. And you, Drayton old dog, dapper as ever."

"Don't you think you're overdoing it a tad?" Theodosia whispered to Timothy as they exchanged elaborate air kisses.

"Not in the least," Timothy hissed back.

Theodosia and Drayton strolled inside to join the two hundred or so guests who were already jostling from room to room, sipping drinks, and marveling over Timothy's home.

"Ah," said Drayton, taking two drinks from the silver tray of a liveried butler. "Mint juleps. Always refreshing."

Theodosia took a quick sip and gazed around. "This is a huge crowd, even by Timothy's standards. Looks like our e-mail invitations, last-minute though some of them were, worked fairly well."

"The better to snare our quarry," said Drayton.

"But only if our quarry shows up," said Theodosia. She paused, bit her lip, and said, "You think we should go take a look?" She was nervous and antsy and eager for something to bust loose.

"You want to view the skull cup?" said Drayton, "Absolutely."

But that was easier said than done. Because first they had to negotiate the center hallway, which was elbow to eyeball with chattering guests.

"Plan B," said Drayton, ducking into the front parlor. "Maybe it's easier if we navigate through the side parlors."

Theodosia followed on Drayton's heels, impressed once again by Timothy Neville's flawless taste. There were Hepplewhite furnishings, glittering crystal chandeliers, and a carved walnut mantelpiece signed by the Italian master Luigi Frullini. The china displayed in the built-in wall case was genuine Spode, and the oil paintings adorning the walls were by the early American painters Horace Bundy and Franklin Whiting Rogers.

Drayton glanced back at her as he pushed through. "You still coming?"

"Lead the way."

They continued through a second parlor and ducked out into the center hallway. From there it was just a few steps to the back of the house, then down a wide stone stairway and out into Timothy's Chinese-style garden. Though the garden had once been a classical Charleston courtyard garden, it had taken a decided Chinese turn over the years. Now there were enormous trees meticulously trimmed and sculpted into the Chinese *pen-jing* style, as well as tall thickets of bamboo, stands of lady fern, and fluffy beds of Korean moss. A long, rectangular pond was lush and fragrant with Asian water plants. Large stone Buddhas and Chinese lion-dog statues stood guard along the various paths and walkways that led into the depths of the garden.

"There it is," Drayton said, under his breath. "The skull cup."

Theodosia took a few dainty steps along a slate walkway lined with bright green moss, and then she was standing directly in front of the skull cup. The bizarre object was the sole occupant of a tall, thin, cylindrical glass case with three built-in pinpoint spotlights shining down upon it.

Under such direct overhead lighting, the polished silver gleamed brightly, while the skull face itself was shrouded in shadows. Eye sockets looked menacing, and the skull's teeth appeared ready to snap.

More than a few fascinated guests had followed Theodosia and Drayton outside. A few moved in closer to take a better look, then stepped back immediately, a little cowed by such a strange object.

"Impressive," breathed Drayton. He was thrilled that Brooke had been able to create this replica in just a single afternoon.

"And daring," said Theodosia, referring to their plan.

"Are you two *still* mooning over that stupid skull cup?" came Delaine's strident voice. They turned and found her clinging tightly to the crooked arm of Dougan Granville. Dressed in a black lace dress with a daring, deep V that showed off ample cleavage, Delaine looked sexy, stylish, and just a tiny bit dangerous.

Granville stared at the skull cup with open and unbridled desire. Clearly, the man coveted the object for his personal collection even though his words dripped with sarcasm. "I can't believe they showed a phony skull cup at the Pirates and Plunder show this past week," Granville scoffed. "One certainly expects more than fakes from an outfit that claims to be a *Heritage* Society. Just not sporting at all!"

"But wasn't it lucky they displayed a copy?" said Theodosia, interceding. "Because now we have the pleasure of viewing the authentic skull cup."

Delaine narrowed her eyes as she peered at it. "Now that I see the real one, there's simply no comparison. Any fool can tell this is authentic. Just take a gander at that diamond—absolutely stunning!"

Reluctantly, Granville pulled his eyes away from the skull cup. "Not as stunning as you are, my dear."

"Oh, you do go on," Delaine fluttered, obviously thrilled to death with her new boyfriend.

"How's Nadine feeling?" asked Theodosia.

"Much, much better," said Delaine. "In fact, she's here tonight." Delaine made a pro forma show of looking around and gave a tiny shrug. "Somewhere."

"Your sister's suffering no ill effects, I hope?" said Drayton.

But Delaine was far more focused on Granville. Looping an arm around his neck, she said, "I think we should go back in and join the party."

Granville smiled down at her. "Anything your little heart desires," he told Delaine. "Anything at all."

Taking her cue, Delaine held out her almost-empty champagne glass and wobbled it back and forth. "As long as you're asking . . . more champagne?"

"Bubbles for my bubbles," said Granville. He planted a big kiss on Delaine's cheek and led her back inside.

"I think I'm going to be ill," said Theodosia.

Drayton gave a shudder. "And did you see how poorly Granville was dressed? The man makes even a Savile Row suit look cheap."

"As a couple, they're a little tedious," admitted Theodosia.

"On the flip side," said Drayton, "since Delaine has obviously staked her claim firmly on Granville, doesn't that leave you free to . . . ?"

"Play musical chairs with boyfriends?" said Theodosia. She sighed. "I know where you're going, but I'm just not ready to discuss it." Max was still an unknown quantity. For now. For a while anyway.

"Not ready," said Drayton, "or unwilling?"

"Both," said Theodosia.

"As you wish," said Drayton. As he moved around to inspect the back of the case, Theodosia followed him. "Do you suppose Tidwell's man is already in position?" he asked, glancing over his shoulder. "Crouching behind the bamboo and shrubbery?"

"Let's hope so," said Theodosia.

His gray eyes flicked across the tops of the bushes. "I don't see anyone."

"Isn't that the general idea?"

"Mmm," said Drayton, "I suppose you're right."

"What we should do," suggested Theodosia, "is scout around the party. See if Thomas Hassel and Scarlette Berlin have shown up yet."

"And if they have?"

"Then we keep a sharp eye on them."

What a party it was. A string quartet played in the solarium, and an enormous buffet table was arranged in the dining room.

"That's also on our agenda," said Theodosia, nodding at the lovely bounty. "Food."

"Will you take a gander at that raw bar!" Drayton exclaimed. One long table featured an enormous ice sculpture of a giant clam shell. Beneath it was a sparkling mound of crushed ice on which was heaped a huge assortment of oysters, crab legs, succulent pink shrimp, and small lobster tails.

"Since we didn't stop at the Buzzard Bar this afternoon," said Theodosia, "I think we'd better help ourselves to a few of these oysters."

"I couldn't agree more," said Drayton.

They picked up plates and utensils, then got in line. Halfway down one side of the raw bar, her plate practically filled with oysters, hot sauce, and a dab of horseradish, Theodosia reached in to grab a particularly tasty-looking crab claw. At the precise moment her fingers were about to pluck it from its bed of ice, another hand shot in from the other side of the table and snatched it. Peering past ice shards and a mound of cherrystone clams, Theodosia saw Burt Tidwell. He was the person who'd one-upped her!

"I was wondering when I'd run into you," she said to Tidwell.

"Funny," said Tidwell, "I wondered the same about you."

"We were just out in the back garden," Theodosia told him. "Taking a look at the skull cup."

"A most unique piece," Tidwell said, his lip curling.

"Is your . . . ?" began Drayton. Then he quickly stopped.

"Yes," said Tidwell. "He is."

"Excellent," said Theodosia.

"Maybe for you," Tidwell snapped, as they all came together at the end of the table. "I'm still convinced this entire plan is madness. Do you know Timothy Neville even asked me to check on some other poor character that you deemed suspicious?"

"Check on who?" asked Theodosia.

"A certain Professor Irwin Muncie," said Tidwell. He pinched an oyster between his thumb and forefinger, lifted it to his lips, and gave a loud slurp.

"What did Timothy want to know about him?" asked Drayton.

Tidwell gulped, then frowned. "Whether the man was ever involved in buying or selling illegal antiquities, that type of thing."

"And what did you find out?" asked Theodosia.

"Not a thing," said Tidwell. "Muncie's record was clean as a whistle except for two speeding tickets. No, the only thing I found out about your Professor Muncie is that he's divorced, is going through phased retirement at the College of Charleston, and lives out on Wadmalaw Island."

"What?" cried Theodosia.

"We were just out there!" said Drayton.

"Do we know if Muncie is here tonight?" asked Theodosia. Muncie's connection to Wadmalaw Island was disconcerting.

"No idea," said Tidwell. "I haven't seen the man. In fact,

I don't *know* the man!" Then he abruptly lurched away, his plate piled high with shellfish.

"Tidwell's upset," observed Drayton. "He thinks we're using him."

"That's because we are," said Theodosia. "Still . . . if Tidwell hadn't tried to stop us early on, if he hadn't waved us off at every step of the investigation, maybe we wouldn't be in this predicament."

"You think?" asked Drayton, giving her a baleful look.

"No," said Theodosia, "not really."

They carried their plates into the library and plunked themselves down on a pair of brocade Sheraton chairs.

"These oysters are wonderful," Drayton marveled. He was just this close to slurping them.

Theodosia nodded. "So sweet and juicy."

"Everyone raves about French Belons," said Drayton, "but I'm getting so I actually prefer our own mid-Atlantic mollusks."

Theodosia nudged Drayton with an elbow. "Look over there," she said under her breath. "Scarlette Berlin."

"All our suspects coming together," said Drayton.

"You think Thomas Hassel is here, too?" Theodosia asked. She was suspicious of Hassel, but more and more her thoughts circled back to Muncie. After all, the man lived on Wadmalaw Island, and he seemed to relish anything and everything concerning Blackbeard.

"Oh, I'm positive Hassel will show up," said Drayton. "He has an undisputed reputation as a social climber, so he's not about to turn down an invitation from the likes of Timothy Neville."

"Then let's go find him," said Theodosia.

27

Five minutes later, they were wandering through the crowd, on the prowl and searching for Hassel.

"There's Brooke!" said Drayton. They edged past two waiters and a gaggle of giggling socialites to get close to her.

"What do you think?" was Brooke's first question. She was referring, of course, to her handiwork on the faux scull cup.

"First rate," said Drayton. "Really stunning."

Brooke turned to Theodosia. "But will it draw in your killer?" she asked in a low voice.

"Hopefully it will," said Theodosia. "Tidwell's here, his man is in place. The real question is . . . will our guy show up?"

"Maybe he's here now," Brooke said, quietly. At which point they all turned slowly and ran their eyes over the crowd.

Theodosia saw Nick Van Buren schmoozing his way through the crowd and Tidwell glowering at her. Oh, well.

"Just have to wait and see what happens," said Drayton, finally. He gave a perfunctory smile, then said, "Theo? Brooke? May I fetch you ladies a glass of champagne?"

"Please," they said, almost in unison, which sent Drayton off through the crowd that seemed to be growing larger and more boisterous with each passing minute.

"Theodosia!"

Theodosia glanced around and spotted Haley edging toward her with a happy-looking Peter Grace in tow. "You made it," said Theodosia, aiming her inclusive smile at Grace. Then she made a quick introduction of Peter to Brooke.

"Where's Drayton?" asked Haley. She looked adorable tonight in a short, midnight-blue cocktail dress. Her hair was twisted up in a creative side knot that looked both fresh and a little messy. But cute messy.

"He's on a champagne run," Theodosia told her.

"I've got Drayton's birthday gift outside," Haley bubbled.

"You didn't wrap it, did you?" asked Theodosia. She wanted to do a fun presentation to him later on. If all went well.

"No," said Haley, "the teapot's au naturel. I tucked it on the back wall right by the garden gate. That way you can easily grab it when the time is right."

"I think we might have disturbed someone when we came in the back way," said Grace.

Theodosia threw him a questioning look.

"He means that police guy," Haley whispered. She winked at Theodosia. "Don't worry, Peter's in on it. He knows there's someone out back playing *Crouching Tiger, Hidden Dragon*, and keeping an eye on things. In fact, Peter's ready to pitch in and help if any thieves show up."

Theodosia smiled at Grace and her lips moved in a silent *Thank you*. She just hoped he wouldn't be called upon to apprehend his beloved professor.

"So if you want to check on the teapot . . ." said Haley.

"No," said Theodosia, "I'm sure it's fine. She smiled at Grace. "Do you know, is Professor Muncie here? I'm sure he'll be excited to see the authentic skull cup."

Peter nodded. "We just ran into him." He twisted his head, looked puzzled, and said, "Well, he *was* here."

"Great," said Theodosia. "Drayton and I wanted to chat with him." She glanced at Haley, wondering if she'd told Peter that Muncie was under suspicion. Then she decided no. Haley wouldn't spill the beans like that. She was a smart girl who knew how to keep a confidence.

"I bring three glasses of champagne," said Drayton, "and see that I really need five." He passed champagne flutes to Theodosia, Brooke, and Haley.

"I'll get a couple more," Peter volunteered, then took off.

"Does he know Muncie's under suspicion?" Drayton asked in a low voice.

Haley shook her head so vigorously her silver earrings lashed against her neck. "No. Of course not. He doesn't even know the skull cup is fake."

"Good," said Theodosia. "Let's keep it that way."

"Shouldn't someone be keeping an eye on Muncie?" asked Brooke.

"I'll go grab him and steer him our way," said Haley, skittering off.

"And I just spotted Thomas Hassel," Drayton told Theodosia. "Chitchatting with Ramona Benson of the Theater Guild and acting as if he's to the manor born." He rolled his eyes in a theatrical gesture.

"I wouldn't be surprised," said Brooke, "if you discovered that Hassel had his grubby little hand in all of this. I don't know much about him, but I trust my instincts. He's simply . . . not reputable."

"Which is why we should keep an eye on him, too," agreed Theodosia.

"Nothing overt," said Drayton, "but let's just keep him in our field of vision."

"Good luck," said Brooke.

But before Theodosia and Drayton could move off, Delaine, in a surprise move, suddenly took center stage.

"Excuse me!" Delaine's shrill voice rang out above the chatter of the crowd. "I have a very special announcement I'd like to make!"

Delaine stood in the grand center hallway, flanked by Nadine and Bill Glass. All around them, guests quieted down and turned attentively to hear what she had to say.

"Where's Granville?" Theodosia whispered.

"I don't know," said Drayton.

"As many of you know," began Delaine, "my dear, dear sister Nadine has been living here in Charleston for the past few months. And she's gotten quite close to many of you."

There was a spatter of applause.

Then Delaine drew in a sharp breath and smiled until her dimples practically puckered. "In fact, one person in particular has pretty much captured my dear sister's heart." She grabbed Nadine's hand, then reached over and grabbed Bill Glass by the hand. "Which is why I have the profound pleasure of announcing . . ."

A sudden crash shattered the night and caused the overhead chandeliers to tinkle and shake.

Theodosia gasped, suddenly on full alert. She glanced at Drayton, who muttered, under his breath, "The trap's been sprung!"

All around them guests wore puzzled, slightly embarrassed looks. One man called out, "There go our drinks."

Delaine looked stunned and angry, as if her great moment had suddenly been destroyed.

As nervous laughter seeped out to fill the air and the moment seemed to pass, Theodosia hastily elbowed her way through the crowd and dashed down the back stairway into the back garden.

Her first impression was complete and total darkness. *Lights in the case smashed out? Oh, yeah.*

In fact, the entire case had been toppled backward. The fake skull cup was nowhere to be seen, while shards of glass flashed angry sparks in the dim light. The trap had worked, but it had been obliterated in the process!

And where was the guard? And where was Tidwell when she needed him?

Drayton, who'd been a few steps behind Theodosia, suddenly caught up to her.

"Good heavens!" Drayton exclaimed. He stood poised on the patio, still as a statue and looking slightly bereft. "It's gone, it's all gone!"

"But gone where?" Theodosia yelped. *And where's the police officer who's supposed to be on guard?*

The answer to that question came in the form of a low moan.

"Do you hear something?" Drayton asked, in a hoarse whisper. He seemed beyond stunned.

Theodosia scurried a few steps down a narrow garden path. It didn't take long to find a pair of feet sticking out from a thicket of tall bamboo.

"Drayton!" she cried. "Over here!"

Drayton lurched down the path toward her. "Oh my goodness!" he exclaimed, when he finally saw the pair of black brogans. Then he was stumbling into the thick bamboo, batting at branches, trying to locate the downed officer and help him to his feet.

Slowly, gradually, with Drayton's help, the officer was hauled to an upright position. He stood unsteadily, a blank look on his face as he tried to focus.

"What happened?" Theodosia demanded.

The befuddled officer shook his head and let loose a shaky sigh. "Someone hit me . . . came up behind . . ." He made a futile hand gesture at the back of his head, and then his arm flopped to his side. The man was injured, loopy, and sheepish, all at the same time.

"But who?" Theodosia pushed. "Who hit you?"

The officer once again attempted to rub his injured head while he struggled to dredge up the precise words. "I remember a blond girl . . . long hair."

"Haley!" said Theodosia.

"Guy was dragging her," stammered the officer, as he tried to focus, tried to remember more. "And she was . . . um . . . fighting him."

"Oh, dear Lord," said Theodosia. She turned to Drayton, a look of fear slashing her face and panic rasping her voice. "Professor Muncie must have grabbed the skull cup and taken Haley along as hostage!"

"They couldn't have gotten far!" Drayton cried.

"We've got to . . . !" said Theodosia. She cartwheeled for a split-second, then spun wildly and dashed for the back gate. As she threw herself against the tall wooden structure, her fumbling, nervous fingers closed around the old wrought-iron handle. Theodosia jerked hard as the gate creaked and groaned. But it wouldn't budge!

Theodosia clawed frantically at the handle. "Drayton, help me!"

Drayton released his hold on the injured man and sprang to her side. He grabbed the door handle and fought to wrench it open. "It's stuck!" he gasped. "Someone's jammed it from the other side!"

As if to punctuate his sentence, there was the low, throaty whine of an engine revving up out on the street.

Theodosia heard the sound and knew instinctively it was Muncie trying to make his getaway. She let out a low, angry growl. Turning fast, she searched for some sort of weapon. Then her hand closed on the first thing that met her eyes. Drayton's teapot.

Clutching the teapot close against her body, Theodosia lowered her head, aimed a shoulder at the thick hedge that ran the perimeter of Timothy's backyard, and rammed her way in!

It was like hitting a wall of needles. Sharp branches ripped at her face and tore at her clothing as she tried to fight her way through. Protesting mightily, the greenery sprang and slashed at her, bouncing her backward. Still Theodosia continued to push with her legs and claw her way through the thick, dense foliage. It was painful, it was awkward, but she finally made it!

And just as Theodosia popped out the other side, still clutching Drayton's teapot, a black car roared toward her.

"Muncie!" she screamed at the blurred face in the windshield.

Without thinking, Theodosia hurled the teapot just as the car flew past her. It struck the rear window with a mighty whomp, chipping out a good-sized divot and sending a myriad of cracks skittering across the smoked window. The car bucked and swerved, clipping the rear fender of a parked yellow convertible. Then Muncie seemed to gain control and correct his steering. There was one slight fishtail, and then his car accelerated, the taillights fading to a wild blur of red.

Falling to her knees in the middle of the street, frustration pent up inside her, Theodosia screamed at the top of her lungs, "Haleeeeeey!"

Suddenly, the gate flew open and Drayton lurched out. He saw the anguish on Theodosia's face and cried, "Where is she?"

"Muncie took Haley!" Theodosia cried, heaving herself to her feet, her tear-streaked face staring after the car.

Drayton took a single stuttering step, and his face assumed a strange, uncomprehending look. Finally he was able to stammer out, "But he's . . ."

Theodosia spun around fast and found herself staring into the anxious face of Professor Muncie.

"Here," finished Drayton.

"Then who took Haley?" Theodosia screamed. "Who could have . . . ?" She shook her fists in frustration.

And then the answer bubbled up inside Theodosia's brain like saber tooth tiger bones being spit from the depths of the La Brea tar pits. Two hoarse words escaped her throat. "Peter Grace!"

Has to be!

Professor Muncie gaped at her, utterly stunned, reacting as if someone had slammed him in the head with a two-by-four. "Peter?" he cried. "Oh, no, Peter wouldn't hurt a fly!"

Tires screeched behind Theodosia as another car came up fast behind her. She jumped onto the curb just as a burgundy Crown Victoria rocked to a stop next to her. The passenger door flew open and Tidwell's loud voice rumbled, "Get in."

But Theodosia had already determined her course of action.

Without warning, Theodosia launched herself at Professor Muncie. Grabbing him by the lapels, she shook him so hard, his teeth rattled in his head and his head bobbled from side to side. "Where does Peter live?" she demanded.

Stunned at being physically manhandled, Muncie gaped at her and stammered out, "Apartment. On campus."

"No!" Theodosia snarled. "There must be another place. Think! If he were running from the police, where would he go? Who would give him shelter?" She shook Muncie again, as if she could physically extricate the correct answer from him.

"He . . . he . . ." stuttered Muncie. "His family . . . uh . . . owns a fishing shack out on Johns Island."

"What's the address?" She was about to shake Muncie again, but Drayton put a trembling hand on her shoulder.

"Let him go," said Drayton.

Theodosia let Muncie go free, but stayed in his face. "I need an address!"

"I can get one . . . at my office!" babbled a terrified Muncie.

Theodosia jammed an index finger in Muncie's face. "I'll call you at your office in twenty minutes. Be there!"

Spinning on her heels, Theodosia scrambled into Tidwell's car. Just as Tidwell tromped down hard on the accelerator, she managed to pull the door shut. And, like a harried passenger giving directions to a taxi driver, she barked out, "Johns Island!"

28

❧

"*Do you know where* on Johns Island?" Tidwell screamed as they hurtled down the street. Yellow streetlamps flashed by like strobes, as live oaks formed a dark tunnel.

"No! No!" Theodosia cried. "Peter Grace took off with Haley in his car, but I don't know exactly *where* he's taking her. We have to call Professor Muncie in a few minutes for directions!"

They flew down Tradd, cut over on Rutledge, then careened out Highway 30 until they hit the Maybank Highway. Theodosia's teeth chattered as she shouted out directions. Tidwell didn't need directions, but he let her rant anyway. He figured it was what she needed to help burn off excess adrenaline.

Finally, on a long stretch of quiet road, he said, "You're bleeding."

Theodosia wiped absently at her face. "Hedge."

"In the glove box," said Tidwell, "you'll find a first-aid kit."

"Don't need it," said Theodosia. There was only one thing on her mind. Find Haley.

"But you do," Tidwell said, his tone a little gentler this time.

Theodosia popped open the glove box and pulled out a small metal box. She dug inside for a tube of antiseptic cream, found it, and squirted a small puddle of white goop into the palm of her hand. "Okay," she said, her mind still in a turmoil as she daubed it on her face.

Were they too late? How were they going to find them? Would Muncie have the address?

"You know," said Tidwell, "I tried very hard to persuade Timothy to abandon this foolhardy plan."

Theodosia ground her teeth together. This was the last thing she wanted to hear.

"It should have worked," Theodosia said, finally. "The bait was there, the trap was set. All we needed was for the rat to spring it."

"Which he did," said Tidwell. "Though these things rarely go as planned."

When the sign for Johns Island flashed in their headlights, Theodosia punched Muncie's phone number into her cell phone.

Muncie answered breathlessly on the first ring. "Yes!" Obviously, she'd gotten through to him.

"What have you got?" Theodosia asked, without preamble.

"I don't have an address per se," Muncie stuttered. He sounded discouraged and upset, practically on the verge of tears. "But I looked through Peter's desk and found a packet of old photos. I think they're . . . his place."

"Tell me exactly what you see in the photos," Theodosia demanded. "Maybe we can somehow . . . find it." She shook her head, angry with her own thought process. No, that wasn't right. Not maybe, they *would* find his place!

"It's a small beach house," said Muncie. "Really just a shack. Peeling white paint, sandy yard, that type of thing."

"You have to be more specific," Theodosia told him. There

were hundreds, maybe thousands of beach houses around that loosely fit that description.

"Uh . . ." said Muncie.

Theodosia heard an urgent exchange of voices, and then Drayton was on the phone.

"Theo?"

"Drayton," said Theodosia, breathing a huge sign of relief. "Tell me what you see."

"A white beach house . . ."

"Beach house or fishing shack?"

"Could be either," said Drayton. "It's nestled in the sand with three rickety steps leading up to it. Flat roof, plain front door, two windows on either side of the door."

"What else?" Theodosia asked. She was beginning to paint a mental picture in her mind. A picture that would have to . . . guide them.

"A rain barrel sitting on the right side, as you view the place from the street."

"Trees?"

"No," said Drayton. "At least I don't see any. So it's possibly quite close to the ocean. Maybe on the ocean."

"Any other details?" asked Theodosia. She'd repeated each description to Tidwell, who was nodding his head, even as he turned onto Bohicket Road.

"Not really," said Drayton. "Sorry."

"Stay there," said Theodosia. "Keep this line open."

"Will do," responded Drayton.

When they got to the more populated, beachy areas, they crept along, keeping a sharp eye out for a small, dilapidated fishing shack. Ten minutes passed. Then fifteen. Then thirty. They eased along narrow roads, always keeping the shoreline in sight. They saw plenty of beach houses and fishing shacks, but none that matched the exact description Drayton had given them.

"We're getting nowhere," said Tidwell. Frustration was evident in his voice.

"We have to keep looking," said Theodosia.

"It's like trying to find a needle in a haystack," rasped Tidwell. "This is madness. We should get his plate number and put out an APB. Call in local law enforcement. Follow protocol!"

"Three more blocks," begged Theodosia. "Just give me that."

Tidwell pursed his lips, but he slowed down, cruising along a line of small beach houses that seemed to hug the curve of the shore.

"We don't even have a landmark to guide us," he fussed.

"Please keep driving."

"I'm turning around," said Tidwell. He slowed and swung the car around in a wide arc. As his headlights flashed across buildings, Theodosia suddenly stiffened.

"There it is!" she cried. A rickety old shack was set twenty feet in from the road. Paint peeled from the wood, one shutter hung at a lopsided angle, and a single dim light burned inside. "That has to be it!"

Tidwell reached for his radio.

"What are you doing?" Theodosia cried.

Tidwell hesitated. "Calling for backup."

"No! By the time you call and we wait, it's going to be too late!"

Tidwell grimaced. "What do you want to do?"

"Are you armed?"

"Of course."

"Then let's go in!"

"It doesn't work that way."

"Sure, it does," said Theodosia. She pushed open the door and leaped out.

"No!" called Tidwell.

Theodosia whirled. "Come on! Back me up!"

Tidwell pulled himself from his car and crept after her.

"You're insane!" he muttered, his voice barely audible over the hiss of the surf.

Theodosia put a finger to her mouth. *Shhh.*

Together, they tiptoed toward the front door.

"Maybe we should go around back," whispered Theodosia. "Try to peek in a window or something."

Tidwell shook his head. "Better we—"

A piercing scream rent the darkness. It rose higher and higher, a terrifying wail that built in agonizing intensity.

"Oh, dear Lord," Theodosia cried, "he's killing her!"

Tidwell made an ungainly sprint for the front door and pounded on it with the butt of his gun. "Open up!" he demanded in a loud, authoritative voice. "Police!"

A light snapped on in the front of the house.

"He's coming to the door!" said Theodosia. Maybe Haley's scream had jolted some sense into Grace. Maybe this could be resolved peacefully, after all!

The door creaked open and a middle-aged man stuck his head out. He was unshaven and sleepy looking, wearing a lank T-shirt and board shorts. "Huh? What's wrong?" he asked, in a bewildered tone.

"Grace?" Tidwell demanded. "Peter Grace?"

The guy was still stunned at the interruption. "What? No." Then he scratched the side of his face and looked thoughtful. "Um . . . down the road, I think." He added a halfhearted gesture.

"What was that scream?" Theodosia demanded.

"Peacock," said the man. "Missus keeps it in a pen out back. Ain't it awful?"

29

❧

Moonlight dappled the road ahead as it curved away from the water. They rolled past a couple of dilapidated wooden warehouses locked up tight for the night and old boats jacked up on wooden rigs that sat in the parking lot.

"Nothing down this way," Tidwell muttered.

"One more block," Theodosia begged him through clenched teeth.

The shoreline had morphed into salt marshes here. Salt-tolerant grasses and plants grew out of brackish water and soggy soil known as pluff mud. This mud flooded and drained each day courtesy of the shifting tides and served as the provenance for crabs, snails, and countless insects.

"What about . . . that?" said Theodosia, pointing.

Set back against the edge of the salt marsh was a small wooden shack. It was fronted by dunes, marsh grass, and a small turnaround littered with crushed shells.

"There's a car there," Theodosia hissed as they crawled toward the place. "A dark car."

"Does it belong to Grace?" asked Tidwell. "Were you able to get a good look at his car?"

"If the back window's shattered," said Theodosia, "it's his." She squinted at the car. "Is it broken? Can you tell?"

Tidwell slid quietly past, his head rotating like a periscope. "It is."

Theodosia swiveled in her seat and gazed at the shack. It was a small place, located at the end of a long, meandering boardwalk that snaked through dunes and marsh grasses.

"You see anything?" asked Tidwell.

"No. But she's in there. I can feel it."

"Well, we can't just go creeping up that boardwalk," said Tidwell. "Whoever's in there will see us coming a mile away."

"But Haley's inside!" Theodosia pushed open the car door and started to slip out. "She needs our help!"

Tidwell held up a big paw. "Wait!"

"Wait?" said Theodosia. "Wait for what?"

"I really *do* have to call for backup this time. We can't just go charging in and . . ."

Theodosia suddenly bent down and picked something up off the ground.

"Get back in the car," Tidwell ordered.

Theodosia held her hand up. A silver bracelet dangled from one finger. "It's Haley's charm bracelet," Theodosia said, her face beginning to crumple. "She dropped it. Or left it as a clue. It was just lying here in the sand."

"All the more reason to call the sheriff's department for backup. After all, I don't have jurisdiction here."

"But I do," said Theodosia, setting her jaw. "Peter Grace kidnapped Haley and that's probable cause for going in after her!"

"He'll kill you!" warned Tidwell. "He's already killed one person and practically disabled another."

"If you bring in more police, Grace will just use Haley as a shield to get away!" She glanced toward the beach house and watched it slowly disappear as the moon slipped behind a bank of clouds.

"Stay!" hissed Tidwell.

"Okay," said Theodosia. Still standing next to Tidwell's car, she quietly kicked off her shoes. "Make your call."

"Now you're talking sense." Tidwell reached for his radio and hit a couple of buttons. There was a burst of static and a voice answered, "Law enforcement center." And just as Tidwell launched into a rapid explanation, Theodosia slipped away.

She ran lightly up the boardwalk, bare feet skimming rough wood, keenly aware of the cool, salty breeze that streamed her hair out behind her. As long as the moon stayed hidden behind that big bank of clouds, Theodosia figured she was practically invisible. Which might just give her the necessary edge to figure out what was going on. To try to negotiate some sort of rescue.

Theodosia's hand was almost touching the doorknob when she hesitated. What if Peter Grace was waiting inside? Crouched down in the dark, with a gun aimed at the front door?

Did he even have a gun? She didn't know, but she wasn't willing to take that chance.

Jerking her hand back, Theodosia stepped off the front deck. Now warm sand shifted beneath her bare feet as she crept silently around the little shack.

There was the barrel sitting alongside the house, just as Drayton had described it from the photo. So . . . this was it!

The wind picked up and now Theodosia could smell brackish water nearby. Had this been the same brackish water that Nadine had slogged through?

Tiptoeing softly around the barrel, Theodosia scanned for another door, a window, anything. Toward the back, she found a small window, half open, no screen.

Now what?

Crawl in? Shout Haley's name? Go back and get Tidwell?

She had to decide. And she had to decide fairly fast!

Theodosia put her lips together and let loose a low whistle. Then she held her breath and waited.

Nothing. Peter Grace's head didn't pop up, his arm didn't poke out to fire a weapon at her.

So . . . nobody in there?

Had Grace come and gone? Had he dumped his car and taken off? If so, where was Haley?

Theodosia rested her fingertips on the window sill. Then, ever so slowly, she pulled herself up to eye level. She waited patiently until her eyes became accustomed to the dark interior, and then she looked around quickly. The interior of the place was a combination living room and kitchen. A door led to what was probably a back bedroom and bath.

And there wasn't a soul in sight.

Theodosia decided that Grace had to have taken off again. Or maybe he had a second vehicle or even a boat. In this part of the country there were hundreds of small streams and inlets that snaked through the tangle of salt marshes. He could disappear in a matter of seconds.

Being ever so careful, Theodosia jacked one foot up onto the window ledge, grasped the sill with her hands, and pulled herself through.

Her bare toes hit a threadbare carpet as the smell of coffee, mildew, and fish assaulted her nose.

Now what? Now that she was inside, what was her next move?

She tiptoed to the back bedroom. Somewhere, in a cop show probably, she'd seen how officers had cleared the scene. So that was what she did. Checked carefully, made sure nobody was hiding anywhere.

Nobody was hiding. And a good thing for that.

So the next thing . . . where was Haley?

"Haley!" Theodosia called in a hoarse whisper. "Are you here?" She checked a front closet, then looked behind a sagging old sofa.

"Haley!" she called again, this time a little louder.

A noise overhead. A kind of thump. Then a voice.

"Theodosia!"

Theodosia's head cranked back, and she scanned the ceiling. *A crawl space. Has to be a crawl space.* "Haley? Are you up there?"

"Help!" came Haley's faint voice. "Get me out of here!"

"Haley," said Theodosia, "where's Grace? Is he up there with you?"

"Outside!" came Haley's cry. "I think he went outside."

"First things first," said Theodosia. "Let's get you down from there."

Standing on her tiptoes, Theodosia lifted her arms in the air and felt around. As she batted the air, a rope swished against her forearm. Quick as a snapping turtle, Theodosia grabbed the rope and gave it a good yank. Slowly, a narrow wooden stairway dropped from the ceiling.

Theodosia was up the stairs in a matter of seconds.

Haley was curled up on a dirty mattress, hands tied behind her. She was shaking and making little mewling sounds, though she was probably unaware she was doing so.

"Got to get these knots undone," Theodosia said, picking at them frantically. But Grace hadn't tied Haley with ordinary rope; he'd used some kind of plastic cord. Which meant the knots were tight and the cord was slippery.

"Hurry!" urged Haley.

"Working as fast as I can, honey." Theodosia struggled with the knots, worrying about Peter Grace, wondering about Tidwell. She fumbled in the dark, frustrated and nervous.

"Plan B," said Theodosia. "We're leaving right now." She helped Haley to her feet and then down the stairs, hands still tied behind her back. The important thing, she decided, was o get outside, get into Tidwell's view so if anything happened, he'd have their back.

"Where's Grace?" Theodosia asked as they hit the last step.

"I don't know," Haley whimpered. "He went running out of here like five minutes ago. I think he's got a boat out back. Maybe even a shrimp boat? I crawled over to the upstairs window and peeked out. I think I saw one of those boats with the big riggers and nets."

Could Grace have taken off in a boat? Theodosia wondered. *Absolutely, he could have. He could be making his way down the coast right now, running silently, floating along on the currents. Or he could be pushing further inland, where streams led to more turgid, blackwater swamps.*

Theodosia tiptoed to the open window and looked out. Where the heck was Tidwell? What was taking him so long? Did he call for backup or was he *waiting* for backup?

Maybe, instead of leading Haley out the front door, she should stash her somewhere. Keep her safe for the time being, until she located Tidwell.

"Change of plan," said Theodosia. She pushed Haley into the tiny space behind the kitchen door. "Stay there, and don't make a sound no matter what!"

Padding softly to the open window, Theodosia gazed out. Her eyes were much more accustomed to the dark now, her night vision almost perfect.

There was Tidwell, standing not twenty feet away from her, talking softly into his cell phone. She opened her mouth to call out, her tongue curling to form a T—when a shadow seemed to flicker within her range of vision.

Theodosia blinked, wondering if she'd really seen anything at all, or if it had been a trick of moon and clouds.

And then she saw Peter Grace, right hand extended low, gripping a pistol and slowly sneaking up behind Tidwell.

Theodosia sucked air in sharply. What to do? If she yelled,

Grace would turn and fire at her. Then he'd probably spin and shoot Tidwell as well.

But she had to do something—anything!—to stop him!

Her eyes lit upon a rusted harpoon mounted to the wall. A weapon. Then they flicked to the bookcase next. Two skull cups rested there side by side! But which one was the real skull cup and which one the fake?

Didn't matter. Theodosia snatched the nearest one and balanced it in her right hand for a split second. Then she coiled like a major league pitcher and let loose her best fastball.

The skull cup rocketed out the window, tumbling end over end, evil eye winking back at her.

And just as Peter Grace brought the gun level with Tidwell's head . . . just as he was about to pull the trigger, the skull cup smacked him in the side of the head.

Whack!

And shattered into a dozen pieces.

Stunned, his jaw fractured instantly, Grace threw his right hand straight up into the air. He fired a single, ineffective shot, then dropped like a sack of potatoes.

30

❧

Theodosia leaned over the handcuffed form of Peter Grace.

"I'm going to drag your sorry carcass to hell," she snarled at him. She was angry as a rabid dog, shaking like a frightened rabbit. "You're going to pay for what you did to Camilla and Rob!"

"Stop," Tidwell warned, "it's over."

"It's not over," Theodosia protested. "It's not!" She was bubbling and seething, feeling as if molten magma might explode from inside her at any moment. She was prepared to grab a dull butter knife and disembowel Peter Grace if necessary!

It wasn't necessary.

Detective Tidwell really did have things under control. Along with his brothers in blue from the Johns Island Sheriff's Department.

Handcuffs rattled and shotguns racked amid the red and blue pulsing lights of a half-dozen official vehicles. Grace was transported, mumbling and moaning, but securely handcuffed to a gurney, into a waiting ambulance. The ambulance roared away with little fanfare.

Of course the event was capped off with a good amount of hand shaking and back slapping among law enforcement.

Hoo-ya, Theodosia thought, standing on the narrow boardwalk with Haley and feeling utterly drained.

Ten minutes later, they were bumping their way back to Charleston. Theodosia, Haley, and Tidwell. Nobody said much on the drive back, though Theodosia and Haley sat in the backseat and held hands.

In fact, nobody uttered a peep until they pulled up to the side portico of Timothy Neville's grand home.

Theodosia peered out sleepily. "Why are we stopping here?" She was so exhausted she felt like she was *talking* in slow motion.

"We've been summoned for a command performance," Tidwell told her. He'd ridden all the way back with a cardboard box sitting on the passenger seat beside him. Contents: one skull cup and the fragments of one completely destroyed skull cup.

"Summoned here?" said Haley. She, too, looked puzzled.

"There are, apparently, people who are concerned about you," said Tidwell. "People who care." He let loose a delicate snort that could have been a legitimate sinus issue or a Tidwellian put down.

Then Drayton was pulling open the car door and helping Haley out. He hugged Haley tightly, then handed her off to Brooke, who immediately swept her into her arms. Then he reached in to assist Theodosia.

Theodosia crawled out gingerly.

"Back again safe and sound," exclaimed Drayton. He look rattled but infinitely relieved.

"Safe," said Timothy Neville, gazing at a somewhat dazed Haley. "I don't know how sound they are."

"I'm okay," said Haley, who promptly broke into tears.

"Dear girl," said Timothy, "shall I call my personal physician?"

Haley sniffled loudly, then wiped at her eyes and shook her head. "You know a doctor who makes house calls?" she croaked. She remained shaken but awfully impressed.

"If you need him, he certainly will," said Timothy. He peered at her carefully. "Do you need him?"

"No," said Haley, in a small voice.

"Inside, then," said Timothy, trying his best to shuttle everyone into his home.

"I'm sorry about your birthday present," Theodosia told Drayton. "Sorry about your Fitz and Floyd teapot."

"I'm sure we'll find another one," said Drayton.

"Looks like the party's over," Theodosia said, as they stepped inside. She was still agitated, and exhaustion was closing in on her fast.

"Not for you, it isn't," Drayton murmured.

Theodosia tottered down the center hallway, her brain running a constant loop that asked, *Where'd all the people go? Where'd they go?* Clearly the party was over, save for a few of the catering staff who were busily cleaning up.

"There's someone here who urgently needs to see you," Drayton told her.

Theodosia stopped in her tracks. "You're not going to make me talk to Nick Van Buren right now, are you?" It was the last thing she wanted to do.

"Theodosia!" called a voice, soft and urgent. Then an amazing-looking man emerged from the side parlor.

Theodosia was pleasantly stunned and suddenly alert. "Max?" she said. She ducked her head and looked at Drayton. "Why is Max here?" she asked.

Drayton gave a genial shrug.

Theodosia switched her gaze to Max. "Why are you here?"

"Drayton called me," said Max. With a minimum of

effort, he looped an arm around Theodosia's waist and gingerly helped her into the front parlor. Whispering softly, he treated her as if she were a priceless Dresden figurine.

"I thought you might need help getting home," Drayton explained as he followed them in. His expression was one of pure innocence, but his voice held a hint of merriment.

Easing Theodosia down onto a damask-covered sofa, Max settled in next to her and fixed her with a loving but worried gaze. "When Drayton called me," he said, grasping Theodosia's hand, "and told me about your ordeal . . . I was stunned! I had to come over . . ." He gazed at her earnestly. "I had to make sure you were really okay."

She gazed at him with tenderness. "Thank you. I am okay."

"Ah," Timothy exclaimed with gusto, as Tidwell strode into the room carrying his cardboard box. "Our prodigal piece has been returned to us."

"What I really want to know," said Haley, trying to stifle a yawn, "is which skull cup did Theo hurl at Peter Grace? The real one or the fake one?"

"Yes," said Brooke, who'd just heard the whole story firsthand from Tidwell, "which one?"

Timothy whisked the box out of Tidwell's hands and grasped it with his bony fingers. He cocked his small head to one side and said, "Does it really matter? Since everything is being returned to storage immediately."

"All of it?" said Haley.

Timothy nodded. "Absolutely. First thing tomorrow."

"The whole enchilada?" Brooke murmured.

"Every single fragment," said Timothy, a mirthless grin splitting his face.

"So the skull cups will never be heard from again?" asked Drayton. He seemed unsettled by Timothy's decision.

"Not for another forty or fifty years," Timothy assured him. "Not until one of my successors pulls this box out one day and wonders what on earth this skull business was all about." He rapped his knuckles on the top of the box, as if to reinforce the finality of his decision.

"Then what about the treasure?" asked Drayton, unwilling to let the subject matter go.

"Probably lost forever," said Timothy. "Lost to the ages."

"You think that's wise?" Drayton asked. "To simply deep-six everything?"

"Of course it is," said Tidwell with a big cat growl. "Because the case is closed." He laced his hands in front of his stomach, looking pompously pleased. "The murder's been solved."

"What do you think?" Drayton asked Theodosia. "About banishing the skull cups to storage?"

"I think," said Theodosia, snuggling closer to Max, "it has all the makings of a good old-fashioned mystery!"

The Indigo Tea Shop

Chilled Peach and Ginger Soup

3 ½ lb. fresh peaches, peeled, pitted, and chopped
1 tsp. ground ginger
1 ⅓ cups heavy cream

PURÉE the peaches and ginger in a food processor. Then slowly add the heavy cream. Chill and serve cold.

Haley's Proprietary Lemon Scones

3 cups all-purpose unbleached flour
1 Tbsp. baking powder
½ tsp. baking soda
¼ tsp. salt
Zest of 1 lemon
½ cup sugar
1½ sticks unsalted butter, cut into cubes

½ cup walnuts or pecans (optional)
1 cup buttermilk
1 egg
1 Tbsp. water

PREHEAT the oven to 400 degrees F. Sift together the flour, baking powder, baking soda, and salt in a large bowl. In a separate bowl, combine the lemon zest and sugar, using a spoon to firmly grind it all together. Add the sugar to the flour mixture and mix well. Cut the butter into the mixture until you get an even, crumbly consistency. Mix in the nuts, if using. Pour in the buttermilk and stir thoroughly until the mixture forms a dense dough. Take a good-sized lump of dough and gently form it into a triangular scone shape. Place the scone on a baking sheet lined with parchment, then continue forming scones until the mixture is used up. Whisk the egg with the water to form an egg wash, then brush the egg wash on top of each scone. Bake for 15 to 20 minutes or until golden-brown.

Easy Chai Tiramisu

1 can (14 fl. oz.) sweetened condensed milk
1 package (3.3 oz.) white chocolate instant pudding mix
1 cup cold water
8 oz. cream cheese, softened
8 oz. whipped topping
1¼ cups chai tea
¼ cup Kahlúa
1 Sara Lee pound cake
¼ cup unsweetened cocoa powder

COMBINE the condensed milk, pudding mix, and water, then let chill for 30 minutes. When the mixture is chilled, beat in the cream cheese, then fold in the whipped topping. Combine the chai and Kahlúa and reserve. Slice the pound cake into ½-inch slices and place one layer in a large glass bowl. Add a layer of the chai mixture, then layer in the pudding mixture. Then sprinkle on some unsweetened cocoa. Repeat the layers, then cover and chill for at least 6 hours. Enjoy!

Tomato and Basil Dip

1 ½ cups fresh basil, finely chopped
2 tomatoes, finely chopped
2 cups fine, dry bread crumbs
2 garlic cloves, mashed
½ cup olive oil
Salt and pepper, to taste

IN a medium bowl, combine the basil, tomatoes, bread crumbs, garlic, olive oil, salt, and pepper. Cover and refrigerate overnight. Add a little more olive oil if needed for a creamy consistency, then serve with your favorite chips or crackers.

Cheesy Bruschetta

3 Tbsp. olive oil
4 tomatoes, seeded and chopped

3 Tbsp. fresh basil, chopped
8 oz. cream cheese
4 oz. herb and garlic feta cheese
1 loaf sourdough or Italian bread, thickly sliced
8 oz. shredded mozzarella cheese

HEAT the olive oil in a saucepan, then add the tomatoes and basil. Sauté lightly until slightly tender. In a small bowl, blend the cream cheese and feta cheese. Place slices of sourdough bread on a cookie sheet and toast very lightly under the broiler. Remove the toast from the broiler and spread with the feta cheese blend, then top with the tomato-basil mixture. Sprinkle with mozzarella cheese and toast under the broiler again until bubbly. Serve immediately.

Miss Dimple's Favorite Tea Cakes

1¾ cups sugar
1 cup butter
2 eggs
3 cups all-purpose white flour
½ tsp. baking soda
¼ tsp. salt
1 tsp. vanilla extract

PREHEAT the oven to 325 degrees F. Cream the sugar and butter, then add the eggs, one at a time, beating after each addition. Add the flour, baking soda, salt, and vanilla and mix to form a dough. Knead the dough on a floured board, then pat it out gently to ½-inch thickness. Cut out the tea cakes with a cookie cutter or glass. Bake for 8 minutes on a greased baking sheet. Serve hot with butter and jam.

Goat Cheese Truffles

> 6 oz. goat cheese
> 1/4 cup chopped almonds
> 1/4 cup chopped dates
> 1/4 cup chopped fresh basil

MAKE 36 small 3/4-inch rounds of cheese using a melon ball scoop. Then roll 12 of them in the almonds, 12 in the dates, and 12 in the basil. These are a great accompaniment to tea sandwiches or mini quiches. *Note:* You can use any type of soft cheese, including cream cheese or Rondelé, and you can substitute chopped pecans for the almonds.

Couscous Salad

> 1/2 cucumber, chopped
> 1/3 cup diced red onion
> 1/4 cup white wine vinegar
> 1 cup boiling water
> 1 cup couscous
> 1 Tbsp. chicken stock
> 2 Roma tomatoes, diced
> 1/4 cup olive oil
> 1/2 cup feta cheese, crumbled
> Salt and pepper, to taste

MIX the cucumber, onion, and vinegar in a bowl and let marinate for 20 minutes. In a second bowl, add the boiling water to the couscous and chicken stock. Mix well and let cool. Once the couscous is cool, add the cucumber mixture, tomatoes, and olive oil. Gently stir in the feta cheese and add salt and pepper to taste.

Old-Fashioned Crumpets

2 tsp. honey
½ cup warm water
1 Tbsp. active dry yeast
2½ cups all-purpose flour
1 tsp. salt
½ tsp. baking soda
1½ cups milk

IN a large mixing bowl, stir the honey into the warm water. Sprinkle the yeast in and let it sit for about 5 minutes, until it bubbles. Stir in the flour, salt, baking soda, and milk. Cover and let sit for 30 minutes in a warm place. Grease a frying pan as well as several round cookie cutters or biscuit cutters. Place the cutters in the pan and preheat. Pour 2 to 4 tablespoons of batter into each cutter and cook over medium-low heat until set, about 10 minutes. When the top is full of holes, the crumpet is ready to turn. Now carefully turn the crumpet and brown the other side for about 1 minute. Repeat the process until all of the batter is used up. Serve warm with butter and jam or slice the crumpets and fill with chicken salad. Makes about 14 crumpets. *Note:* These are also known as griddle scones.

Creamy Dreamy Parfait

1 can (6 fl. oz.) frozen orange juice concentrate
8 oz. vanilla yogurt
1 cup milk
1 Tbsp. granulated sugar
½ tsp. vanilla extract
3 ice cubes
Orange slices and cookies for garnish

BLEND the orange juice concentrate, yogurt, milk, sugar, and vanilla in a blender on low speed until smooth and creamy. Increase the speed to high and drop in the ice cubes, one at a time, keeping the top of the blender covered. Blend until the ice is crushed. Pour into parfait glasses and garnish with orange slices and your favorite cookie.

Lemon Chess Pie
(Courtesy of baking great Carroll Pellegrinelli)

2 cups sugar
¼ cup butter, melted and cooled
5 eggs, slightly beaten
1 cup milk
1 Tbsp. flour
1 Tbsp. cornmeal
Zest and juice of 3 lemons
1 9-inch pie shell

PREHEAT the oven to 375 degrees F. Combine the sugar, butter, eggs, milk, flour, cornmeal, and lemon zest and juice and pour into the pie shell. Bake for 30 minutes. Remove from the oven and tent the crust edges to prevent overbrowning. Bake for another 15 minutes or more—or until the middle of pie no longer jiggles.

Bridal Shower Tea

Polish the silver and pull out all the stops for this elegant tea. Think cream-colored tapers, white linen tablecloths, and your best china and tea ware. Your menu might include chicken à la king in puff pastry, pineapple cream cheese tea sandwiches, strawberries dipped in chocolate, and cranberry orange scones. Serve a black Ceylonese tea as well as a spiced plum infusion. Don't forget to play a little classical music interspersed with Beyonce's "Single Ladies."

Sip for the Cure

Think pink for this tea—pink tablecloth, pink napkins, pink flowers for your centerpiece, and pink floral dinnerware. Pass out pink ribbons to all your guests and swag pink ribbons around the backs of chairs. If you want to tie your tea into a fund-raiser, pass out pink envelopes and let everyone make a donation. And be sure to keep the menu pink, as well. Your choices could include raspberry tea, crab salad tea sandwiches, cranberry scones, and strawberry shortcake. Ceylon Silver Tips tea also yields a pale pink liquor.

Letter-Writing Tea

Aren't you tired of texting and e-mail? Wouldn't it be fun to compose an old-fashioned letter? Round up some quill pens, ink, and fancy stationery, and invite your friends to a letter-writing tea. Put on some relaxing music and let everyone jot a letter or a few thoughts while enjoying an afternoon of tea. Oolong is a thoughtful blend that goes nicely with quiche, citrus salad, and lemon scones. If you want to give your guests favors, think pretty pens and tiny notebooks in net bags.

Scottish Tea

Arrange a wooden table in front of a crackling fire and put out your pewter ware and candlesticks. Serve fresh baked bread with a platter of sliced meats and cheeses. For a good, strong Scottish blend of tea, try Brodies or Taylors Scottish Breakfast Tea. Be sure to include shortbread, gingerbread, and pots of lovely jams and jellies. For entertainment, think Scottish music or even Scottish poetry. After all, who doesn't love Robert Burns?

Big Hat Tea

Tell your friends to wear their biggest, boldest go-to-church hats! Serve smoky Lapsang souchong tea from China along with a Brie cheese omelet, cheese and fruit plate, and lemon poppy seed tea bread. If the weather is nice, there's nothing more spectacular than big hats in a garden setting.

Stitchers Tea

For your centerpiece, arrange a big bouquet of flowers in an antique sewing basket. Fill other baskets with embroidery floss, needles, and tea towels to work on while you sip. Serve Assam tea with hearty vegetable soup, melted cheddar and turkey on toasted English crumpets, and coconut macaroons.

Shabby Chic Tea

Pull out a floral tablecloth, set the table with mismatched dishes, and use whatever mismatched silverware and serving dishes you have. Got an old wire egg basket? Fill it with flowers. Grab an old ceramic flowerpot, rub on some white paint, tuck in a napkin, and pile up your scones. Repurposing is the name of the game with shabby chic, so get creative. For your menu, think about popovers stuffed with walnut and tarragon chicken salad, a fruit salad, and some chocolate chip scones.

TEA RESOURCES

TEA PUBLICATIONS

Tea: A Magazine—Quarterly magazine about tea as a beverage and its cultural significance in the arts and society. *Tea Poetry*—book compiled and published by Pearl Dexter, editor of *Tea: A Magazine*. (www.teamag.com)

Tea Time—Luscious magazine profiling tea and tea lore. Filled with glossy photos and wonderful recipes. (www.teatimemagazine.com)

Southern Lady—From the publishers of *Tea Time* with a focus on people and places in the South as well as wonderful tea time recipes. (www.southernladymagazine.com)

Tea House Times—Dozens of links to tea shops, purveyors of tea, gift shops, and tea events. (www.teahousetimes.com)

Victoria—Articles and pictorials on homes, home design, and tea. (www.victoriamag.com)

The Gilded Lily—Publication from the Ladies Tea Guild. (www.glily.com)

Tea in Texas—Highlighting Texas tea rooms and tea events. (www.teaintexas.com)

Fresh Cup Magazine—For tea and coffee professionals. (www.freshcup.com)

Tea & Coffee—Trade journal for the tea and coffee industry. (www.teaandcoffee.net)

The Leaf—Tea magazine. (www.the-leaf.org)

AMERICAN TEA PLANTATIONS

Charleston Tea Plantation—The oldest and largest tea plantation in the United States. Order their fine black tea or schedule a visit. (www.bigelowtea.com)

Fairhope Tea Plantation—Tea produced in Fairhope, Alabama, can be purchased though the Church Mouse gift shop. (www.thechurchmouse.com)

Sakuma Brothers Farm—This tea garden just outside Burlington, Washington, has been growing white and green tea for ten years. (www.sakumamarket.com)

Big Island Tea—Organic artisan tea from Hawaii. (www.bigislandtea.com)

TEA WEBSITES AND INTERESTING BLOGS

Teamap.com—Directory of hundreds of tea shops in the United States and Canada.

GreatTearoomsofAmerica.com—Excellent tea shop guide.

Cookingwithideas.typepad.com—Recipes and book reviews for the bibliochef.

Cuppatea4sheri.blogspot.com—Amazing recipes.

Seedrack.com—Order *Camellia sinensis* seeds and grow your own tea!

Friendshiptea.blogspot.com—Tea shop reviews, recipes, and more.

Theladiestea.com—Networking platform for women.

Jennybakes.com—Fabulous recipes from a real make-it-from-scratch baker.

Teanmystery.com—Tea shop, books, gifts, and gift baskets.

Allteapots.com—Teapots from around the world.

Fireflyvodka.com—South Carolina purveyors of Sweet Tea Vodka, Raspberry Tea Vodka, Peach Tea Vodka, and more. Just visiting this website is a trip in itself!

Teasquared.blogspot.com—Fun, well-written blog about tea, tea shops, and tea musings.

Bernideensteatimeblog.blogspot.com—Tea, baking, decorations, and gardening.

Tealoversroom.com—California tea rooms, Teacasts, links.

Teapages.blogspot.com—All things tea.

Baking.about.com—Carroll Pellegrinelli writes a terrific baking blog complete with recipes and photo instructions.

Lverose.com—La Vie en Rose offers book gift baskets paired with the perfect tea and CD.

Teawithfriends.blogspot.com—Lovely blog on tea, friendship, and tea accoutrements.

Sharonsgardenofbookreviews.blogspot.com—Terrific book reviews by an entertainment journalist.

Teaescapade.wordpress.com—Enjoyable tea blog.

Lattesandlife.com—Witty musings on life.

Napkinfoldingguide.com—Photo illustrations of twenty-seven different (and sometimes elaborate) napkin folds.

Worldteaexpo.com—World Tea Expo, the premier business-to-business trade show, features more than three hundred tea suppliers, vendors, and tea innovators.

Sweetgrassbaskets.net—One of several websites where you can buy sweetgrass baskets direct from the artist.

PURVEYORS OF FINE TEA

Adagio.com

Harney.com

Stashtea.com

Republicoftea.com

Bigelowtea.com

Teasource.com

Celestialseasonings.com

Goldenmoontea.com

Uptontea.com

Heartoftea.com

Turn the page for a preview of Laura Childs's
next Scrapbooking Mystery . . .

POSTCARDS
FROM THE DEAD

Coming October 2012 in hardcover
from Berkley Prime Crime!

A dazzling night filled with gigantic floats, silver beads, dizzying lights, fire-twirling *flambeaus*, and a crowd that was fueled by too much Dixie beer and Southern Comfort. This Wednesday evening, the Loomis Krewe's parade was rolling through New Orleans's historic French Quarter, pumping out all the brazenness and utter abandon they could muster. And the city of New Orleans fairly sizzled, caught as it was in the throes of another fantastical Mardi Gras celebration, beginning with the Epiphany and ending with the crazy-costumed, over-the-top super finale known as Fat Tuesday.

Smack-dab in the middle of it all, Kimber Breeze, the perky, Botoxed blond reporter from KBEZ-TV, stood on a delicate wrought-iron balcony outside the Hotel Tremain. Three floors above Royal Street, she chirped happily into her microphone and smiled broadly at the cameras as she interviewed various French Quarter denizens and broadcast parts of the parade spectacle live.

Inside, in the Bonaparte Suite, fifty costumed revelers

sang and danced and whooped it up. Most were there for the free booze; only a few had been invited for actual interviews.

Carmela Bertrand, owner of the Memory Mine scrapbook shop in the French Quarter, was one of those waiting her turn on the balcony. Carmela wasn't a big fan of Kimber Breeze, but she knew a photo op when she saw one. And her business, still not fully recovered from that enormous hiccup known as Hurricane Katrina, could always use a punch of publicity.

"This is taking forever," Carmela drawled to her best friend, Ava, who had come along to keep her company. Having taught a morning class on stencils, then spent the afternoon unpacking boxes filled with new mulberry and banana leaf papers, Carmela wasn't in the mood for the zydeco music and the fever pitch energy that pulsed through the room. Carmela would have preferred to be tucked snugly into her little French Quarter apartment, watching *Wheel of Fortune* and enjoying a calm, relaxing evening with her two dogs, Boo and Poobah.

"C'mon, *cher*, enjoy the party!" urged Ava. Ava was a party girl and former Southern beauty queen, while Carmela was clearly the laid-back cocooner. "Loosen up and live a little!"

Carmela smiled tolerantly and smoothed back a strand of honeyed blond hair from her short, choppy bob. Not quite thirty, Carmela was lithe and youthful-looking, with eyes the same flat blue-gray as the Gulf of Mexico and lush lashes that tipped up slightly at the ends. Though her peaches and cream complexion rarely saw the need for makeup, she did enjoy the natural hydrating properties of Louisiana's industrial-strength humidity. Carmela was also the one who favored more classic (okay, conservative) clothing in colors of navy and camel, while Ava, always willing to push the envelope as far as humanly possible, loved to dress in black leather pants and tight, low-cut tops.

"Tonight's a school night," Carmela joked. She knew that

tomorrow morning, come nine o'clock, she had to be primed and ready for the onslaught of customers that would pour into her shop. Most would be frantic to grab reams of paper, rubber stamps, and rolls of purple and green ribbon. All the better to create Mardi Gras menus, party place settings, and scrapbook pages.

"Oh my gosh!" Ava suddenly screeched, "I don't believe it! There's Sugar Joe!"

Carmela stood on tippy-toe and tried to peer over the heads of the costumed crazies. "Where?" Sugar Joe Panola was the best friend of her ex-husband, Shamus Meechum. But where Shamus was a rat fink of the first magnitude, Sugar Joe was actually a pretty nice guy.

"On the monitor, on the monitor!" cried Ava, pointing.

Carmela swiveled her head to where Raleigh, one of KBEZ-TV's camera guys, sat at a portable console. "Let's watch," she said. "See how it goes for him." *Maybe see what's in store for me.*

Over the years, Carmela hadn't enjoyed a particularly warm relationship with Kimber Breeze. Truth be told, whenever they'd had dealings with each other, Kimber had pretty much tried to sandbag her. But Carmela didn't hold with harboring old hurts and grudges. After all, what good did it do to hang on to them? Nothing, really. Unless, of course, it was a grudge over an ex-husband. Then it was perfectly legitimate.

Threading their way through the rambunctious crowd, Carmela and Ava eased up to Raleigh and his equipment. Raleigh, who was middle-aged and favored khakis and T-shirts, seemed to have a perpetual hunch from lugging around battery packs, cables, and camera gear. And trailing after Kimber. And listening to her shrill, domineering voice.

"How come you're not out there with Kimber?" Carmela asked him.

"No room," said Raleigh, as his fingers worked the dials.

"That balcony is a tight squeeze even for two people. So I've got one camera locked on Kimber, another one on the parade below, and one running in here." He waved a hand. "Which means besides being camera man, I get to play floor director tonight."

"What does that mean exactly?" asked Carmela.

Raleigh shrugged. "Switching between camera A, camera B, and camera C."

"And all this feeds directly back to the station?" asked Carmela, indicating the monitors. She found this technical part fascinating, akin to assembling a video scrapbook.

"That's right," said Raleigh. His brows beetled and he was suddenly on alert. "Oh hey, here we go."

Carmela and Ava watched the monitor as Kimber interviewed Sugar Joe. Which, for the preening Kimber, pretty much turned into a flirtfest.

"Maybe she'll flirt with you," Ava said to Carmela, then giggled wickedly.

"Maybe she'll turn tail and walk away," said Carmela. She wasn't sure what Kimber's reaction would be. Stamp her foot and refuse to do the interview? Could happen.

In the monitor, Kimber gave Sugar Joe a warm hug, then a few seconds later Sugar Joe came bounding in from the balcony. Sugar Joe was tall, with buzz cut blond hair and a broad, open face. When he saw Carmela and Ava he broke into a grin.

"Carmela!" Sugar Joe cried out. "And Ava!" He spread his arms wide open, the better to hug them. "You ladies look ravishing!" Sugar Joe told every woman within a two-mile radius that she looked ravishing. And he greeted each and every woman with, *Hello, beautiful!* Carmela decided Sugar Joe's boundless enthusiasm for the fairer sex wasn't the worst thing in the world.

"You looked mighty handsome on camera, Sugar Joe," cooed Ava. Ava had a way with the opposite sex, as well.

But Carmela was more interested in the broadcast. Raleigh had switched to the parade feed now to capture an enormous pirate ship that was gliding by, illuminating the night with thousands of white twinkle lights.

"Now this feed's going to the station?" she asked Raleigh.

"It's going there, but not live," he told her. "It's being automatically archived for later."

"But a portion of this broadcast will be live?"

Raleigh glanced at his watch and seemed to tense up. "Oh yeah. In about eight seconds." He slouched forward and spoke into his microphone, "Okay, Kimber, time to cut in for station ID." He paused while he twiddled a dial on his console. "Kimber?" he said again. "Better be on your toes, girl, because I'm coming to you live in five." Raleigh stole another quick glance at his watch, then began his countdown. "Five, four, three, two . . ."

But when Kimber's monitor came on, no one was there.

"Crap!" whooped Raleigh. He frantically keyed her microphone. "Kimber," he hissed, "you're *on*!"

A blank screen. Still no Kimber.

Suddenly a blur of motion flashed across the screen, then Kimber's face was pressed tightly against the camera's lens in grotesque grimace.

"What?" cried Raleigh. He jerked back. "Oh man, now the lights went out! Jeez Louise, I gotta switch my feed!" His fingers quickly pushed buttons, cutting over to the parade that was lumbering by below them.

Was Kimber just goofing off? Carmela wondered. Was she being a pill and trying to rattle poor Raleigh?

But something didn't sit right with Carmela. From her perspective, Kimber had looked . . . terrified. "No, put the balcony feed up on the other monitor!" she cried to Raleigh. "Something's wrong!"

He shook his head. "Can't. The Klieg's down. No light out there."

Carmela stood motionless for one more second, knowing it wasn't her place to interfere. Then she quickly reconsidered and pushed her way through the impervious, partying crowd and out onto the balcony.

Arriving slightly breathless on the little half-circle balcony that hung out over the street, Carmela stopped dead in her tracks. Bizarrely, Kimber was nowhere to be found.

Huh? Where on earth did she disappear to?

Carmela blinked and glanced around again.

Kidnapped by aliens?

She saw only two cameras, locked in place, their dark lenses and all-seeing red eyes staring directly at her.

As Carmela fought to figure out what strange trick had just been played, shrill screams echoed from the street below. Startled now, she turned and glanced down. An enormous pink-and-gold dragon float was rolling by, the dragon's ten-foot-wide gaping mouth spewing smoke and shooting sparks while its enormous tail wagged back and forth across the entire width of the street. Perched high atop the dragon's spiky back were at least forty white-robed krewe members tossing strands of silver beads to the screaming, deliriously happy crowd.

But still the screams persisted. And now the crowd wasn't just crying out for beads! Now, horrified faces were upturned.

Looking at me?

Puzzled, Carmela glanced down and saw a fat black cord snaked tightly over the balcony railing.

Leading to . . . ?

Her heart did a slow-motion flip-flop. Then, with a feeling of dread and a swirl of vertigo, Carmela leaned farther out over the narrow wrought-iron balcony and gazed straight down.

That's when Carmela saw Kimber's lifeless body dangling ten feet below her. Kimber's face was a massive purple clot.

One slender high heel hung from her foot, and the other foot was completely bare. Then a spotlight from the dragon float suddenly angled its bright light upward, revealing Kimber's twisting body, and Carmela's scream rose in a frantic plea, mingling with the hysterical shrieks from the crowd.

WATCH FOR THE NEXT
TEA SHOP MYSTERY

Agony of the Leaves

A catered party at Charleston's Neptune Aquarium sends a loved one tumbling overboard in a troubling and particularly gruesome murder.

AND ALSO THE NEXT
SCRAPBOOK MYSTERY

Skeleton Letters

Business is humming at Memory Mine as Carmela offers lessons in calligraphy and plans an extravagant wine-tasting party. But when a friend is murdered and a valuable crucifix is stolen from a church, the intrepid scrapbooker takes matters into her own hands.

BE SURE TO WATCH FOR THE
NEXT CACKLEBERRY CLUB MYSTERY
BY LAURA CHILDS

Stake and Eggs

A bizarre murder leaves the townsfolk of Kindred badly shaken. And inquiring minds want to know—will the ladies of the Cackleberry Club jump in to solve this one, too?

FIND OUT MORE ABOUT THE AUTHOR
AND HER MYSTERIES AT
WWW.LAURACHILDS.COM
VISIT LAURA CHILDS ON FACEBOOK
AND BECOME A FRIEND.

Indigo Tea Shop owner Theodosia Browning finds herself in hot water when a body surfaces at the grand opening of Charleston's Neptune Aquarium—her ex-boyfriend Parker Scully . . .

FROM *NEW YORK TIMES* BESTSELLING AUTHOR
LAURA CHILDS

AGONY OF THE LEAVES
• A Tea Shop Mystery •

When Theodosia notices what look like defense wounds on Parker's hands, she realizes that someone wanted him dead, but the local police aren't keen on hearing her theory. She knows that if she wants Parker's killer brought to justice, she'll have to jump into the deep end and start her own investigation . . .

Includes delicious recipes and tea time tips!

laurachilds.com
penguin.com

M983T0911